A DOVE AGAINST DEATH

Also by Christopher Wood

FIRE MOUNTAIN
DEAD CENTRE
TAIWAN

Christopher Wood

A DOVE
AGAINST DEATH

THE VIKING PRESS   NEW YORK

With love and thanks
to Marjory Chapman

LIBRARY OF CONGRESS CATALOGING IN PUBLICATION DATA
Wood, Christopher, 1935–
  A dove against death.
  I. Title.
PR6073. 0 576D6 1983   823'.914   82-19991
ISBN 0-670-28066-6

Printed in the United States of America
Set in Baskerville

ONE

The early morning mist closed in and Lieutenant Poynter checked the impulse to swing his arms across his chest against the cold. They were due to attack in ten minutes and he could see no more than a few yards in any direction. Their target, Ndinga Mountain, was totally obscured.

How ironic, after all these days of approaching it across the sun-scorched plain. The crags on the squat monolith gleaming temptingly like precious stones. Jewels on a crown awaiting a hand bold enough to snatch it from the Germans. Now the prize only remained as an image shimmering against the retina of the eye.

What a strange war, he thought, this West African affair. A few hundred white men playing murderous chess on a board twice the size of the United Kingdom. Marching forward, sideways and backwards past bewildered natives whom they press-ganged into service as levies or carriers. Advancing, retreating, killing, dying. Always at the mercy of the climate, the terrain and the flies.

He looked into the tense black faces about him; men thinking of wives, children, sweethearts, other places, better times. Perhaps most difficult of all, trying to think of nothing; making the mind a vacuum that starved out fear.

A horse whinnied at its picket and Poynter spun round as the naval six-pounder loomed out of the mist. This was the weapon that had been brought up from the coast in pieces to blast the Germans out of their heavily-fortified position. Each barefoot gun carrier in tunic, shorts and puttees responsible for a wheel or part of the breech mechanism carried on his head.

The blacks were pushing the gun under the diligent eye of

7

a grizzled petty officer and a rating no bigger than a whippet. Poynter observed the little man. His round nondescript face was like that of a cloth doll with buttons for eyes. Now it was almost totally obscured beneath his pith helmet. His naval uniform had been exchanged for army clothes, so large that they made him seem even smaller than he was; as if he had shrunk inside the voluminous shirt and shorts that brushed the tops of his puttees. He sang tunelessly and raucously when he was happy, which was most of the time.

The rating looked up and caught Poynter's eye. His name was Smith.

Smith looked at Poynter and saw a spindly, sharp-featured young man who was probably the same age as himself but appeared even younger. There was a pink, child-like bloom to his skin that the fierce African sun had not succeeded in taming. He stood self-consciously with his cane held behind his back, his chest thrust out, his thin frame trying to impose itself on its surroundings. An officer, who at all times must be a buttress, a rallying point, a presence. As Smith's gaze examined him he turned away.

The British force and a small support company of French from Chad were spread out amongst the giant boulders at the foot of the mountain. The British had entered the Cameroons after a journey of five hundred miles from the coast on the Nigerian side of the border; by stern-wheeler, dug-out canoe, foot and pony; along great rivers as wide as lakes with the jungle choking the banks in a jostling welter of steaming foliage; above the falls where mists of spume were hung with rainbows, through narrow jungle paths where the sun was shut out and the mosquitoes clustered round men's heads like a fine, black mesh.

And the plan. The master plan that they were seeking to achieve; Major Liddell, Captain Cunningham, Lieutenants Fox and Poynter, Sergeants Brown and Taylor, the naval gun crew, the French tirailleurs and the motley collection of Hausa, Yorubas, Fulani and unclassified pagans under their

8

command. That was no less complicated than the terrain.

If Ndinga fell, men could be liberated to attack the main German stronghold to the south east at Yaunde. With the fall of Yaunde, Douala, the great deep-water port and coaling station wrested from the Germans in 1914, would be safe. Whichever side controlled Douala held the key to naval supremacy in the South Atlantic. As the British High Command saw it, Ndinga Mountain was the first in a line of dominoes that would topple backwards to smash German resistance in the Cameroons for ever.

Poynter looked up. Above his head was a luminous circle which showed where the sun was trying to break through the mist. The summit of the mountain was probably already bathed in brilliant sunshine. The defenders would be scanning a sea of white, waiting for life to crawl from it. On sunny days you could see the flash of their binoculars. He took a deep breath and smelt a scent brought by memory. When he had arrived by ship earlier in the year the coast had been concealed behind a curtain of mist and it had been the mysterious, intoxicating odour of unseen flowers, palm oil and damp vegetation that had been his introduction to the country. Now he could smell it again across the border in this desert fastness of the German Kamerun. But the sweetness and the allure had gone. Now the smell was musty and dry. It made him think of a crypt.

Smith drummed his fingers against the breech of the six-pounder and hummed to himself. The lieutenant was talking to his Hausa sergeant. Soon they would be on the move. He watched Poynter step back and wipe his upper lip. There was a rattle of steel and bayonets were fixed. Smith caught the eye of one of the gun crew and winked.

'In good heart, young 'un?' Captain Cunningham had appeared at Poynter's elbow. There was a difference of two years between the two men. 'The Old Man seems to think that the mist is going to be a blessing. We'll be in position and raining down shells on the Hun before he knows what's hit him. Hope the old cuss has put the mist in the picture.'

Cunningham was a tall, graceful young man with a blond moustache that trailed down languidly on either side of his sensual mouth. Poynter suspected that the moustache had been grown to make the wearer look older and more ferocious. It had not succeeded. Cunningham had been an officer in the Royal Horse Guards before volunteering for service in the WAFF – The West African Frontier Force. Poynter had never felt completely at ease with him. It was not merely a question of age and rank but the fact that Poynter's regiment, The Somerset Light Infantry, was a comparatively humble one compared to the dashing 'Blues' and, even more important, his own lack of worldliness was sadly inferior to the style of his brother officer. Cunningham glided through life as if it was a subservient machine needing only an occasional drop of oil to make it run smoothly. On the journey up the Niger he had stepped ashore at Lokoga and played a memorable game of polo with the garrison. Poynter's presence on the field had barely been noticed.

'I thought we might wait until the mist had lifted,' said Poynter. 'I mean, the gun can't come into action until we can see the target. There's a risk of us getting separated.'

'Just shepherd 'em up to the edge of the boulders. There's plenty of cover and they've got the elevation. I've had a pow-wow with the senior matelot and he's happy – well, as happy as he'll ever be when he hasn't got the briny beneath his feet. I'll be ahead with the dashing major. I'll send a runner back if we need you.' Cunningham patted the lieutenant on the shoulder. 'Good luck, young 'un. I've got a flask of brandy in my saddle bag. We'll have a snort or two on the summit.'

'Splendid,' said Poynter, wishing immediately that he could have injected more assurance into the word.

Cunningham disappeared into the mist and could soon be heard briefing his troops. He was going to be the first man into the enemy position. If there was going to be a first man.

Poynter signalled to the petty officer and the gun began to grind into the murk.

The mist could be friend or enemy. Often it lifted with the speed of a silk handkerchief being snatched into the air. The Germans had no artillery but had proven themselves deadly marksmen with Mauser and machine gun. Patrols had come under withering fire. Poynter thought of the steep, exposed slopes and licked his lips. Oh to be like Cunningham, dashing and fearless.

The giant boulders were scattered around the foot of the mountain as if they had rolled down its sides like malformed marbles. In the mist their lumpen shapes were ghostly and menacing, sour food for the imagination. The gun wheels creaked and the men strained. The surface was rock, sometimes smooth like the inside of an oyster shell but more often broken by fissures and falls of stone. There was no easy passage and shoulders scraped against angled door posts of granite.

Poynter removed his pith helmet and mopped his brow. His hair was damp and clung to his forehead. Ahead, the rocks were closing in. His eyes probed for a way through.

'On the wheels, boys.' Muscles bulged on black arms; there were gasps and sighs, stretched lips, clenched teeth, trembling limbs. The wheels ground and scraped. Smith threw his weight behind the gun with the blacks. Poynter hesitated, wondering whether to do the same. Better not. Such a gesture would belittle his rank. Automatically he found himself thinking what Cunningham would do.

The mist was clearing. Poynter could see his sergeant and two men beyond him warily picking his way through the rocks. He felt an almost dream-like sense of distance from the scene. He might have been studying a detail in a painting.

The wheels grated, the men grunted. The spokes jerked round like the arms of an overstrained windlass. Poynter sweated and glanced at his watch. Cunningham would be half way up the ridge on the north side of the ravine. At least there had been no shots. A wheel slipped into a crevasse and the six-pounder tilted clumsily. Poynter knew that he was beginning to hate it. In pieces it had become imbued with the personalities of the men who carried it, almost an extension of their cheerful, nimble selves. Now, assembled, it was a cold, brutish mass; crude, cumbersome, lifeless but life-taking. A wheel scraped against rock and the parched husk of sound skittered away like a stone thrown across ice.

'Sergeant!' Poynter hissed the word as he jerked his arm up and down. The men were advancing too fast. They must stay with the gun. The mist was closing in again, the sun was no longer a myopic observer. Poynter felt increasingly uneasy. He had reconnoitred a way through the rocks but now nothing seemed familiar. He waited a few more minutes and then approached the petty officer. 'On the right track do you think?'

'Over to the left,' said Smith.

Poynter ignored him. 'Well?'

The petty officer reflected uncomfortably. 'I think he may be right, sir.'

'I'll take a look,' said Poynter. 'You stay here.' He withdrew his pistol and moved forward with two men. The rocks were damp and patterned with graffiti of white lichen that might have been applied with a paint brush. The mist sucked and swirled like smoke at the corner of a pipe smoker's mouth. Poynter brushed his hand against the white, expecting it to come off like paint on his fingers. It felt like the fur of a dead animal. His eyes strained and a shape took form through an archway of rock. His arm jerked forward and then fell. It was no more than a column of stone clothed by the mist. The porcupine tingle along his spine subsided. Move! He stepped forward and dislodged a small flurry of stones, the sound running on like a warning signal. He crouched and the Hausas' bare feet slapped against rock as they darted to take up firing positions. Silence.

Seconds passed. Poynter could smell the fear in his sweat. He edged forward and approached the arch. A single shot rang out followed by a volley of rifle fire. The sound was muffled but deafening. It seemed to come from all around and crashed on like a stone bouncing inside a revolving tin drum.

Had they come under fire? The Hausas' heads were darting like storks as they sought the unseen enemy. Cunningham must have engaged the German position. But why wasn't the sound of firing coming from above? More shots, and he tried to pinpoint their source. Again the sound roared and echoed. Nobody was firing at them. The sound was coming from behind. From the direction of the six-pounder. 'Double!' Poynter ran back the way they had come.

Everything looked different; the bands of white lichen, the witch locks of moss. A bullet screamed off the rock and he ran down a narrow defile hearing the men's bayonets clattering against the rock. An opening yawned and he burst through it and nearly fell onto the six-pounder. The petty officer lay beside it with Smith trying to stem the flow of blood from his throat. Men were scattered amongst the rocks, some firing haphazardly into the fog. Poynter looked for his sergeant. The man lay sprawled with a bloody mess where one of his eyes had been. He was dead. Above the scream of bullets came the demented neighing of the stallions as they fought to break free from their pickets. Poynter crawled to the nearest boulder and slowly raised his head. Something moved and he fired two pistol shots before a rifle bullet scored the rock beside him. He dropped down, shattered, confused. What the hell should he do? Rally his men and charge or stay where he was with the gun? He changed position and raised his head again.

The mist swirled and wide shafts of sunlight broke through like probing torch beams. There was a shout and figures rose up from behind the rocks. They wore red fezzes. Poynter raised his pistol and then hesitated, seized by a terrifying thought: the French native soldiers wore red fezzes. They had lost their way in the mist and were coming under fire from their allies. Horrified, he stood up. 'Hold your

13

fire!' he shouted. A man's face turned up to his, the eyes wide with bewilderment.

'*Anglais!*' shouted Poynter. '*Ne tirez pas! Nous sommes vos amis.*'

The soldiers continued to advance, thrusting their rifles out before them. A bullet whipped through Poynter's shirt sleeve. What was happening had the ponderous momentum of a nightmare. The figures were still coming, still firing.

'*Anglais!*' screamed Poynter. '*Anglais!*'

And then he stopped. An officer had appeared in the middle of the advance. He carried a pistol and wore a spiked brass helmet. Their assailants were not Fuzellier's tirailleurs but the enemy who had launched a daring counter attack. No sooner had the awful realization struck Poynter than there was a violent explosion and he was hurled forward into unconsciousness.

TWO

'I think he's coming round, sir.'

Poynter heard the words and wondered who they referred to. He was an eavesdropper on this conversation, his mind still blundering through the swirling mist. He opened his eyes and quickly closed them again as the brilliant light scorched his eyeballs. A mirror image of Smith continued to shimmer against the smoke blue darkness.

'You're all right.'

Poynter was inclined to doubt it. He prised open his gummed eyelids and saw a roof of palm fronds cut short by an expanse of dazzling blue sky. His memory began to filter information through layers of pain. Unless he was in some state of purgatory he must be alive. Wounded but alive. He could feel something pressing around his head. He raised his fingers gingerly and touched coarse bandage.

'Steady on, young 'un.' That was clearly Cunningham's voice. 'Nothing too serious. You fielded a rock with the back of your head.'

Poynter looked up and saw Cunningham staring down at him, his handsome face grazed and blackened by powder. He moved his head and groaned. 'What happened?'

'Double-distilled disaster. The Hun was too clever for us. Didn't wait to be attacked but used the mist to outflank us. Shot us to pieces on the slopes.'

Poynter felt a new pain. 'The gun?'

'Captured.'

A terrible guilt descended. 'I thought they were French,' he said faintly.

'What?' Cunningham glanced at Smith for confirmation.

'I think he's still a bit dazed, sir,' said the rating. He looked at Poynter. 'We're the only ones left, sir. They came round the back of us with bombs.'

'But the others,' said Poynter. 'Major Liddell and the French.'

'I don't know,' said Cunningham. 'Withdrawn probably. Those that are still alive. I got separated from my section and took a purler. Woke up a guest of the Kaiser.'

'Haven't seen other prisoners,' said Smith. He followed Poynter's wandering eyes. 'We're on top of the mountain.'

The lieutenant hauled himself up and saw that the crude shelter above his head formed a belvedere affording a panoramic view of the desert. There was a low stone parapet and an almost sheer cliff-face that dropped to steep boulder-strewn slopes pressing in like petrified waves. A dark shape dropped through his vision and drew his eye to what lay below. He craned forward and winced. A flock of vultures were tearing at a man's body. 'There's a man –!' He broke off. The man was not crawling to find cover amongst the rocks. He was already dead. Only the clumsy scrabbling of the thrusting, rending birds lent his corpse movement. A puppet arm flapped and there was a disgusting glimpse of bone and scarlet entrail being tugged out like string. The newcomer thrust its way into the squabbling horde and Poynter turned away. So much for the attack on Ndinga Mountain.

'Major Liddell will be back when he's re-formed,' said Cunningham.

'He's not going to get much chance unless he brings a twelve-pounder with him,' said Smith. 'And he'll need to go to Lagos or Douala for that.'

Cunningham's expression suggested that he did not care overmuch for the rating's observations. He picked up a gourd and thrust it into the little man's hands. 'Go and find some water.' He waited until Smith had reached the native guard watching them from the shadow of a stone redoubt. 'Basically a good sort but a trifle too free with his opinions. How're you feeling?'

'All right.' But Poynter was thinking of how Smith had tried to protect him. 'There's something I think you ought to know –' he began.

Cunningham laid a hand on his sleeve. 'Plenty of time for that, young 'un.'

There was a clatter of boots against rock and Smith reappeared with a stocky German, wearing tunic, shorts, ammunition pouches and a battered helmet that looked as if it had saved its wearer's life on more than one occasion. He had the complexion of a hay-maker and a fair thatch of moustache on his upper lip. Poynter looked at him, feeling a strange sense of identity and yet of distance. The man might have been a British soldier. Even his khaki uniform was similar.

Smith handed over the gourd and Poynter drank the cool water greedily.

The German watched impassively. '*Kommt mit. Der Hauptmann* wishes speak with you.'

Cunningham ignored him giving all his attention to Poynter.

'*Kommt!*'

Poynter started to pull himself to his feet. 'I can manage.'
'Take your time,' said Cunningham. 'Mustn't let these
people get the idea they can push us around.'
'What else can we do?' said Smith.
'When I want your opinion I'll ask for it,' said Cunningham. 'And you will continue to address me as "sir".'
'Yes, sir.' Smith's voice was resigned rather than chas-
tened. He offered Poynter an arm. 'Need a hand, sir?'
'Thank you.' Poynter swayed and closed his eyes until the
nausea had passed. The glare was blinding even beneath the
shade. He felt the bandage at the back of his head and his
fingers came away damp and red. There was a swelling the
size of a small apple. He took some deep breaths of the heavy
air. What must it be like down on the plain? His eyes strayed
towards the death-infested slopes and quickly jerked
away.

From the perimeter defences they were led towards the
centre of a small plateau that formed the summit of the
monolith. On the right, a col ran towards two diverging
ridges and Poynter saw how narrow the German position
was. It was sited along the edge of a truncated cone and the
ridges that fanned out on either side suggested that they
might form the remains of a caldera, the crater of an exploded volcano. Possibly, two volcanoes had once stood side
by side. He looked along the col and screwed up his eyes
against the sun. There appeared to be some kind of man-
made structure rising from the distant caldera. He blinked
and looked again. Perhaps it was his imagination or a trick of
the heat. There were strange menhir-type stones that rose
like Cleopatra's needles, possibly formed by the wind un-
countable ages ago. He had seen them around the base of the
mountain. But these columns were different. Taller, more
delicate. Almost like slender ferns. The rock fell away before
him and revealed where the stone had been quarried. It lay
in slabs like slices of a giant cut loaf amidst swirls of glittering
dust.

In the centre of the depression was a cluster of stone buildings. A native soldier, a Yaunde, stood on guard outside the largest and, with a stab of unease, Poynter recognized the red fez the man was wearing.

A second figure emerged from the building like a bear from its lair. He was a huge man whose square head seemed to have been driven down into his shoulders with a mallet so that his neck had disappeared. He wore a familiar German spiked helmet and the insignia of Korpsgendarm, a sergeant major in the Imperial Army.

As Poynter looked into the man's face he felt a surge of shock and disgust. Some terrible accident or act of war had warped his features so that they resembled a mask of rage melted by fierce heat. The man barely glanced at them before disappearing amongst the buildings. What lingered behind him was not so much the jolting hideousness of his appearance but the message in his small, cold eyes. It said simply: You are scum.

Their guard jerked an arm and Poynter followed Cunningham into the building. It was dark after the bright sunlight and it took him a few seconds to focus clearly on the figure sitting behind a table at the far end of the room. The man was tall, his features aristocratic. He sat back in his chair and lazily tapped his fingers on the helmet of his solar topi like a drumbeat heralding the build-up to a difficult trick. His hair was almost unnaturally white and shaven close to his head, his mouth a thin, straight line beneath his aquiline, predatory nose and his eyes a blue so pale that the irises seemed almost to melt into the whites. A monocle glinted against his chest and a pair of field binoculars rested beside his solar topi on the table. He wore an Iron Cross at his neck, and a captain's insignia on his tunic. At a guess he was nearer thirty than twenty, though in a face so bleached of emotion it was difficult to read years.

Seconds passed and the silence became a weapon. Then the German stood up and approached them round the table, his head nearly brushing the ceiling. He paused before

Cunningham and his eyes narrowed slightly. The beginning of a smile plucked at the corner of his mouth.

'Good heavens,' he said in flawless English. 'Alistair Cunningham.'

THREE

Cunningham stared. Then he slapped his thigh. 'Of course, Max von Graben. We've played polo together.'

The German nodded. 'At Oxford. My last year, your first.'

'That's right.' Cunningham reflected. 'Balliol, wasn't it?'

'Christ Church.'

'Of course.'

A silence followed the interchange and a small lizard ran across the wall like a shadow. Poynter looked towards Smith and wondered if the man's expression of incredulity matched his own. What he had just heard seemed more appropriate to the smoking room of a gentleman's club than to a remote corner of war-torn Africa.

Cunningham cleared his throat and turned to his two companions. 'Lieutenant Poynter and – er Able Seaman Smith.'

Von Graben's strange luminous eyes turned on them as if looking inside their heads for secrets. 'It must be clear to you all that your presence here is an embarrassment.'

'Perhaps we won't be here for very long,' said Cunningham.

Von Graben did not smile. 'Perhaps. I rather tend to believe that that will depend upon the duration of the war in Europe. Our position here is unassailable.'

'Come now,' said Cunningham. 'Even if that were true, we could still starve you out.'

Von Graben was unimpressed. 'You don't possess the resources. There are natural springs on the mountain and our relations with the local natives are excellent. We have considerable supplies of food and ammunition and we can obtain more.' He let his conqueror's gaze fall upon all three men. 'I think this morning's exercise must have demonstrated to you our capacity for movement.'

'No denying that,' said Cunningham grudgingly. 'Impressive show.'

Smith made a noise between his teeth.

Poynter felt uneasy. Part of him sympathized with Smith. The memory of the man's body covered with vultures and of the dying petty officer with blood pouring from his throat did not make it easy to bestow congratulations for a job well done. However, there was also the training of his modest public school which taught that you were gracious in victory and, in the unlikely event of defeat, sporting and uncomplaining. Smith had clearly lacked the opportunity to be exposed to such concepts.

Von Graben turned on the heel of a well-polished boot and walked briskly to his makeshift table. 'We have no facilities for prisoners of war. I must therefore ask for your word as officers and gentlemen that you will not try to escape.'

The faintest of smiles illuminated Smith's gnome-like face as if he was wondering whether the category of "gentlemen" was included for his benefit.

'The alternative is that I would have to keep you cooped up in one of the blockhouses. I would prefer not to do that.'

Poynter noted that von Graben's eyes rested only on Cunningham. A faint feeling of resentment stirred inside him. Cunningham considered for a moment and then nodded briskly. 'You have our word.'

'I take it that – er – we'll be able to move around within the defences,' said Poynter.

Von Graben looked at him sharply. 'For the sake of our internal security I would prefer that you remain in the immediate vicinity of this position. It will be less confusing for

20

our native soldiers, and safer for you if there is another attack.' Poynter said nothing. The German native soldiers had seemed perfectly disciplined on his limited exposure to them. The reply made him wonder again about the strange objects in the central crater.

'I am afraid you will all have to share the same accommodation,' said von Graben.

'That's all right by me,' said Smith cheerfully.

Cunningham's mouth tightened.

'I would like to have a word with you, Alistair,' said von Graben. 'Your comrades may be dismissed.'

Cunningham seemed almost relieved. 'I'll talk to you both later,' he said. 'Better go and lie down, Poynter, you look jiggered. Keep an eye on Mr Poynter, Smith.'

Poynter noticed that he was not addressed as 'young 'un' in front of von Graben. Perhaps this casual intimacy would have suggested a familiarity that Cunningham was not keen to parade before his fellow Oxonian. Perhaps he was being sensitive.

Von Graben snapped out some orders in pidgin German and Poynter and Smith were led out into the fierce sunshine and towards a conical stone structure formed by filling in the gaps between three almost contiguous boulders with off-cuts of quarried rock.

As they approached, two sweating blacks emerged stooped through the one narrow opening. They staggered under the weight of a huge coil of copper wire. Poynter was intrigued. What was it doing up here? Trip wires might well be used as part of the defensive system, but why copper wire?

Their guard gestured towards the strange troglodyte dwelling and Poynter ducked and entered. At least he was out of the sun. The bandage round his head felt as if it was shrinking and itched unmercifully.

Smith studied the three crude palliasses that had been placed on the floor in the company of a threadbare blanket. 'Which one do you want, sir?' He enjoyed watching Poynter grapple with the decision.

'Best to leave the one near the doorway for Captain Cunningham. I'll go in the middle.'

Smith clicked his tongue. 'Proper turn up for the books, him being at Oxford with Hauptmann von-whatsit, eh? Makes you wonder what we're all doing here.'

Something of the sort had been going through Poynter's mind but he felt disinclined to share his thoughts with a naval rating. One, moreover, who had already established a kind of unwanted intimacy by preventing him from blurting out the blunder he had made on the plain. He must make quite sure that there was no confusion about their relationship. 'A word of advice, Smith,' he said, sensing how pompous his voice sounded. 'I think Captain Cunningham's taking none too kindly to some of your observations. Best to keep your lip buttoned, especially in front of the Germans.'

The little man nodded to himself as if confirming some private thought. 'Not to let the side down.' There was no hint of mockery in his voice.

'Precisely.' Poynter tried to think of something more positive to say. 'We may have been taken prisoner, but we can still do something useful. Take a note of all the German defensive positions, the arms they have, how many white men there are. All that kind of thing.'

'What's the good if we can't tell anybody?'

'I'm certain Captain Cunningham did what he thought was best,' said Poynter, again feeling a strange sort of resentment against Smith for raising a point that had been troubling him. The dull ache inside his head flared up and he sank onto the nearest palliasse. 'I think I'll try and sleep for a bit. If you could find me some water.' He closed his eyes and heard Smith whistling as he went.

When he woke up it was to find Cunningham looking down at him. There was no sign of Smith. 'How are you feeling?' Cunningham sank to his knees and Poynter was surprised to smell brandy on his lips. Could this be the brew promised for their triumphal arrival on the summit?

'Bit shaky. Where's Smith?'

Cunningham frowned. 'I sent the little bounder away with a flea in his ear. Heaven knows what Max thought of his behaviour. Must have got a pretty rum idea of discipline in the British army. I spelt that out to him.'

'D'you think he understood?'

'Difficult to say. He's one of those barrack room lawyers if you ask me. Got a chip on his shoulder. I told him I wasn't going to stand for any of his nonsense.' Cunningham looked round the dingy enclosure disapprovingly. 'Awkward us all being together.'

Poynter helped himself from the calabash of water he found beside his palliasse. 'I think there's some kind of structure in the central crater. Did you see anything?'

'Like a series of tent poles? I thought they were putting up a building.'

'Seems strange. I saw an enormous roll of copper wire as well.' He waited for a reaction from Cunningham. 'It was being stored where we are now. I think we ought to find out what's going on, don't you?'

'Definitely got to keep our eyes open.' Cunningham sounded slightly uneasy.

'Try and get along the col and look down into the crater.'

'A bit ticklish that. We did give our word that we'd stay where we were.'

'We gave our word that we wouldn't try and escape – or rather you did. Von Graben said that he would *prefer* us to stay where we were. That's not the same thing.'

Cunningham flushed. 'Dammit man! You're sounding like Smith. Max – I mean, von Graben, didn't press the point because he was speaking to gentlemen – to two gentlemen at least.'

Poynter's head was starting to ache again. He rubbed his eyes. 'Honestly, Cunningham, I don't think we can have a moratorium because you were at Oxford with von Graben. Whatever the Germans are up to here we've got to find out and get the word back to Douala.'

'I'm not going to break my word. Frankly, I'm surprised

23

at you, Poynter. I thought you had standards.' He turned to
see that Smith had reappeared in the doorway. The sight
clearly irritated him. 'What are you staring at?'

'Nothing,' said Smith. 'I mean, nothing, sir.'

FOUR

The trigger was pulled and the black head jerked back.
Poynter recoiled with it and awoke nursing a crick in the
neck. The night was full of dark phantoms and the sweat that
soaked through to the thin blanket was not only caused by
fever. How clear the image had been: the pistol held to the
head of the wounded man, the blood darker than black, the
twitching body, the bare toes scoring the dust. And, in the
background, the six-pounder being dragged away.

Poynter twisted his head and breathed deeply. Cunningham was snoring softly and somewhere there was the drone
of a mosquito. Each sound had a reassuring reality that shut
off the mayhem of the inner mind. Poynter turned again and
looked towards the entrance. A figure stood in the doorway.
It was Smith peering out into the night with a mosaic of stars
about him. He seemed like an icon. Then he was gone.

Still not certain whether he was dreaming, Poynter peered
towards the straw mattress in the darkest recesses of the
chamber. Smith wasn't there. Doubtless he had gone to
relieve himself.

Seconds passed. Poynter sat up and felt the back of his
head. The swelling had diminished. The bandage seemed to
be serving no useful purpose so he removed it, leaving a piece
of dressing sticking to the dried-up wound. He could move
his head without feeling dizzy. Where was Smith? Was he
trying to escape? Poynter considered waking Cunningham
and then decided against it. His unquestioning reliance on
Cunningham was beginning to waver. In a strange way his

Want the America's Best Hospitals issue?

ORDER BEFORE: 6/15/02

☐ **52 issues (1 year) $34.97**
Only 67¢ an issue

☐ **26 issues (6 months) $17.97**
Only 69¢ an issue

The Case of the Missing Intern

U.S.NEWS
& WORLD REPORT

EXCLUSIVE RANKINGS

America's Best Hospitals

A guide to the nation's finest healthcare

Plus: Great advances in transplants

NAME _____
(please print)

ADDRESS _____

CITY _____ STATE _____ ZIP CODE _____

EMAIL _____

☐ Enter E-mail address to receive information about *U.S. News* products via E-mail.

☐ **Payment enclosed.** ☐ **Bill me later.**

U.S. News publishes weekly except for 5 special double issues per year.

62F1LE

U.S.NEWS
& WORLD REPORT

Offer valid in U.S. only. Canadian and other foreign rates available upon request. Please allow 4-6 weeks for first issue to arrive.

sympathies were drifting more towards Smith.

Poynter had been born at Uphill, a village not far from the town of Weston-Super-Mare in the county of Somerset. His father had been a solicitor and he had been raised to believe himself a gentleman. However, at an early age he had ridden to hounds and realized even then in that paradigm of society that there were gentlemen and gentlemen; that society stretched to Heaven and even, in the case of its upper level, slightly beyond.

Poynter listened and heard a dog barking in the distance. The sound must come from one of the villages that lay in the foothills on the north side of the mountain. Warily he peeled back the blanket and rose to his feet, muscles creaking. Cunningham still slept, the moonlight slanting in on his handsome face, a crimp of petulance pinching the corner of his patrician mouth. Poynter stepped over his body and peered from the doorway. There was no light from von Graben's redoubt. He waited a few moments and then pulled on his boots and stepped out into the night.

Clinging to the shadow of the rocks he approached the north side of the plateau. In the distance was the uneven black line of mountains and a pinpoint cluster of lights that must denote a village. To his left he could see the roof of one of the strongpoints sticking up above a slab of rock. He listened and heard a clinking noise like a rifle barrel striking stone. A sentry. He shrunk closer to the rock. On the right the col stretched away towards the central caldera, its steep side intermittently streaked with moonlight. Poynter looked and then looked again. What at first he thought was an animal had emerged from a patch of darkness and was moving along below the ridge and parallel with it. Almost capering, the small figure traversed the dangerous moonlight and disappeared from view.

Smith.

What the devil was he up to? He was heading for the caldera. Poynter hesitated and moved quietly towards the beginning of the col. Anyone walking along the path would be clearly visible from either end. He would have to follow Smith's route. A glance over the low parapet and his stomach muscles tightened. The angle of descent was precipitous and the shale of rocks and small boulders balanced precariously. It would not need much to send them crashing down the mountainside. He swung a leg over the parapet and hesitated. The palms of his hands were damp and he rubbed them against a smooth stone. His headache seemed to be returning. Fever, fear. He thought of the comparative safety he was leaving behind.

There was a sound of a man clearing his throat and he jerked his head sideways as a native soldier stirred in a crevasse a few feet away. Poynter slid over the parapet and dangled with his feet desperately trying to find a foothold. He heard the sentry sneeze and the rattle of his rifle. Poynter struggled to improve his grip and felt the stone he was clinging to move its position. At any second he might bring the whole parapet down on top of himself. He twisted his head sideways and glimpsed a shadow. The sentry was standing directly above him. If he chanced to look down he must see Poynter dangling in space.

Poynter grit his teeth and waited for the shout and the bullet. His fingers were growing numb and he knew that he could not hang on much longer. His toe-caps probed the side of the mountain but the face was smooth. Sweat stung his eyes and he felt as if he was on a rack, his arms being slowly wrenched from their sockets. He closed his eyes and then glanced sideways again. The shadow had disappeared. He clung on and tried to count to ten. At seven he could bear it no longer. All sensation died above his elbows and he dropped into the unknown. For a split second there was the terror of feeling nothing and then his feet struck rock and his desperate hands clawed the cliff face. The pain of scraped flesh flared up like an igniting match and he slid to a halt amongst a miniature avalanche of falling stones. He listened to them tumbling away into the darkness, not daring to move. At least he was in shadow.

26

Above, there was an exclamation and the sound of a bolt slamming home. If they fired a flare . . . To his right there was a skitter of stones and a glimpse of something moving fast through a patch of moonlight. Some foraging dog or jackal that had been searching for scraps. The sentry saw it and heaved a rock down the hillside. Poynter heard the grunt and the yelp of fear as the animal took off. He closed his eyes in relief. Thank God for the distraction. He waited several minutes and rose slowly to his feet. The dizziness had returned. He shook his head and took deep breaths of the cool night air. Ahead, the side of the col stretched away like a steeply curving beach. The moon was high and tipping shadow over the lip of the pathway like thick black sauce. Poynter clenched his fists and began to move. Each step was measured, each breath controlled. His fingers brushed the hillside as if the act of touching it had some magic power that would save him from plunging into the abyss. Above, the heavens were bright with a billion stars, ahead the caldera loomed like a squat black mountain sending out shoots.

Fifty paces and he heard something. Footsteps. Somebody was approaching along the path above his head. A black shadow rippled across the pool of moonlight. Then the footsteps stopped. Poynter shrank closer to the hillside feeling unseen eyes probing his flesh. There was the sound of a throat being cleared and a gobbet of spittle sailed into the darkness. The footsteps continued and died away. Poynter's breathing returned to normal.

When he reached the side of the caldera there was no sign of Smith. The ground was soft and powdery and there was a distinct smell of sulphur. He sank to one knee as a shooting star scored across the crowded heavens.

All was still except for a strange whirring noise. At first he thought it was inside his head, a singing in the ears caused by his injury. Then he realized that it came from above, from within the caldera, the noise that a hive of bees might have made on a summer's day.

Apprehensive, but excited, he began to creep forward,

skirting the side of the cone so that he would not be visible from the col. After about a dozen yards he was out of sight and saw a trail of footsteps rising diagonally across the smooth, dark crust that led to the edge of the crater. This was the route that Smith must have taken. Carefully, Poynter followed the footsteps. The droning noise grew louder. Poynter's eyes were trained upwards and he ducked as a shape loomed into view above him. It was the tip of a vertical mast, a lattice-work of metal supported by diagonal wires like the threads of a spider's web. The mast seemed to be humming as if it was alive.

Poynter continued to climb and saw Smith lying on the rim of the crater a few yards away. He was staring down totally absorbed. Poynter dropped to his knees and crawled towards him, the sulphurous powder brushing against his chest and pricking his nostrils. Smith's narrow shoulders were before him and he eased himself forward and stretched out his hand. At that second, Smith turned and his fist flew back. He recognized Poynter and the two men faced each other, the strange whispering noise in the background.

Poynter eased himself forward and looked down. The depression descended to a depth of a hundred feet and in its centre was a large, single-storey building with wide windows through which could be glimpsed rows of marble boards covered with switches. Two dim lights glowed and Poynter could see men with headphones sitting before the boards. They were white and they were talking in German. Not only could he hear their voices but a disembodied babel of other languages piled on top of each other as if the whole crater was full of gabbling, muttering, whispering spirits convened from every country in the world.

Around the building, nine huge masts rose in the air so that they protruded from the crater like gun barrels. The intricate arrangement of supporting wires that Poynter had glimpsed when approaching the summit of the cone was continued at ground level and there were fresh slabs of marble and giant coils of copper wire to suggest that the work was not completed.

Poynter looked at Smith and the two men's gaze returned to the crater. 'Must be the biggest blooming wireless station in Africa,' murmured Smith.

FIVE

'I'm putting you on a charge,' said Cunningham.

It was the following morning and they were standing on the plateau looking along the route that Poynter and Smith had followed the previous night. Now the mountain range showed itself as successive layers of purple, blue and black gaining in clarity as the soaring sun sucked away the pools of mist.

'You might as well put me on a charge as well,' said Poynter.

Cunningham sighed. 'Dammit. What's got into you fellows?'

Poynter hesitated. 'You're aware that the Germans had a huge wireless station in Togo.'

'Of course I am,' snapped Cunningham. 'At Kamina. They destroyed it before they surrendered.'

'Well, they've built another one here. Even bigger from what I've seen. The old one could communicate direct with Berlin and relay messages to every German ship in the Atlantic. With Kamina destroyed the German fleet was operating in limbo.'

'We'd already cut the German cables in the English Channel,' chipped in Smith. 'I was on the ship that did it.'

'It seems to me we've stumbled on something pretty important here,' continued Poynter. 'This new station is invisible from the plain. You have to be up here to see it.'

'And they don't exactly pipe you aboard,' said Smith.
Cunningham considered. 'Major Liddell will be back.'
Poynter shook his head. 'Not necessarily. Certainly he
won't be encouraged to without the six-pounder. He'll get
word back to Douala and await instructions. He may be told
to pull out, he may be told to leave a detachment here and
report back if the Germans try to break out. But they won't
break out. We think we've got them pinned down whilst
they're secretly doing exactly what we're here to stop them
doing: passing on information that can lose us the war.'

There was a silence whilst Cunningham tugged at his
moustache and looked uneasily towards the tips of the
wireless masts now appearing like the combed antennae of
giant moths. 'I gave my word that we wouldn't try and
escape,' he said.

Poynter stuck doggedly to his self-imposed task. 'We're at
war with Germany. Every day that we sit here doing nothing, the Germans are pumping out messages that could be
sending our men to the bottom of the ocean.'

'They're arming merchant vessels and liners all over the
world,' said Smith. 'Most of our fleet's off Scotland. The
rest's strung out like washing on a line and could be picked
off just as easy.'

Cunningham sighed and looked down towards the plain.
The curve of the mountain hid all but a scattering of the
boulders and beyond them the sand stretched away in a
series of shallow, wind-formed ridges only occasionally pock-
marked by a scrub of spikey vegetation. There was no sign of
human life nor of anything to support it. He rubbed his hand
across his cracked lips as if the sight was already making him
thirsty. 'Dammit!' he said eventually, 'Dammit, young 'un.
You're right. I was a fool. Allowed Max to make me feel that
I was back at Oxford.'

'So what are we going to do?' said Smith. His own eyes
travelled across the desert. 'It must be thirty miles to the
Nigerian border.'

'More like forty,' said Cunningham. 'We'd never cover it

all in one night. Not on foot. We'd fry once the sun came up.'

'There's always the chance we could catch up with Major Liddell,' said Poynter.

'Thin chance,' said Cunningham. 'Needle in the haystack variety.'

There was a long silence and Poynter's gaze drifted down the steep slopes to where bars of shadows turned the re-entrants into long black furrows. Hundreds of feet below something moved and caught his eye. A pony trailing a picket was making its way along a narrow ledge. Behind it followed another, and then another. They moved from shadow into light and then into shadow again. All three must have escaped when the Germans attacked.

A plume of dust arose and the leading horse kicked up its heels and began to gallop. The others followed. The dust drifted across the hillside like the smoke from a locomotive and suddenly stopped. Poynter peered closer. All three horses were together, jostling shoulder to shoulder, their heads bent as if thrust into the ground. They must be drinking. Down there on the mountain side there must be a spring.

Before Poynter could point out what he had seen there was the 'thwack, thwack' of bare feet approaching. The native soldier who had conducted them to their quarters halted before them and slapped the butt of his Mauser in salute.

'*Kommt mit. Hauptmann von Graben,*' he said.

Poynter felt the fear of a small boy with crimson fingers and a pound of stolen strawberries in his belly. He was certain that von Graben had learned of the previous night's exploit.

One glance at von Graben's face was enough to convince him that he was right. His monocle was held in place by a frown and his cold eyes gleamed with anger. He stood in the dark, stone chamber with his hands clasped behind his back and his legs apart. His voice had a cutting edge.

'One of our forward defensive posts saw movement

31

around the edge of the central crater last night. They assumed that it was a patrol from another section and took no action. I have made enquiries and found that none of our men left their posts. An attack from outside is inconceivable so there is only one possible alternative.' He paused and glared into Poynter's bruised face. 'You have been doing some exploring, gentlemen. In direct contravention of our agreement. Is that true?'

There was an embarrassed silence and then Cunningham and Smith spoke at the same time.

'No', said Cunningham.

'Yes,' said Smith.

Von Graben's lip curled. 'I won't strain your powers of invention further. Your privileged prisoner status has been withdrawn. From now on you will remain in your quarters until I grant you leave to move. A guard will have instructions to shoot if you take one step outside. I hope that is clear?' There was silence from the trio and he nodded brusquely to the guard and rapped out an order in German. He had turned his back before they left the room.

SIX

'Dammit,' said Cunningham. 'Why couldn't you keep your mouth shut?'

Smith looked apologetic. 'I thought I ought to take any blame that was going.'

Cunningham ground his teeth. 'Let me remind you once and for all that I am the senior officer present. I am our spokesman with von Graben or anyone else. Is that understood?'

'Yes, sir,' said Smith.

'You no longer have to worry about breaking your word,' said Poynter.

Cunningham digested this remark in a silence broken only by the drone of a lone mosquito. The roof above their heads was covered with its more diffident companions waiting for dark.

'So what are we going to do?' asked Smith.

Cunningham stopped to glance out of the doorway. Their Yaunde guard was polishing the bayonet of his Mauser with a piece of stone. The steel gleamed like silver. Cunningham's eyes began to roam the chamber. Two of the irregular walls were formed by boulders and against one of them a black line showed where the adjoining stones in their crude mortar had shrunk away from the rock as the bond dried. The narrow gap was less than a finger's width. 'I wonder how thick that wall is?'

'We'll need a tool,' said Poynter.

Smith's hand slid beneath his tunic. 'I hung on to a spoon.'

'Good man,' said Cunningham. 'We'll wait till nightfall.'

Poynter remembered what he had seen from the parapet. 'I saw three of our ponies down the mountainside. I think there's a spring. If we can catch them we've got a chance.'

'They could be wild.'

'They were trailing pickets.'

'It's a long shot but we don't have much choice. Right, I say we try and get some sleep.' Cunningham stretched out on his palliasse and put his hands behind his head. 'You're right about this wireless station. It is thundering important. We've got to get word back.'

At six o'clock they were fed a thin mealie stew and marched to the cliff edge to relieve themselves. Behind them three helmeted NCOs were putting thirty native troops through their paces on the flat ground near von Graben's bunker and the sight was impressive. The drill was good and the turn-out impeccable.

Poynter turned away from the slamming rifle butts and found his eye drifting down the steep slopes. He expected to see exposed bones, a few tatters of cloth that had once been a uniform. But there was nothing, no trace of a human presence.

The sun slid behind the horizon and the light faded from the sky with the speed of a lamp wick being turned down. An invading tide of shadows raced across the plain and filled the shallow valleys between the ridges with pools of dark light. A palette of blues and mauves deepened into black and the dying sun appeared as a single candle flame held beneath the lip of the world. Lamps were lit and the faces of sweating men glistened in the artificial light. Still the drill continued and harsh German voices shouted orders that echoed from the crags. A native soldier let his rifle slip from his hands and was punished with three savage cuts of the cane across the back of the thighs. He made no sound.

The man who delivered the strokes was the Korpsgendarm glimpsed outside von Graben's headquarters. He clearly relished his task and his grossly swollen neck bulged out from beneath his helmet as if under pressure. Throughout the drill he bellowed orders and strode up and down the lines of kepied soldiers stinging their faces with his spittle. Poynter heard one of the Unteroffiziers address him as Schutz and was grateful that he had not fallen into his hands during the events of the previous night. The man inspired terror.

Their ablutions finished, they were marched back to their stone cell and a new guard took over. The noise from the drill square continued for another half hour and was superseded by the sound of native voices chanting. Then the singing stopped abruptly as if a curfew had been imposed. In the distance the same dog could be heard barking mournfully. Cunningham positioned himself just inside the doorway and peered out. The guard was sitting against a rock with his knees drawn up against his chest and his rifle and a lamp nearby. He produced something from beneath his tunic and began to chew.

'Right, lads,' breathed Cunningham. 'Let's go to it.'

Smith was already kneeling beside the far wall. He inserted the handle of his spoon into the crack between the

34

stones and the boulder. A black shape flew across the floor of the chamber and he started back as a large, evil-looking spider fled under Cunningham's palliasse and was eventually stamped into oblivion by Poynter.

Responding to the noise, the guard stopped chewing and seized his rifle. He approached the entrance, lantern in hand, to find the trio lying on their beds and the remains of the spider exposed to view.

The guard grunted and went back to his rock. Cunningham waited until he had relaxed and started chewing again before whispering an all clear.

Smith ran his spoon gingerly up and down the crevice with the air of a man passing a naked flame over a stick of gelignite.

'Get on with it!' urged Cunningham.

After an hour's probing, the spoon had broken and blisters had been rubbed from their bleeding hands. Four stones had been removed leaving a hole eighteen inches wide and a foot deep. Poynter slumped back and felt the sweat running down beneath his armpits. The room stank. He made way for Cunningham and crawled to the entrance for the balm of cool night air. The guard sat with his knees drawn up and a blanket around his shoulders and legs. A trail of mist wafted across the rock. There were no stars to be seen. Smith grunted and there was a sudden noise of falling stones and a muffled exclamation from Cunningham. Poynter looked anxiously towards the rear of the chamber and then back towards the guard. The Yaunde's head which had been rocking towards his knees jerked upright.

At the same moment there was the sound of boots ringing out against stone and a glow of approaching light. The guard rose unsteadily to his feet as Korpsgendarm Schutz swaggered into view. Poynter shrank back and scrambled onto his bed, pulling the blanket over his body and wiping the sweat-lathered dust from his face. He could hear Smith and Cunningham struggling to sort themselves out in the background. The air was full of dust.

An angry German voice suggested that Schutz was displeased. There was the sound of a blow being struck and a snort of pain. A lamp filled the entrance to the chamber and Poynter received his first close-up view of the Korpsgendarm. The eyes were small and glacial and buried in swollen flesh that gave the man the appearance of having a perpetual toothache. He had not one small pouting chin but several, layered on top of each other in thick folds that started at his Adam's apple and bulged upwards to a mouth that at first glance seemed to be permanently twisted in an idiot's grin. The left side of his mouth had been obliterated and the lips were represented by horizontal smears of blanched flesh. Pulled tight, the opening had formed a drooping pocket on the right from which ran a permanent dribble of saliva. At this moment it glistened on the swollen cheeks and small bubbles formed like mucus in the folds of the dewlaps. This crazed, lolling mouth might have been ludicrous but beneath the angry, staring, wild boar eyes it took on a chilling nightmare reality like the carving of a hobgoblin.

Poynter saw the eyes stare at him with unconcealed loathing and then quickly transfer their poison to the furthermost recesses of the chamber. Smith sat upright with his back concealing the hole in the wall. His face was smeared with sweat and dirt but his mouth hung open in a yawning rictus and his head toppled towards his shoulder. His eyes were closed and he emitted a guttural snore that sounded as if it could cut through soft wood.

Schutz took in the sight. In this skinny, unwashed specimen he clearly saw the product of an inferior race. With another grunt, he jerked the lamp away and the room was plunged into darkness. He directed a flurry of words at the guard and the creaking leather of his well-waxed pistol belt disappeared into the distance. Cunningham raised himself on one elbow and wiped the sweat from his forehead with his blanket. 'Jolly good, Smith. That was splendid.'

Poynter's eyes were still directed out into the night. The guard was mumbling to himself and pacing to and fro before the entrance. He was in a bad humour but his anger seemed external to the prisoners he was guarding. Schutz's visit might actually have done something to help them.

Shortly before the sun rose to send threads of red and yellow light across the darkened plain, a last stone was extracted and a breath of air fanned Poynter's face. They were through the wall. Pressure on supporting stones showed that they would yield and that, barring a fall of rock, a breach could be made that would be large enough for a man to wriggle through. But not for another fifteen hours. All three were now too exhausted.

The stones were replaced and packed with a loose mortar of earth and pebbles. Dust and rubble were swept beneath the palliasses and the men collapsed on them wearily. When the guard changed and the new sentry peered into the chamber they were still sleeping soundly.

Smith was the first to awake. The heat was intolerable. He felt as if he was being baked alive. The water container was near the door opening and he crawled to it and looked out. Their new guard sat hunched up in the shadow of the nearest boulder throwing stones at lizards. He saw Smith and gestured to him to move back. Smith waved cheerfully and withdrew.

Poynter slept with his mouth slightly open and his sandy hair flopping over his eyes. Even in repose he looked as if he was under strain. His mouth twitched as if he was grappling with a decision. Smith examined the contrast with the calm, patrician features of Cunningham and smiled. Officers amused him. Their posturing and their frailties. Sometimes the two pips on the lieutenant's shoulder seemed to weigh a ton. And Cunningham. Almost more at ease with von Graben than he was with his own men. Rum companions.

Smith drank a small amount of water and returned to sleep.

At nightfall they were fed a meal of stringy plantains and

37

marched to the cliff face. The air was still warm but after the suffocating heat of their prison like a draught of fresh spring water.

Von Graben was watching the evening drill and nodded to Cunningham coldly. Poynter noted the slight tremble that passed across the Englishman's face and wondered if above a certain level of society the frontiers that divided nations ceased to exist. His own father had crumpled up his *Times* at the outbreak of the war and denounced it as an insane folly being fought for no other reason than to swell the pockets of international speculators. Was not the Kaiser Wilhelm II Queen Victoria's grandson? Why were families who attended each other's weddings at each other's throats?

A glance at the brutal, brooding bulk of Korpsgendarm Schutz provided one answer. There was no sense of a shared history here. This dark, satanic force had emerged from the central European swamps with its destiny pre-formed: the expansion and aggrandizement of Germany's global ambitions no matter what the cost. Anything that stood in its path would be crushed and for too long the British flag had tempted and taunted in every corner of the world. Now was the time for the sun to set on it for ever.

Poynter watched the tiny beacon slide beneath the rim of the world and splashed water on his face. Already there were pools of mist forming on the plain. They stole silently towards the mountain like silent avenging ghosts and Poynter saw in the advancing swirls the bodies of his fallen comrades. He turned away hurriedly to see that Schutz had disappeared. The rifle butts still crashed against the rock but one of the Unteroffiziers was shouting orders.

Their ablutions completed they were marched back to their cell. Schutz was standing outside. There was no evidence that he had searched the chamber but his gaze singled out each one of them. Poynter could still see the small, piercing eyes as he entered the encroaching darkness. They hung before him like lantern slide representations of his worst fears.

Smith looked towards the wall. Their work seemed undisturbed. Schutz's footsteps could be heard retreating into the distance.

Cunningham let out a sigh of relief. He spoke softly. 'Right! Let's get on with it.'

'What about Schutz?' asked Poynter.

'Let's hope he's seen enough of us for one day. Anyway, we'll have to risk it. We must cover as much ground as we can while it's still dark. If we can lay our hands on those nags we could be across the border by daybreak.'

'I've never ridden a horse,' said Smith.

'No better time to learn,' said Cunningham. 'With our friend Schutz on your heels it'll turn you into a Derby winner overnight. He's got the right build for it, don't you think, young 'un?'

Poynter tried to inject some enthusiasm into his response. Inside him, the dull, persistent ache had returned.

Cunningham kept watch and Poynter and Smith set to work. Now that he had something to do the lieutenant felt better. The remaining barrier to the far side of the wall was revealed and a hole the size of a man's fist appeared with the night behind it. Slowly and carefully the last large rock was levered free and allowed to topple into space. Smith managed to sneeze loudly to conceal the sound of its fall. There was a clatter and a rattle of stones that to Poynter sounded like a landslide but the guard did not react.

They were ready to move.

SEVEN

Poynter and Smith arranged some of the fallen stones and Cunningham covered them with a blanket to give the impression of a sleeping body sprawled just inside the entrance.

39

The mist was now swirling across the plateau and their guard invisible a dozen yards away.

Cunningham nudged Smith and the little man wriggled through the opening without mishap. Poynter followed and collapsed untidily onto a rock damp with mist. Feeling tense but exhilarated he breathed in fresh air and listened. The only sound came from the distant dog.

Cunningham was the biggest of the three and found it the most difficult to manoeuvre. His shoulders wedged in the hole and he was quickly trapped. Seconds passed. At any moment the guard might take it into his head to peer into the chamber. Smith made a yanking motion and the two men tightened their grip. A vicious tug and Cunningham was free. But a large stone fell noisily.

Poynter helped haul Cunningham to his feet and led the race to the parapet. His foot flew over the side and he leapt into the void. His feet struck shale and he rolled several painful yards to land in a hissing avalanche of stones. Hardly had he picked himself up than Smith tumbled into his arms and there was a shout from above. A native voice began a continuous bellow and Cunningham crashed out of the mist.

'Stick together!' Barely pausing, Cunningham continued down the mountainside precipitating a small landslide, and the mist swirled before their eyes. Smith fell, blundering into Poynter. Cunningham could be heard crashing on ahead. Above them, men were shouting and a light glowed dully through the mist soon joined by another. Poynter disentangled himself and continued slithering and sliding in an attempt to keep up with Cunningham. A machine gun opened up on their left and there was a terrifying yammer of bullets spraying the slopes. Poynter sprinted until the ground disappeared beneath his feet and he tumbled into a narrow gully beside Cunningham.

'Will they come after us?'

'Of course they will. Now that we know about the wireless station they can't let us escape. Where's Smith?'

'Here.' Smith shook himself free of a pile of falling stones.

40

Cunningham peered down the slope. 'Where's your spring, young 'un?' A loud explosion drowned Poynter's reply and the three men huddled together in the bottom of the gully, heads pressed against the earth. A patter of stones from the bomb fell against their shoulders. The machine gun continued to rake the slopes.

'Two hundred yards, three maybe. Over to the left I think.' Another bomb exploded, further away this time, and Cunningham moved forward with shoulders stooped. 'Right,' he said. 'We'll go like blazes. If one is hit the others don't stop. Somebody's got to get through.' He did not wait for a reply but launched himself down the steep descent like a mountain goat. Poynter listened to the unseen machine gun and choked back fear. At least while it was firing nobody would be coming after them. He pulled Smith by the arm and leapt forward.

Ten feet from the end of the gully they dropped from the mist leaving it hanging above their heads like a smooth white ceiling. The moon glowed and by its ghostly light could be seen what lay below. A series of deep ravines and gulleys scoring the side of the mountain like the claw marks of some huge animal. There was no obvious sign of the path the horses had taken nor of the position of the spring. Above them the machine gun had stopped firing.

Poynter scrambled down to where Cunningham was waiting in the mouth of a ravine. He was almost too exhausted to speak. Smith dropped to his knees. Cunningham hissed, 'Keep in the shadow. They'll search the upper slopes before they get down here. Follow me.' He moved forward, seemingly hardly out of breath.

Poynter again hauled Smith to his feet. 'All right?'

'Yes,' said Smith. He sounded unconvinced.

They plunged on down the slope and for the first time encountered a sparse vegetation, thick and stumpy like cabbage stalks. The strange growth brushed against their legs and then gave way to a grove of spikey plants that curved away from the hillside to a height of three feet. The spines

41

scored their bare flesh and ripped through their tunics to inflict more pain. Poynter fell and slid down the steep ravine feeling needle points of fire ravaging his shoulder. He picked himself up and stumbled on at the mercy of the steep descent. One of the gourds of precious water that he had been wearing round his neck had split and was flapping hollowly against his face. When the ground suddenly levelled out, he was thrown to his knees.

Cunningham crouched beside him. 'Catch your breath, young 'un. It should be around here. This vegetation must be sucking moisture from something.' He moved forward to peer over a ridge of rock and returned almost immediately. 'There's some kind of track below or I'm a Dutchman. The ground's all scuffed up between the rocks.'

Once again he was off with barely a glance behind him. A narrow gap showed itself between two rocks and the ground dropped sharply. Poynter followed Cunningham and felt the earth soft beneath his feet. A path followed the contour of the mountainside. Cunningham seized Poynter's arm.

'You were right, young 'un.'

Poynter wiped the sweat from his eyes and saw the dried crusts of horse droppings following the line of the path.

'Now, which way's the spring?'

Poynter said nothing. He had lost all sense of direction. What lay above them was now obscured in mist and darkness. There was no sound and even the barking dog had stopped as if frightened by the volley of shots.

'I don't know.'

'We'll try this way.' Cunningham's verve was undiminished. With one quick glance to see that his followers were still capable of movement he led the way along the mountain, his stride scarcely shorter than when they had set out. On each side large white stones loomed up and the way was narrow.

Poynter followed. What was happening above? Were the Germans climbing down the slope after them or would they stay where they were until daybreak? There was a sudden rattle of movement to his right and his heart jumped before he realized that it was some snake or lizard probably more terrified than himself.

A stone that gaped like a vertical split log loomed before them and beyond the ground levelled and widened to become a small sloping enclosure surrounded by stones that rose to a height of seven feet. Underfoot the surface had been pummelled into a circular track by the pressure of pounding hooves. Poynter saw a dark stain against the rock of the mountainside and heard the unmistakable sound of trickling water. Some subterranean spring had chosen this spot to emerge from its labyrinthine meanderings. Cunningham's hand touched the moist rock and he rubbed it across his lips. He dropped to his knees and splashed water like a playful child.

'By jingo, we've done it! Fill your bellies. I'm going to have a look round.'

He returned after making a quick circle of the rocks. 'I think we're in luck. These rocks are tight as a set of teeth. They make a natural paddock with only one entrance: the one we came in by. When the ponies come to drink we'll let them in and then jump down into the opening. If they're trailing their pickets they should be pretty easy to nail.'

'It would be better if we could block off the opening,' said Poynter.

'Of course it would, but can you see anything to do it with?' Cunningham continued briskly. 'The first stallion through will be the leader. I'll take him. You take the next one, young 'un, and you –'

'I'll take all the rest,' said Smith.

'That's right.' Cunningham clapped him on the shoulder. 'Now we'll get on that big split rock and lie doggo.' He led the way back and helped Poynter and Smith up beside him. 'They may smell us, but I'm relying on the scent of water being more irresistible.'

Smith jerked his head over his shoulder. 'What about them?'

Cunningham's mouth set hard. 'If we don't get the nags we're done for. We'll stay here as long as we can. Sleep if you want to. I'll take first watch.'

Poynter stretched out across the smooth surface of the rock and suppressed a groan. There was no chance of his falling asleep with the pain in his shoulder. He moved his hand and tried to pull out the spines. Time passed and his senses remained keyed up as he waited for the sounds of pursuit down the mountainside. The stinging in his shoulder had subsided to a dull ache. Beside him Smith slept with his cheek flush to the rock and a small pool of spittle dribbling from his mouth. His expression seemed almost serene and there was a suspicion of a snore in the rhythmic cadence of his breathing. Poynter was envious. Even without the ache in his shoulder he would have found it near impossible to sleep. He was too afraid. His joints stiffened, and the cold entered into his body. Would the ponies ever come back? They might have perished in the desert, found another spring or even been captured by natives from one of the local villages. Their vigil seemed more and more pointless, almost a meek capitulation after their precipitous descent of the mountain. Soon, the sun would rise, the mist be snatched away and their recapture made a formality. Korpsgendarm Schutz would already be preparing his welcome.

Cunningham squeezed Smith's ear lobe. The little man twisted and then froze. From somewhere to their left came the sound of falling stones and an abrupt whinny that seemed almost directly beneath him. The lead stallion paused at the approach to the spring. Poynter clenched his fists and willed him to go on. He could hear the other ponies jostling impatiently. Another whinny and the stallion surged forward. They heard the rhythmic sucking of water.

Hardly had the first note met his ears than Cunningham was vaulting down into the gap between the split rock and he was following him. The horses swung round and a grey pony dropped its head as if to charge and then veered away and stretched its forelegs towards the far rocks. The others set off in pursuit as if in a circus ring.

'Hold still, young 'un!' Cunningham braced himself with arms apart and Poynter tried to help him fill the gap. There was a thunder of hooves and a cloud of dust rose in the air. The ponies raced round the natural amphitheatre, the leader occasionally checking his stride as a possible escape route loomed up. Each time they surged towards the opening and then veered away to circle again as the three men held their ground. Poynter saw the pickets dancing at the end of the ropes and the eyes wide with fear. The grey unleashed a piercing whinny and accelerated round the rocks as if picking up speed for a final attempt at escape. Dropping his head he charged towards the human barrier and reared up, feet flailing.

Cunningham launched himself forward amongst the hooves and snatched the picket line. He hurled himself sideways and pulled the maddened stallion with him, hauling in on the rope until his hands were almost against its teeth. Enraged, the grey lashed out with its hind legs and tried to twist free. Cunningham clung on for his life and then, with the skill of an expert horseman, twisted again to spring onto its back and stay there clinging to the mane until the pony had ceased to buck and was under his control, pacing nervously sideways with head held high.

At the capture of their leader the other two mounts abandoned the fight and allowed their lines to be seized without a struggle. Cunningham patted his pony's neck and spoke to it reassuringly before sliding from its back and leading it towards the shallow spring. Its head went down immediately. 'Let them drink their fill and then we'll drink ours and be on our way.'

'That was damn fine,' said Poynter admiringly. He would have said more but there was a clatter of stones from up the mountainside and the sound of an order called softly in German. The mist was breaking and he could see an isolated crag silhouetted against a sky touched with pink. Nearer,

45

much nearer, dark figures were spread out like wraiths, picking their way down the mountain in an untidy line.

Poynter drew back under the shelter of the rocks and plunged his remaining gourd into the water between the thrusting muzzles of two ponies. The noise of their drinking must have been audible fifty yards away. Cunningham's face was tense. He seemed to be counting the seconds before he pulled a pony away and beckoned Smith to mount it. 'Hang on to the mane and grip with your knees. Don't worry about anything else.'

He heaved Smith onto the beast's back like a sack of potatoes. The pony veered away and backed crab-like into the centre of the open space. Almost immediately there was a shout of recognition from up the slope and an isolated rifle shot. Cunningham was on the grey's back in an instant and hunched low as he wrenched the pony's head from the water and kicked its flanks towards the opening.

'Come on, young 'un!'

The words were not hushed but shouted at the top of his voice. A clarion call to action, a challenge to the enemy to do their worst and be damned for it. The grey thundered through the cleft rock and Smith's mount followed it with the little man bouncing like a lone pea in a pod. Poynter hauled himself across his mount and set off in pursuit. Bullets cracked above their heads and the narrow defile suddenly opened up into a hillside scattered with boulders. The sun was coming up and ahead of them lay the desert.

EIGHT

Crack! The lash fell across the Yaunde's back and his body convulsed. He was a brave man but his response to the pain was a reflex action that could not be controlled by pride. He lay spread-eagled on the rock with four of his fellow blacks

46

each pinning down an arm or leg. Crack! Schutz had turned his attention to the buttocks, leaving the back awash with sweat and blood. Each stroke was measured to a millimetre, calculated to lie in the same bed as its predecessor and inflict the maximum amount of pain and healing time. There were few duties that Schutz performed with more attention to detail.

Crack! Von Graben's jaw tightened as another blow bit deeper into the flesh, carving an angry red line spurting like a razor slash. There was repugnance in his gaze, because he suspected that the Korpsgendarm was receiving a vicarious pleasure from performing his duty. The native soldier merited his punishment for his part in the escape of the prisoners but there was no excuse for revelling in it. Maximilian Joseph Rupert von Graben was a proud young man forged in the mould of his illustrious Junker forbears and he did not believe in the infliction of pain for its own sake.

Crack! Another blow fell, this time across the thighs. Schutz's strength did not seem to have abated. At a glance it would have seemed that a cutlass blade had sliced the flesh at shoulder, buttock and thigh. The sight reminded von Graben of the duelling scars more honourably received at Heidelberg. Honourably, but in his view, misguidedly. If your cheeks were scarred it meant that you were clumsy enough to be hit. His cheeks were still smooth and barely lined even by the passage of his twenty-five years. Only around the eye that held his monocle were there horizontal furrows. The monocle he had cultivated at Oxford as a private joke to compensate for his fellow undergraduates' disappointment at his lack of duelling scars and in order to offer them something that satisfied their vision of a young Prussian nobleman. They had thought him a bit of a prig but not a bad fellow and nicknamed him Fritz.

Von Graben tried to remember how many strokes had been administered. It would be foolish to render the man incapable of performing his duties. The position although virtually impregnable was not overmanned and in the pursuit of the escapees he was going to have to further reduce the garrison.

He stepped forward as Schutz's arm rose again. 'That will be all, Korpsgendarm.'

Schutz's head turned and he looked at von Graben like a dog being ordered away from its meal. Then he took a grudging step backwards and saluted. The Yaunde was dragged to his feet by his comrades and half-carried away. Where he had been lying there was a damp patch on the rock which began immediately to dry. Schutz wiped the sweat from his forehead with his finger and flicked his switch through the still air to release the last drops of blood.

'*Danke schön*, Korpsgendarm,' said von Graben. 'Fall in the patrol. We will move out as soon as the horses arrive.'

Schutz clicked his heels and strode away, moving lightly for a man of his bulk. His face appeared even more bloated, as if puffed out by his displeasure.

Von Graben walked to the parapet and looked down towards the foothills and the nearest native village. What appeared to be a line of ants showed him that a string of horses had been rounded up from their grazing and were approaching the nearest mounting point. They would be able to set off within the hour.

His eyes drifted out towards the horizon. There was little hope of survival for the Britishers in the great, flat sandy waste that stretched to the Nigerian border they were surely making for. Their undernourished mounts would wilt under the pitiless sun and they themselves would be hard-pressed to survive for more than a few hours without water or shade. It was hardly worth setting out in pursuit. And yet von Graben knew that he could leave nothing to chance. It was in his nature and it was also to do with the nature of the men who had escaped. The British were never more dangerous than when they appeared to be on the brink of defeat. Von Graben's time at Oxford had shewn him this, and his father who had sent him there had often spoken in respectful terms of the men he was now fighting against.

But most important was the secret that the Englishmen now knew and which must not be allowed to get back to the British forces clinging to the vital port of Douala. They would stop at nothing to destroy the wireless station, and it would be better from all points of view if they never learned of its existence. With the station beaming out vital information to the fast-growing German Atlantic fleet, the war in Europe would be over that much quicker and relations between Germany and England could return to normal; only with Germany now in the ascendant position. The likes of Alistair Cunningham would be making the pilgrimage to Heidelberg.

Von Graben looked out across the glowing desert and frowned. He would prefer to recapture Cunningham rather than find his bleached bones. They were Oxford men who had played polo together. He tried to form a picture of Cunningham as an undergraduate. Bluff, gregarious, possessed of an odd sense of humour like so many Englishmen; a member of the Bullingdon – von Graben still smarted that he had not been invited to join this exclusive club – a man like himself who waited for others to open doors. Why then had he broken his word? There was something demeaning about this particular conflict, battling away with hordes of savages as pawns. It was not gentlemen's warfare. But dammit! – von Graben clenched his fists – all the more reason why gentlemen should honour the code.

'Herr Hauptmann, this message has just arrived.' Von Graben turned to see the pasty face of one of the wireless operators who toiled almost incessantly in the rapidly expanding station. He took the scrap of paper and read it swiftly before looking again towards the Nigerian border. An expression of grim satisfaction settled over his handsome, austere features. Now, Cunningham and he would surely meet again.

49

NINE

Cunningham turned as Poynter's horse faltered, stumbled and began to totter sideways. The lieutenant clung on in a daze and then slid from its back a split second before it crashed to the sand. Its head twisted in one frantic, wild-eyed movement and a tremor ran through its bony flanks. Its rear hooves scrabbled momentarily against the sand and then lay still. The eye turned towards the burning heavens was made of glass. Only a faint stirring along its flanks hinted at the last vestiges of life.

'Poor devil.' Cunningham quickly dropped from his own lathered pony. 'Wish I could put him out of his misery.' He saw the expression of disgust on Poynter's face as the lieutenant turned away. God forbid that the man should crack. He was more of a liability than Smith. What had they said about him in the mess? 'The greenest thing in the desert.' On all sides the undulating sand stretched away into haze. There were no landmarks and no signs of life save for the black dots circling watchfully above their heads and pinpointing their position to any distant observers.

'We'll walk the ponies from here,' said Cunningham firmly. He pushed his mount's makeshift bridle into Poynter's hand.

'How much further?' asked Smith. His solar topi was wedged over his eyes like a button mushroom.

'About two miles less than when you last asked me. You might as well save your breath.' Cunningham slapped his pony on its rump and it jerked Poynter with it. The lieutenant's eyes were still fixed on his own mount as if he was waiting for it to come to life.

50

Cunningham strode ahead. The inside of his mouth was dry as a corn husk. It was painful to swallow and his lips were cracking. He knew how the others must feel but there could be no letting up. Fifty paces from the dead pony and there was a noisy clatter of wings. Cunningham turned his head and told the others to keep moving. The first vulture had arrived. It hopped onto the carcass and began rending the flesh in greedy beakfuls. Within seconds, half a dozen of the hideous birds were jostling and squabbling, engaged in a grisly tug-of-war over the tripes.

Seen from Ndinga Mountain the desert was flat but in reality it rose and fell in a series of shallow ridges formed by the wind. Sometimes there was a sparse stubble of spiky vegetation that promised moisture but this died out as swiftly as it appeared. At the summit of each ridge Cunningham shaded his eyes and scanned the horizon but there was no hint of distant verdure. Only another shallow trench seeming to act as a magnet to the sun.

Poynter could see two suns. They existed inside his mind, glowing dimly through a hot, swirling mist. The sand was getting deeper. Without water they were not going to be able to last much longer. Already the flies were beginning to treat him like a corpse. They did not scatter at the approach of his hand but had to be smeared away in clusters. The remaining gourd that hung around his neck mocked him with its emptiness. He raised it to his lips, willing that there should be one last drop of water but there was not even the vestige of its odour; not even its cool, dark pigmentation to act as a sop to his senses.

Smith saw what Poynter was doing and the sight increased his own pangs of thirst. He brushed against his own mount's slavering jaws and felt the wet foam against his dry skin. Almost involuntarily his hand stole out and transferred the white foam to his mouth. He began to suck his fingers greedily.

Poynter turned and his eyes narrowed. Smith said nothing but continued to wipe the moist curd into his mouth. Poynter staggered backwards. He shook his head and, as if awoken to the realities of survival, raised his hand to his pony's mouth. Slowly he scooped the foam into his own.

On the ridge ahead, Cunningham lay flat as if picked off by a bullet. He turned and beckoned urgently. Poynter thrust his bridle at Smith and stumbled forward, scrambling the last few yards on hands and knees so as to keep below the skyline. Cunningham's face was a sandy mask but his eyes gleamed. 'What do you make of that?'

Poynter raised his head slowly and peered over the ridge. Before them the country became more undulating and sand-hills took on the form of small hillocks with occasional outcrops of red sandstone. In the distance four figures on camels were approaching. A cloaked rider with a turban led the way and he was followed by what appeared to be a man in the garb of a European soldier and two other natives. The three natives had rifles slung over their shoulders. Poynter saw the sun glint from the helmet of the European. 'German scouts,' he said.

Cunningham nodded. 'With a German force behind them. But where's it come from? They must have pushed up from Garoua on this side of the border.'

'Then surely they'll have met up with Major Liddell and the rest of our party.'

Cunningham looked grim. 'That's what I'm afraid of, young 'un. I think we've suffered another mauling. Whatever's happened it's not going to make it any easier for us to get back to Nigeria.' He glanced up at the sun and groaned. 'Even without them we'd be hard pressed to keep going much longer.' He raised his head slowly and Poynter narrowed his eyes and peered over the dune with him. The leading man was just disappearing from sight behind a hillock. One by one the three camels followed him, moving with slow, bobbing grace as if attached at intervals to a halter.

Suddenly Cunningham stood up. 'There's nothing for it. We'll have to attack.'

Poynter looked up at him as if he were mad. 'We haven't got any weapons.'

Cunningham appeared totally unmoved by this argument. 'That's how we'll get some,' he said. 'We'll flog the nags over to the ravine. That's where they'll come out into the open again. We'll scramble up the side and surprise them.'

Poynter stared across the expanse of sand, struck speechless by the audacity of the plan. There was now no sign of the scouting party. 'Stay here and we're dead,' said Cunningham simply, and he started to run back towards the two ponies.

Poynter followed him trying to reassemble his senses. The sudden challenge of danger concentrated the mind wonderfully. At least this was death with some life in it. Better the bullet than the lingering agony of thirst.

Cunningham hauled himself onto Smith's mount, its eyeballs rolling in the last stages of exhaustion. 'Smith rides with me. He can't weigh more than a sparrow.' He tossed the picket line to Poynter and waved impatiently at the little man. 'Come on! They'll be out in the open before we're mounted.' He helped Smith scramble up behind him and the pony valiantly struggled forward over the ridge.

Poynter threw a leg across the pony and immediately sensed that the poor brute was going to collapse. He felt it sway beneath him, its hooves sinking deeper into the sand. Hating himself, he drove his heels against the skinny flanks. Nothing happened. He drove again but harder and the pony shuddered and then started forward. It cleared the ridge and set off in pursuit of Cunningham's mount, emitting a ghastly rasping wheeze that could only be a death rattle. Half way across the open space it stumbled and collapsed on its knees. Poynter pitched forward and hot sand stung his face. He rolled over and pulled himself up to stagger after his two comrades. Their mount had carried them to the foot of a tall dune that flanked one side of an opening in the sandstone. Irregular footsteps of rock broke through the sand like the backbone of some prehistoric animal. Cunningham was beginning to scale the steep side of the dune with Smith following him. Their pony toppled onto its side and lay still.

A black mist hung before Poynter's eyes and a ball of nausea wedged itself in his throat. The dune towered above him and he started to scramble up it, the sand hot as ash against his hands. Somewhere nearby he heard a low bellow like the moo of a cow. He saw Cunningham pause and crouch closer to the dune. He drew nearer hearing a dialect that he did not recognize and a voice that was speaking in what sounded like pidgin German. It seemed as if the men were conferring only a few feet away.

Cunningham looked from Poynter to Smith. Two parched, exhausted men fighting to control their breathing. Did they have it in them. Too damn late to do anything about it if they didn't. He made a pouncing motion with his hands and crawled forward towards the edge of the dune feeling the fire of battle flare up in his veins. This was more like it. Galloping out for the final chukka against Cambridge. Scores level and everything to play for. Scores not level this time. The Hun definitely a few goals ahead. Just have to play all the harder. His eyes moved down from the smooth sandstone wall opposite to the rolled turban of a native scout with a rifle resting against his shoulder. The man sat at ease on his camel as if in a favourite armchair. The beast moved and three more men came into view down the narrow ravine, two blacks and a German NCO who held his helmet in one hand and mopped his face with the other. The German raised his head to put on his helmet and his eyes stared. Cunningham leapt with a shout. Snatching at the cameleer's rifle he brought the man crashing to the ground. He tore the weapon free and swung round as two pistol shots spat past his ears. The German surged past on his long-striding camel and fired again at Poynter and Smith. Cunningham calmly swung up his rifle and dropped the man with a shot between the shoulder blades. The camel continued to gallop into the desert.

'Cunn –!' He ducked with Poynter's shout as a black shadow materialized to his left. There was a flash of steel and a sword blow nearly struck the rifle from his hands. He sprang back and fired from point blank range. The black head jerked and a spurt of crimson gushed from the forehead. The sword dropped and in his loose robes the man collapsed slowly like a tent being struck. Cunningham was turning away before the body had hit the ground.

Another shot rang out and there was a long anguished scream of pain. A panic-stricken camel strode past dragging its rider beneath its hooves. The last cameleer shook off Smith, buffeted Cunningham aside and galloped into the desert. Swinging round in a flurry of sand he disappeared behind a dune. Cunningham cursed and threw himself at the remaining camel. With the stench of its rancid breath in his nostrils he yelled at Poynter and Smith to catch the beast dragging its rider into open desert.

Poynter discarded his rifle and charged in pursuit as the wounded cameleer was shaken free. He leapt over the man and launched himself at the strip of trailing rope. High-stepping legs lashed out and yellow teeth snapped viciously. He lunged again and was able to drag the beast to a halt. A shout made him spin round. The wounded cameleer had dragged himself to Poynter's rifle and was taking aim. Smith dived and the weapon was knocked sideways as it fired. Cunningham leapt at the cameleer and after a brief flurry of movement the black lay as still as his fellow. In their flowing robes they seemed like two exotic birds.

Cunningham handed the bridle to Smith and turned over the German NCO with his boot. The man was dead. Poynter struggled to regain his breath. Three men dead. Two camels, two rifles and a pistol captured. All in the space of a few confused and bloody seconds. He looked at Cunningham with renewed respect.

'Well done,' panted Cunningham. 'Damned nuisance about the one that got away but it can't be helped.' He nodded at Poynter's solar topi. 'You're in luck.'

Poynter removed his headgear and saw what he meant. A bullet had passed clean through, just below the crown.

Smith brought a chuggle of water that he had retrieved from one of the camels. The creature sank to its knees and rested impassively, quite unperturbed by everything that had happened. The second camel followed suit.

The three men squatted and drank sparingly, each savouring the moment.

'Well?' said Poynter.

'We move on,' said Cunningham. 'Fast. The Hun will be back with his tail up as soon as our absent friend sounds the alarm. We can't go forward because they're in front of us. No point in going back either. If I know anything about him, my friend Max will be on our heels by now. That leaves north towards Chad and the French, or south towards the jungle.'

'Chad is closer,' said Poynter.

'So we'll go south. The Bosch will expect us to go north.'

'But we'll never reach Douala through the jungle.'

'We won't try, young 'un. We'll stay close to the border and cross into Nigeria further down. We'll head north for a bit though and try and cover our tracks before heading south.' He looked towards the horizon and frowned. 'It may not be necessary.' In the distance the sky was dark and plumes of brown were stretching out from the lowering mass. A sudden gust of wind sent sand skittering up the ravine and stung Poynter's eyes. He paused with the chuggle half way to his lips. 'A sandstorm?'

Cunningham nodded. 'Could be our friend if it's not too violent. Drink up.'

'What about the ponies?'

'If they're on their feet they come with us. If not, we'll put them out of their misery.' He turned to Smith. 'Collect all the weapons you can find and strip the robes off those men. We're going to need them. I'll see to the horses.'

He took a rifle and strode away around the dune. Poynter listened. One shot. Two shots. The ponies would not be accompanying them.

By the time he was mounted up behind Smith the wind was blowing fiercely and what seemed like a moving sea carried the sand across the desert. The men had garments wrapped about the upper halves of their bodies to protect their faces but the sand still fought a way through. Against sunburnt flesh it stung like a million biting insects. There was a noise like a high-pitched human voice crying out in pain and the sky was black with the sun totally obscured. Poynter looked down at the body of one of the men they had killed. It was now totally buried. Only one hand stretched out with a finger pointing as if in warning.

It was an unhappy omen as Cunningham led the way into the screaming wind.

TEN

'No trace,' repeated von Graben, thoughtfully.

'I had not realized that it was so important,' said Major Herrmann. He was a small, bustling man with a walrus moustache and a habit of stroking the insignia at the neck of his tunic when he was talking. He had fought the British in Togoland before the German surrender and made a much vaunted escape through French Dahomey before rejoining the German contingent in the Kamerun after an arduous sea passage. As a professional soldier who had worked his way up through the ranks, he felt himself alienated from the Junker class to which von Graben belonged. 'Happier in a tailor's shop than on the battlefield,' he used to say to his few confidants. He found the sand-encrusted monocle dangling at von Graben's neck faintly ridiculous.

When he had learned that Liddell's contingent had crossed the border and was heading for Ndinga Mountain, Herrmann left the German stronghold at Garoua and marched north to reinforce von Graben. He had not expected to find the British in disarray and semi-retreat. A surprise attack had killed three British officers and had sent the remnants of Liddell's force streaming for the Nigerian frontier under cover of darkness. Von Graben had come upon Herrmann's victorious force as they pressed on towards the mountain and learned of the ambush of the scouting party. The sandstorm had brought them to a temporary halt and they were now bivouacked for the night. Camp fires burned and the ponies stirred restlessly at their pickets. Only the few camels knelt silent and serene silhouetted like sphinxes against the night sky.

'As soon as the Unteroffizier returned with the news we advanced. But the sandstorm was just starting and it was impossible to make more than a perfunctory sweep. All tracks were obliterated.' He looked at von Graben searchingly. 'I suppose these were the men.'

Von Graben watched Herrmann stroking his insignia of rank as if they were jewels beyond price and was shrewd enough to realize that the analogy was not inapt. These coloured blazons were the symbols of everything that Herrmann had achieved, of everything that gave him status.

He jerked his mind back to the question. 'Three men, one very small. Two dead ponies. It must be . . .' He was about to mention Cunningham's name but checked himself. It was something that he did not wish to discuss with Herrmann. Herrmann was a good soldier but a slogger who had probably never heard of Oxford and would most likely have thought of breweries when the name Heidelberg was mentioned.

'It must have been them,' continued von Graben.

'If the sandstorm has not accounted for them.'

'We survived without undue difficulty.'

'We are equipped to survive. They have no food and I doubt if they have any water left.' He studied the smooth impassive features that gazed down on him with a look of near condescension and turned to stare into the spluttering embers of the thornwood fire. What infuriated him was that von Graben appeared to show no genuine feeling of shame or regret for the escape of his prisoners. The whole affair might have been dictated by the will of some superior deity.

'Nevertheless, we cannot afford to take chances – any more chances. You must find these men or prove beyond doubt that they are dead. If they can get into Nigeria or join up with the French then the secret will be out and you will have even more to answer for.'

Von Graben said nothing and the light from the fire revealed that his expression was still devoid of penitence. Major Herrmann was forced to continue, which he did with an increasing edge to his voice. 'Our first priority must be to defend Ndinga Mountain. The garrison cannot repair the damage that has been done. I will take over command. You will take half a dozen men and continue with your search, avoiding contact with all other enemy units. Is that understood?'

Von Graben nodded slowly. 'Perfectly clear, Major Herrmann. I will take Korpsgendarm Schutz, Unteroffizier Neecher and four Yaundes. If you have no objection.'

'Take whom you wish.' Herrmann's fingers closed about his precious insignia as if he feared that they might have been spirited away. 'Only find those men!'

After the sandstorm, the night was without a breath of wind and the moon shone down from a clear sky. On all sides the desert stretched away like a vast, silver, undulating plain. Von Graben stirred the embers of the fire with his foot and turned his head to north and south as if from somewhere in the great emptiness of Africa a sign would come to show him the whereabouts of Cunningham. Reason told him that the British would either try and break through to the Nigerian border or, more likely, attempt to trek to the French base at Fort Lamy in Chad. But he knew that reason was not always a good guide when dealing with the British. He remembered a paperchase at Oxford when he and an Englishman had been the hares, striding out over the bleak fields with a rime of frost on the ploughed earth and the water frozen in the wheel ruts. It had been the Englishman who had suggested doubling back, laying a false trail and then cutting back through a spinney to confuse the hounds.

'I suppose you'll be heading north,' said Herrmann gruffly.

'South,' said von Graben. He rose gracefully from his folding chair and clicked his heels. 'And now, Major, if you will excuse me I will make my preparations.' He did not wait for a reply but turned on his heel and strode away towards the tidy line of tents. Major Herrmann watched him, lips pursed. He had no great belief that von Graben would find anything, but a spell of roughing it in the desert would do the dashing Captain a power of good. Take the shine off his boots and teach him a little humility. As an extra bonus, he might even lose that infernal monocle.

ELEVEN

Poynter's head slumped forward against Smith's shoulder and he jerked upright and tried to shake himself out of the parched trance which seemed to be slowly draining life away from him. He could feel the camel moving beneath him but it was a motion taking place outside the sensations of his own body. All that really affected him was the terrible throbbing in his head and the blinding yellow light that replaced vision and still wrung water from his stinging eyes.

They had survived the sandstorm by sheltering behind their squatting camels and letting them act as buttresses to the wild winds. After two hours of fury they had been half-buried and their faces masked by a quarter of an inch of sand that penetrated clothing to block eyes, mouths and nostrils. It had been too painful to try and scrape the sand away. They had had to breathe through it as best they could. Then mount up and keep going. Through the night and now through the day, with the sun climbing higher and higher but yet seeming closer and closer in its power to maim and destroy.

Poynter knew that the last dregs of his strength were ebbing fast and with them his will to survive. With dehydration came pains that he had never known before; as if his body was buckling under exposure to intense heat. He ached at knee, elbow and hip. His tongue was a stranger to his mouth. A coarse, wooden bung placed at the entrance to his throat. The two figures before him were propped up on their mounts like straw men. Perhaps they were dead. They did not turn, they did not speak.

The sky wheeled before him and Poynter felt a violent blow in the back. His head ached and coloured lights danced before his tightly shut eyes. When he opened them he recognized Cunningham and Smith peering down at him anxiously, their sandy faces looking as if they were covered in fur. He had fallen from the camel.

When Cunningham spoke, his voice came through cracked, swollen lips and was halting and barely recognizable. 'Come on, young 'un. No faltering now.'

Smith knelt beside him and squeezed his arm as if trying to pump life into him. 'It can't be much further, sir.'

What can't be much further, thought Poynter. Did they know what they were heading for? They might even be in Nigeria now for all the good it was doing them. He allowed himself to be hauled to his feet and felt the familiar tremors of nausea threading through his empty stomach. If only the German bullet had been a couple of inches lower. Anything must be better than this.

With Smith supporting him he looked beyond Cunningham and then shaded his eyes and looked again. It must be a mirage or a trick of his deranged imagination but on the horizon was a patch of green. Quelling his excitement he stared into the distant haze. Yellow sand, blue sky. A primitive paintbox must be mixing colours for him. But yet it was so sharp, so defined. 'Look!' he croaked.

'I'll be damned,' said Cunningham. They both turned to Smith for confirmation.

'Green,' he said.

Now there was hope and with it came the strength to scramble back onto their mounts. The sun climbed but the patch of green came no closer. It seemed to bob away from them on the crest of each succeeding wave of sand. Then there was a definite shape and outline to it and other spills of vegetation showed along the horizon as if overflowing from some giant bowl. Poynter clung to his mount and prayed that this was not some strange refraction, a mirage that would always linger temptingly before them. Then the ground began to rise slowly but perceptibly and they saw the first clouds of the day, thin bars of white high in the sky, floating like doves.

More clouds appeared and there was the fuzzy outline of treetops against the horizon. Amongst them, like a welcoming beacon, something shone bright silver in the sunlight. Poynter screwed up his eyes and tried to read meaning into the static, flashing light. At first he thought it must be a heliograph but as they drew nearer, he saw that it was a building. A building made of metal with a sharp soaring spire that looked as if it could gut the heavens. It was a church, fashioned as if by a precocious child. Poynter looked and wondered as the structure took shape before his eyes. Head swimming and exhausted unto death he felt like Christian at the end of 'Pilgrim's Progress'.

'By God,' rasped Cunningham beside him. 'A mission station.'

The jagged outline of a palm decorated the skyline and a tall fluttery tree hung with lianas like a half-stripped Christmas tree. The camels snorted, stretched out their legs and began to pick up speed. A stunted palm tree gave way to a cluster and then, magically, they were in a grove with shade above their heads and the thwarted sun broken into a

62

thousand shimmering shards. Poynter felt exhaustion over-
whelm him. His hand gripped Smith's shoulder and the little
man did not look back but patted it as if comforting a child.
'We done it! We done it!'

Now the path rose steeply and the camels were almost
galloping. Poynter clung on and glimpsed a native child in a
ragged pair of shorts running ahead and shouting excitedly.
A gleaming expanse of silver loomed up and they were in an
open space near the church with hills in various shades of
green rolling away behind. The country had changed with
the suddenness of a colour division on a map. Before them
was a low bungalow structure with a wide verandah surrounding it and another building thatched with palm fronds
and open at the sides. A number of children sitting on
makeshift benches rose as one and ran to the wooden rail as
the newcomers exploded into their midst.

The camels careered across the open ground and dropped
their heads into a large zinc tank that rested against one of
the walls of the bungalow. Poynter had never realized that
water had such a powerful smell but now it seemed to fill his
nostrils. Half falling from his mount he joined Cunningham
and Smith, shoulder to shoulder, as they drank with no less
relish than the camels. Like a plant that has survived a
drought, Poynter felt his body swelling as the water flowed
through it. He lowered his head and let the sand wash away
from his stinging flesh. What balm, what ecstasy. He drank
until he felt giddy and straightened up. The children had left
what must be their classroom and were watching warily from
the nearest clump of trees. A figure disappeared into the
bungalow and he had an impression of a long muslin dress
brushing against the boards of the verandah; blonde, almost
white, hair pulled back into a bun and an erect, dignified
carriage that seemed older than its years. The girl had been
teaching the children. Was she the missionary's wife?

The figure that appeared in the doorway of the bungalow
suggested otherwise. The man was tall and thin and looked
as if he had wasted away inside his baggy white suit. His hair

63

was thinning and he fumbled in his breast pocket for a pair of pince-nez before advancing to the verandah rail. He wore a cross about his neck and a large Red Cross armband. He seemed in his mid-sixties and had an unusually pallid skin for a man who must have spent most of his life beneath a tropical sun. He did not look well and it was perhaps recurrent bouts of malaria that had pinched the corners of his mouth and sunk his eyes deeper into his long cadaverous face.

Cunningham saluted. 'Good day, sir. We are British soldiers. My apologies for our presumption in helping ourselves to your drinking water before introducing ourselves.'

The missionary turned aside and for a moment Poynter thought that he was deaf. Then he heard a few words of German and a woman emerged from the shadows. She was younger than the man but she shared his unhealthy appearance and her hard eyes glistened unlovingly as she looked down at the three men before her.

'Mulder,' she said. 'Leipzig mission. Little English.' She made a circle with finger and thumb to emphasize the last point.

'We will try not to be an imposition, Frau Mulder,' said Cunningham. 'But we are very hungry. I hope that you will be able to provide us with something to eat.'

Frau Mulder nodded without enthusiasm and spoke to her husband in German. He in turn bowed stiffly from the waist and pulled at his armband so that the Red Cross was unmistakably obvious.

Poynter instinctively disliked the cold, distant couple and distrusted them. The missionary had not turned towards his wife when she had been translating Cunningham's words and she had gabbled them as if going through the motions. Poynter suspected that Pastor Mulder understood English perfectly well.

The meal they were served was an unappetizing stew in which stringy sections of plantain were the staple ingredient accompanied by, in diminishing quantities, beans, peppers and scraps of scrawny chicken. But to the starving men it was ambrosia and even the black bread with the consistency of baked cork was devoured with relish.

Cunningham asked questions about the conduct of the war in that part of the country and the proximity of troops from either side. These Frau Mulder fended off to her husband when she was prepared to admit that she understood them. German troops had passed through the area; how long ago neither of them could remember. They were the first British soldiers seen since the beginning of the war. The border with Nigeria was thought to be fifty miles away, maybe further. The Mulders had never been there but had come up from Douala by the railway that ended at Ndala. After that, they had covered the terrain on horseback with carriers bringing their chattels. The Mulders seemed to have little idea of the route they had taken once they had left the railway. It was not surprising. They were Germans. It was natural that their allegiance should be to the Kaiser.

The lieutenant looked round the dark, gloomy room with its shutters drawn against the sun and its heavy crucifixes and engravings of suffering Christs with crowns of thorns and tears of blood escaping from their closed eyes. What a jolly procession the Mulders must have made, coming from the coast. Plodding through the Stygian rain forests to bring joy and insight to the poor savages of the grasslands. He looked at the black servant who pressed his hands together in a prayer-like gesture each time he addressed master or mistress. His shorts were clean and he wore a spotless white shirt. Had his life taken on a new meaning since the arrival of the missionaries? His inscrutable expression revealed nothing. At least there was some reassurance in his calm. The Mulders were on edge. Their eyes were on the door before a servant had set foot through it. Each noise in the yard commanded some of their attention. When a scrawny fowl stuck its head round the door inquiringly, as if searching for its companion in the stew, Mulder barked at it as if its very presence was an affront.

There was no sign of the girl and Poynter was beginning to believe that he had dreamed her existence. But there could have been no confusing that slim blonde creature with the blunt uncompromising lines of Frau Mulder. She must have existed as she almost ran across the verandah, her knees dimpling the sides of her long, flowing skirt. Presumably she was ill at ease and shy in the presence of the enemy. Perhaps Pastor Mulder had told her to remain in her room.

Cunningham continued to question. How many horses did the Mulders have? The answer was disconcerting: none. They were all dead. Frau Mulder imitated a buzzing noise and made a stinging motion with her forefinger to suggest that some insect had killed them. So the Mulders had no transport? They shook their heads and agreed that this was true.

Cunningham listened politely to the few words that they had to say. Eventually he thanked them for the meal and withdrew with his two companions to a corner of the verandah where they could only be overheard by the boldest of the native boys who still hovered like watchful minnows.

'I think we'll take a turn around the property,' said Cunningham. 'Smith, you'd oblige me if you'd tether those camels and keep a look-out across the desert. I'm expecting company.'

Smith nodded. Poynter had never known Cunningham to treat the little man with so much civility.

As Smith departed, carrying the Mauser that had scarcely strayed further than a foot away from him since it had come into his possession, a handbell rang out. Immediately there was an obedient rush to the thatched schoolroom and Poynter turned eagerly, anticipating another glimpse of the girl. He was disappointed. As one of the older boys wearing a military style cap with a high crown and a small brim replaced the bell on the table, Pastor Mulder emerged from the bungalow and walked stiffly to the classroom looking neither right nor left.

66

'Unlovable cove,' observed Cunningham. 'Not so certain that I care overmuch for his lady wife either.'

'I saw a girl,' said Poynter. 'Tall, blonde hair. A regular Brünnhilde.'

'Sure it wasn't the heat?' said Cunningham. 'I doubt if those two old sticks could strike sparks. Come on, let's take a look around.'

They moved to the side of the mission furthest from the desert and Poynter was again astonished by the speed with which the landscape had changed. Although there were patches of sand in the gentle undulating land that lay ahead, the ground was almost heathlike. The grass had been tinted brown by the sun but its predominant colour was green as it stretched away to the horizon like a series of waves immobilized in a Japanese painting. After the harsh glaring light of the desert there was a soporific restfulness about the scene. But the sun was still hot and the insects still droning through the still air as if it possessed some special quality of heaviness that weighed upon their wings.

Poynter stifled a yawn and glanced back towards the mission. The louvred shutters on the windows were each divided into three sections, the top one of which could open like a hatch. The girl with the flaxen hair was watching him through one of them. She was staring at him with an intensity that Poynter found unsettling, as if he was a specimen under a microscope. The hair that had been held tight behind her head in a bun was now hanging down about her shoulders and she was brushing it with long thoughtful strokes that seemed to gain in power as their eyes met.

What made Poynter turn away hurriedly was not only the uncompromising frankness of her gaze but the fact that he could see her exposed bosom through the louvres. Not in detail – but enough to be certain that what he had imagined was indeed there, touched with bars of shadow and golden light. He blushed, feeling guilty for having inadvertently acted the role of voyeur. Guilty also for the excitement that passed through him at the thought of what he had seen. He knew he would think of it again.

'What do you make of that, young 'un?'

Poynter looked up sharply. Cunningham was nodding towards an expanse of flat ground that stretched away towards a slight rise overlooking the grasslands. An area four hundred yards long and fifty wide had been scrupulously cleared of vegetation. 'Looks like a polo pitch,' said Poynter, glad of the distraction.

Cunningham snorted. 'Don't quite see our friend as being the sporty type. Anyway, he hasn't got any nags, has he.' His eyes narrowed. 'Or has he?'

Poynter followed Cunningham's gaze to a clump of palms beside the cleared ground. The earth was churned up and an oil drum appeared to have been half-buried against one of the palms. Cunningham tapped his newly cut switch against his boots.

In the grove there were picket lines slung between some of the trees, a scattering of corn husks and several piles of horse droppings. Cunningham stirred some of the droppings with his toe, disturbing a cluster of busy dung beetles. 'Mulder was lying. Four or five ponies were picketed here this morning. He must have seen us coming and had them hidden.'

'So he wants to keep us here. Because he knows the Hun will be back.'

'Precisely. They could even be stationed here. That ground they've cleared could be a parade ground.'

'Maybe they haven't hidden the horses. Maybe they're out on patrol.'

Cunningham's face clouded. 'Not a very cheering prospect, young 'un.' He gazed from the grassland to the desert as if looking for signs of an advancing enemy. 'We'll have to be on the move again.' He read the despair that Poynter was trying to hide. 'I know. We need rest. Look, we'll finish looking round, lay a false trail and camp a few miles into the grasslands. With any luck, Mulder will send the Hun in the wrong direction. When we've slept we'll head for the border.'

'Fifty miles,' said Poynter wearily.

Cunningham slapped him on the shoulder. 'Probably a lot less. Mulder would lie to discourage us. If we're right about the Hun coming here I wonder where they bivouac. If I threatened to wring our friend's scrawny neck he'd probably spill the beans but I suppose the damn fellow is only doing what he thinks is his duty.' He smiled. 'Nobody's ever told him that God's an Englishman.'

'There's a hut over there,' said Poynter. He wanted to get away from this place. It was not just a desire for sleep or a fear of the enemy but something about the atmosphere of the mission that made him feel ill at ease. Perhaps it was something to do with the girl. He thought of mentioning her again to Cunningham but decided against it. He could never describe what he had seen or thought he had seen through the shutter. At school, boys had talked about that sort of thing after lights out and made jokes about it but Poynter had always turned his back and pretended that he was asleep. He knew instinctively that there was something very wonderful and mysterious about women and he wanted to protect it for himself. It must be amazing, he had thought, when you get married and see a woman naked – the word shocked yet at the same time excited him when he thought about it – for the first time. A woman that you loved.

The hut the lieutenant had seen was huge and thatched with what looked like stooks of corn laid side by side and bound with plaited lianas. The roof came down to within a few feet of the dusty earth and on either side of the small, low doorway were squat wooden figures with swollen bellies and mouths full of carved teeth that stretched to their ears. There was a smell of stale smoke from the interior. Poynter imagined that the building must be a dwelling place for some of the natives who formed Mulder's congregation.

He was about to stoop and follow Cunningham inside when he saw a man watching him from some nearby trees. He was naked save for a scrap of material round his waist and a piece of sharpened bone penetrated the septum of his nose. His face glowered with hatred and he turned on his heel and loped off towards the mission. Poynter's grip tightened on his rifle and he felt a surge of irrational anger that made him long to put a bullet through the man's back. It must be the place.

Cunningham reappeared. 'Come in here, young 'un, there's something decidedly rum.' He ducked back through the entrance and Poynter followed, expecting darkness. But the inside of the hut was comparatively light. Although there were no windows, a large section of the roof and some of the wall had been removed to make way for a large rectangular object resting beside one of the crudely hewn roof supports.

'A packing case,' said Poynter.

'Or I'm a Dutchman!' said Cunningham. 'I wonder what's in it. I'll wager it's not bibles translated into Baminiki.' He stepped forward. 'Look at this!'

Poynter craned forward and saw that some words had been stencilled on the bottom right hand side of the casing: ETRICH TAUBE. 'German,' said Poynter. He looked up at Cunningham but his comrade's expression showed an excitement far greater than that comparatively simple revelation would have warranted.

'A *Taube*, a *Taube*,' repeated Cunningham as if chanting some magic incantation. 'A Dove!'

As if no more words were necessary, he seized Poynter's rifle and inserted the muzzle at a point where one of the planks was standing proud of the others. A sharp twist of the wrists and the plank sprang back with a snapping noise. Cunningham eagerly started on the next.

Bemused, Poynter squinted into the interior of the packing case at ground level and saw a large wire wheel and a mass of bunched wires.

'She's a flying machine, the most beautiful, the best,' exulted Cunningham. 'I've flown one of them – well, I've been up in one of them.'

'An aeroplane?' said Poynter. He remembered a Frenchman called Blériot flying the English Channel in one of them

70

while he was at school. Everybody had thought that it was a jolly brave thing for a 'Froggy' to do and Poynter's mother had written and told him that Selfridges was decorated in red, white and blue in honour of the achievement. There were some American brothers too, called Wright, who had appeared in the newspapers and broken lots of records. 'Madcap tomfoolery,' Poynter's father had called it, a man who, before its departure, was bitterly resentful that his application for a cabin on the inaugural voyage of the *Titanic* had arrived too late.

'But it's German,' Poynter said, thinking out loud.

'Austrian,' corrected Cunningham. 'Your Austrian is often quite a sound chap. This fellow Etrich has a factory at Wiener-Neustadt south of Vienna. The guv'nor took me there after we'd been rambling round the Tyrol. It used to be the thing out there to have a flying machine. Chaps would invent their own specification and talk it through with Etrich. Rather like talking to your tailor.'

Poynter said nothing but peered unknowingly at the fuselage fairing, forward cockpit and bulky six-cylinder Daimler-Mercedes engine that he could see protruding from the cowling. There was no propeller fitted and he was puzzled by the oil tank fitted above what he now saw was a second cockpit. Sections of wing had been packed against the side of the fuselage, presumably awaiting assembly. There was a bewildering array of wires. The whole thing seemed like the chrysalis of some enormous dragonfly. There was even a glossy, translucent quality to the wings. Poynter looked and wondered. Could this mass of wood and metal be turned into something that could fly through the air?

'What's it doing here?' he asked.

'The Hun probably intends to use her for reconnaissance. Just think, a couple of men could patrol the whole area from here to Ndinga Mountain and down over the grasslands. It must be why they've cleared the ground out there. They intend to use it as a landing field.'

Poynter felt a new stab of fear. 'So they'll be back.'

71

Cunningham borrowed Poynter's bayonet to rip away another section of planking. 'Yes, but now with any luck we won't be here.'

Poynter looked down at the shiny sycamore twist of the propeller wrapped in a protective sheet of the same rubberized cloth that was stretched tightly over the fuselage. 'What?'

The rifle butt thudded against the last section of planking and the whole eight-metre length of the Dove was revealed standing on a low four-wheeled chassis. Cunningham stepped back and beamed with satisfaction. 'Yes, young 'un,' he said cheerfully. 'Now we can fly across the border.'

TWELVE

Cunningham stood before the exposed Dove like a fairground barker trying to enthuse a sceptical audience. 'This is what the Austrians call a *Klapptaube*,' he said. 'They can get it ready for flight within an hour, dismantle it in half the time. Remarkable, eh?' He smiled at Smith, willing him to utter an encouraging response.

Smith's wary expression did not change. 'What about the fuel?' Cunningham frowned.

'Dammit, yes, the fuel.' He glanced round the hut and then towards Poynter.

'There must be some around here somewhere.'

'Some oil would be welcome,' said Smith.

'Perhaps the Germans have gone to fetch it,' said Poynter.

'Perhaps,' Cunningham sounded unconvinced.

Poynter felt Smith's eyes on him and turned away feeling a surge of irrational resentment towards the little man.

'There's nothing in here,' said Cunningham. 'We'll take a look round outside.'

No sooner had they emerged than a strutting Mulder appeared with the native who had seen Poynter entering the hut and three companions.

'I wish to protest most strongly,' he said in excellent English. 'The contents of that building are Imperial German Government property and you have no right to enter it.'

'Allow me to congratulate you on the exceptional progress you have made with our language,' said Cunningham drily. 'However, I would like to point out that a state of war exists between our two countries. I am entitled to requisition anything I wish. If I decide to make use of the flying machine, I will do so.' Mulder fumed. 'And I want to know where the fuel for the aeroplane is stored.'

Mulder's mouth set in a thin tight line. 'There is no fuel,' he said stiffly.

The minute he heard the words Poynter felt a small tinge of hope. The man's whole demeanour was shifty and defensive. If there was no fuel, why was he making such an issue of the flying machine? Poynter looked across to the clump of palms where the ponies had been tethered and another thought occurred to him. The sunken fuel drum that had been used to water the horses. Where had that come from?

Mulder stood his ground. The aeroplane carried no armaments and had nothing to do with the war. Cunningham responded that he seemed very well informed for a man of God. As Poynter listened to the exchange, he found his attention being captured by the native with the bone in his nose. The man was gazing at him with an expression that was frightening in its intensity. But it was not hatred that Poynter saw in the eyes but covetousness. The man was looking at the bayonet that Poynter had been using to open the packing case and which was now tucked in his belt. He wanted it.

Poynter began to wonder how far Mulder's influence over his flock extended. He turned back to the greedy eyes and plucked the bayonet from his belt and held it aloft like a prize. 'Man he go find more big tin for dis place,' he cried pointing dramatically to the fuel drum in the grove. 'I go dash him dis knife.'

The effect of Poynter's carefully cultivated pidgin English was remarkable. The native with the decorated nose took only seconds to assimilate the words and then struck two of his companions on the shoulder and began to gabble feverishly. As Mulder tried in vain to intercede, the three men set off towards the mission at a lope.

'View halloo,' said Cunningham. 'I think you've started a fox, young 'un.'

The expression of rage on Mulder's face was more than adequate confirmation. He stumped off after his charges, the three Englishmen half a pace behind.

At the mission an angry Frau Mulder was vainly attempting to stop the natives removing some of the planks that covered the underside of the verandah. These came away to reveal that the whole structure of the bungalow was raised on stilts and that there was ample storage space beneath. Poynter stooped down and saw that two of the natives were already crawling under the flooring to manoeuvre a large drum from its hiding place. There was enough noise to suggest that it did not lack companions.

Cunningham turned to Mulder. 'You will stay in your quarters until further notice. Please make available all the lamps that you can reasonably spare. Smith, you will supervise the collection of these and bring them to the hangar.' He smiled as he said the last word.

Mulder turned away without a word and went into his house. A fuel drum rolled into the open and the native with the bone bounded forward to collect his reward. From his glance at Poynter's rifle it was clear that he was wondering what service would be required to obtain this prize. His fingers stroked the barrel and Poynter was forced to jerk the weapon away and shake his head vigorously.

'Keep your wits about you, Smith,' said Cunningham firmly. 'I don't trust Mulder, and these gentlemen would

clearly eat their own grandmothers as soon as look at them.'
He turned to Poynter.

'We'll check the fuel and then start assembling the Dove.
Well done, young 'un. That was a splendid inspiration of
yours.'

Poynter blushed and prepared to concentrate his mind on
the intricate welter of wires he had glimpsed. 'Can we really
do that?'

'Absolutely. There's certain to be some instructions in the
cockpit and I've had a pretty good look at one. Just got to
make certain that we get the wing bracing right. Two damn
fine pilots, Eckenbrecher and Prinz, lost their lives last year
when their *Klapptaube* folded up in mid-air. Better not
mention that to Smith, I think he's a bit windy already.'

'I won't,' said Poynter, thinking that Cunningham had
clearly over-estimated his own enthusiasm for the operation.
'But surely the aeroplane's just a two-seater?'

'That is a problem,' mused Cunningham. 'But Smith
weighs next to nothing. As a last resort one of us will have to
stay behind. May be a good thing just in case there is . . .' he
hesitated, '. . . a hitch.'

Poynter said nothing. It seemed to him that nearly all the
illustrations he had seen of aeroplanes in the newspapers had
shown them with their tails in the air and their noses buried
in fields. Perhaps he was tainted by his father's scepticism.

When they arrived at the hut it was with a small crowd of
interested natives at their heels. With their help they pushed
the Dove out onto the edge of the landing field and levered it
off its transporter. The native with the bone had now taken
over the role of unofficial foreman and was directing his
labour force with threatening jabs from his bayonet. The
aeroplane was heavy but two men could just move it. Two
men in better physical condition than Poynter and Cunningham.

Cunningham saw Poynter stagger and patted him on the
shoulder. 'Stick it out, young 'un, with any luck we'll get her
ready soon after nightfall. Then we'll sleep and take off at

75

sunrise. We can't afford to wait here a minute longer than we have to.'

Poynter agreed with the last sentiment. He was exhausted but he knew that in getting the secret of the wireless station back to Douala there would be complete expiation for past sins and omissions.

When stretched out and bolted together, the wings of the Dove had a total span of nearly forty-six feet. What astonished Poynter was their apparent flimsiness. Three wooden spars ran from the fuselage with the foremost ferociously curved at its end and forming the wing leading edge. Wing ribs at eight-inch intervals were made of ash with bamboo being used for the tip ribs. The ribs were constructed of two wooden strips that had been steamed to shape and separated by spacer blocks. Towards the wing tips they stretched far behind the rear spar accentuating the impression of a bird's wing in flight. The whole of the wing was covered in rubberized cloth. To Poynter each wing looked like a huge Chinese fan and seemed scarcely more capable of helping to transport a weight of over one thousand pounds through the air. The addition of the wing-stiffening girder was therefore a reassurance. This piece of metal was bolted to the wheel assembly and stretching out beneath the wing to join it at three points with the aid of vertical mountings. Further support was provided by king posts, vertical posts protruding above and below the wings at approximately four feet from their extremity and attached by wires to another post mounted on the fuselage between the two cockpits. These wires gave additional support to the wings and also allowed them to be used to control the direction the aeroplane should take. Cunningham pulled different wires and showed how they drew the bamboo tip ribs together like the fingers of a hand, causing the covering fabric to lift and pucker into a scallop pattern. 'The wind meets this resistance and up she goes,' explained Cunningham enthusiastically. 'Just like a bird.'

Poynter looked at the graceful form that was now taking

shape. At least he could see why she had been called a Dove.

By the time the wings had taken their final shape, it was as if a giant spider had started to spin a web around them. A profusion of wires led to the rear cockpit where the pilot sat behind a wheel and a set of levers and pulleys. On the instrument panel was a compass, a barograph, a tachometer and a water-temperature gauge. Cunningham installed himself in a wicker chair and checked that all the aileron controls were working and the warping wires tightened to the right tension.

Poynter, watching the tips of the wings rising and falling, like those of a disdainful butterfly, began to feel an excitement buoy him up through his tiredness. Cunningham did seem to know what he was doing. What had appeared enormously complicated, now seemed relatively simple.

To Cunningham the work was a recreation. He was in his element. Frequently referring to the instruction manual, which with Teutonic thoroughness had been placed on the pilot's seat, he moved about the Dove with the composure of a man laying out his toilet things on a hotel dressing-table. 'We've just got to get her into the air,' he said, patting the bomb-like protuberances on the engine. 'That's the only difficult part. Once she's there, she'll stay there. A mechanic at Wiener-Neustadt told me that when the delivery pilots brought a *Taube* in over Cologne, they would climb out of the cockpit and lie on the wing roots of their machines. The craft would fly round the airfield in shallow circles without losing altitude.'

'Better not tell that to Smith.'

Cunningham laughed. 'Righto! Now give me a hand with the rudder and the stabilizer.'

He moved to the rear of the craft and the onlookers stepped back respectfully, encouraged by the officious attentions of their bayonet-wielding foreman. Cunningham had nicknamed him 'Boney'.

A vertical rudder post was mounted at the end of the longerons and attached to a hinged rudder assembly that

77

operated above and below the fuselage and terminated in the metal tail skid. The fan-shaped horizontal stabilizing surface started just behind the forward wing housings and swelled out gracefully exactly like the tail of a dove. Again there was an intricate system of wires that allowed the after edge of the stabilizer to be warped for additional control in flight. 'How on earth are you going to remember which wires to pull?' asked Poynter.

'There're only about four main options,' said Cunningham cheerfully. 'If you choose the wrong one you soon know about it – and have time to correct it,' he added quickly, seeing Poynter's expression.

The work continued. Smith lit lamps and the glistening black faces pressed in about them. At last Cunningham was satisfied that the wings, rudder and stabilizer were assembled correctly and turned his attention to the propeller and engine. Eight foot six inches of polished sycamore was manhandled into position and laboriously secured by heavy bolts. The radiators, fixed flat against the fuselage under both wings, were filled with water and Smith organized the transport of a fuel drum and some oil that he'd found, also hidden away beneath the mission.

Even Cunningham was exhausted by the time the oil and fuel tanks above the pilot's seat were filled. His hands shook as he screwed up the last cap and dropped into his wicker seat. 'Just turn her over and we'll join the excellent Mulder for dinner,' he said.

Smith gawped.

'Turn the engine over. Start it. Find some chocks – a couple of rocks – and wedge them under the wheels. They'll stop the machine from running away once we get it going.'

Cunningham turned his attention to Poynter. 'Now, young 'un. This is where you come into your own.' He reached above his head and switched on the fuel. 'I want you to turn the propeller by hand until you feel some resistance. This will mean that the cylinders in the engine are charged with the right mixture of air and fuel to fire it when I switch on the magneto. Got it?'

'No.'

'Just do it. When you feel a resistance shout "Contact" and I'll switch on the magneto and shout "Contact" back to you. That means that the mixture is waiting for a spark to ignite it and start the propeller spinning. You will supply that spark by pulling down on the propeller as hard as you can in a clockwise direction and moving fast to the left. You don't want to lose your head.'

'Blimey.' Smith gazed up at the propeller. 'I'm glad I can't reach it.'

'I'll hold you up if you like,' said Poynter.

'Let's try it,' said Cunningham.

Poynter waved the natives back and grimly positioned himself beneath the propeller. Smith held a lamp beside him in a mute gesture of solidarity. The flame fluttered and hissed and the glass was almost obscured by a scrambling mass of flying insects.

Poynter gripped the propeller and started to turn it. At the third revolution he felt as if another hand was pulling against him. 'Contact!' he shouted.

Cunningham's hand lifted to the instrument panel. 'Contact!'

Poynter closed his fingers about the tip of the propeller in the twelve o'clock position and wrenched down with all his force. He met a violent resistance that jolted him through to the shoulder blades and the engine made a noise like a horse coughing.

'Again,' said Cunningham. 'Try and get a bit more power into it this time.'

'And don't forget to step sideways.'

Smith's advice was unnecessary. The angry snort from the engine had been an ample reminder to Poynter of the force he was dealing with. He felt as if he was about to pluck a hair from a sleeping giant's head. Once again his hands closed round the smooth blade and he gritted his teeth.

'Now!' He swung down with all his might and suddenly the obstacle was surmounted and the propeller seemed to have taken on a life of its own. As he launched himself sideways the engine roared to life and the natives fled with Boney in the van. Cunningham revved the engine once or twice and then eased back the throttle and switched off the magneto. Silence fell save for the dying revolutions of the propeller chopping the still air and the insects returned to swarm about the lamps. Cunningham raised an arm in salute and switched off the fuel supply. 'Splendid! We fly at dawn.'

THIRTEEN

A floorboard creaked and Poynter awoke with a start. For a confused moment he wondered where he was and then it came to him: a room at the back of the mission. Cunningham had insisted on sleeping in the cockpit of the flying machine. Rhythmic snores from the heavy wooden bedstead at the other side of the room told him that Smith was obeying Cunningham's injunction to get a good night's sleep. Poynter turned over and stared towards the strips of moonlight coming through the shutters. He had always slept badly when he was excited or on edge. Christmas, examinations.

The bars of light made him think about the girl. There had been a glow from the window of her room when they came back from the aeroplane but she had not appeared at dinner. Once again he began to wonder if she was a figment of his imagination. He was so tired, so confused, so keyed up. He tried to think about the events of the evening as a form of counting sheep. Dinner had been a strange meal. Not so much the food, which had been exactly the same as when they arrived at the mission, but the attitude of those sitting round the table. The Mulders had not spoken a word. Frau Mulder had barely done more than pat her dry lips with a folded white napkin. It had been left to Smith to break the silence. When a huge sausage fly had whirled round the room several times and crashed into a lamp, he had spoken one word: '*Klapptaube*'.

Cunningham had laughed and then started to outline his plans to keep the Dove as spoils of war. How he intended to dismantle it once they had got to Nigeria and ship it back to England. 'Just think,' he had said. 'When this whole rotten business is over, I'll be able to invite Max von Graben up for a spin. Least I can do, really. After all, his lot did invent the beauty. Of course, you can come too, young 'un. And you too, Smith. Bring the missus.'

Smith had assured Cunningham that he did not have a 'missus' and that one trip in the blooming flying machine would be more than sufficient for his needs. Cunningham, still exuberant, still buoyed up by the spirit of excitement and adventure had finished by inviting the Mulders to join him in the air as a reward for their hospitality. They had looked at him with undisguised loathing.

Crack! Another timber moved and Poynter sat up. Somebody was stirring in the next room. That was the room the girl had been in. He heard footsteps crossing the floor and the creak of a door opening. She had gone out into the corridor. Poynter thought of going out himself but what could he say to the girl? Apart from the truth, that she exerted a strange fascination over him, that he wanted to be sure that she really did exist.

He rose to his feet and crossed to the shutters. He could see through the louvres and across the verandah and over to the shadowy schoolroom. Suddenly the girl went past the window. She carried a lantern and he glimpsed the hair about her shoulders and the intensity of her expression. There was a look of icy purpose in those wide eyes that touched his soul. Where was she going? She wore a long white robe that must be a nightdress. Was she sleep-walking?

Poynter fumbled for his boots. He would go after her. Perhaps he could save her from coming to harm. He could still see those eyes. So deep, so very deep. Drowning pools.

Outside, the night was still, save for the fluted chirp of a million unseen insects. Stars bunched in the sky like clusters of enormous chandeliers and a swelling crescent moon turned clumps of trees into landscapes of broken shadow.

A will-o'-the-wisp of light was bobbing towards the landing field. He followed it, brushing aside the mosquitoes that buzzed about his face. Clear of the trees, the girl was a white shape against the dark mass of the flying machine. She was moving directly towards it; not walking so much as gliding, with her robe flowing away from her body like the tail of the Dove itself. She must be going to look at it. Perhaps she had been intrigued by what she had glimpsed and heard during the day. It was strange though, her coming out at night. Strange as the expression on her beautiful face. Because her face was beautiful. Noble yet yielding like the faces of the women in Pre-Raphaelite paintings he had spun romantic fantasies about.

The fever mounted inside him. He moved on, a white knight picking his way through a thicket. How was he going to approach her, he spoke no more than a few words of German? But there had been something in her eyes when she had gazed at him through the shutters. He began to embroider a more sentimental version of Cunningham's fantasy at the dinner table. He would speak to her and they would exchange a few shy words whilst they walked back to the mission. He would kiss her and promise to come back after the war. She would squeeze his hand in a token of her love and perhaps even give him some simple keepsake. In the morning he would fly away and the last thing he would see as he looked down would be her waving to him from the window where he had first glimpsed her tantalising nakedness.

All this passed through Poynter's young mind as he looked upon the girl with whom he had not yet exchanged a word.

Now she was circling the aeroplane and Poynter wondered if Cunningham was awake to share his enjoyment of this vision. He hoped not; he wanted to keep it for himself. The girl symbolized the spirit of the Dove. She was as graceful. Seen from behind, with her robe flowing out in the moonlight, she was the sister image of the craft. Now she was stooping, the lamp stationary behind her. Poynter was puzzled. He peered forward and then started to run. The girl was pouring something around the aeroplane and moving towards the fuselage.

Poynter shouted and the girl turned and ran towards the lamp. Poynter smelt the fuel as she swept it up and ducked away from him. She made a pass at the grass trying to ignite it and then ran, bringing back her arm to throw the lamp. She was shouting words that Poynter could not understand, brutal words that did not seem to belong in such a mouth. She sounded as if she were mad.

The girl stumbled and dropped the lamp. It hit the ground and broke, sending out a spray of kerosene. A birthday cake of small flames sprang up across the grass and in the same instant the hem of the girl's nightdress caught alight. She screamed and the flames flared up behind her as she fled in panic. Poynter sprinted and lunged out to tear at the burning cotton. The material came away in handfuls and he ripped the fabric from her body. She turned to face him naked and he glimpsed a matted triangle of hair where her legs met. She was still screaming but the danger from the flames was over. She thrust at him and for a second he thought that she was attacking him. Then, wild-eyed, she locked her arms round him and began to rub her body against his with a furious gyrating motion. Her mouth came up and he tasted her saliva as she tried to kiss him. Disgusted, he thrust her away but she was like a leech still clinging to him and still making the obscene motions with her body. Poynter was terrified, confused and shocked. A dream had exploded in his face. The girl was sick. He knew what she was trying to do and it made a cruel mockery of all his dreams. It offended him more

83

than anything he had so far experienced in the whole of his life.

Cunningham appeared to pull the girl away and she sank to the ground sobbing. A lamp swayed under Poynter's nose and he recognized the deranged features of a night-shirted Mulder. Spittle stung his face as the missionary shouted into it. '*Schweinhund! Schweinhund! Schweinhund!*'

FOURTEEN

Korpsgendarm Schutz was the first to see the mission. Despite his scars there was nothing wrong with his eyes. They were sharper than most men's when it came to aiming a weapon or scanning a patch of distant scrub for signs of the enemy. A drunken stepfather who had thrown boiling water in Schutz's face because the child's crying kept him awake had taught Schutz the advantage of having sharp eyes and quick reactions. Schutz had been six years old when the scalding took place and he had never cried again.

Schutz rode back past Unteroffizier Neecher to where Captain von Graben rode hunched in the saddle with his cavalry officer's cape wrapped tight about his body. The nights were cold in the desert.

'Mulder's mission, Herr Hauptmann,' he said.

Von Graben leaned forward in his saddle and peered into the melting darkness. The first red starburst of the dawn was appearing over the Eastern horizon and he could make out a small silver shape like a tiny reflection of the vanished moon.

'How many kilometres, would you say?'

'Six, maybe seven, Herr Hauptmann.'

'Then we will be there with the dawn.'

'And if Mulder has seen nothing?'

'Then we will wait for the patrol from the south.'

'And if they have seen nothing?'

'Then we will go back and look to the north.'

Schutz nodded emphatically as if to indicate that this was what he would have done in the first place. 'Yes, Herr Hauptmann.'

He spurred his weary mount forward to leave von Graben with his thoughts. These were not particularly flattering to Schutz. He found the man a malodorous brute with ambitions above his station. But he put the fear of God into the natives and would keep going until the boots rotted from his feet. He made an excellent bloodhound. If Cunningham were alive they would surely track him down.

FIFTEEN

'It wasn't your fault,' said Cunningham. 'The poor creature is depraved. Come on, young 'un, you've got to forget it.' As he spoke he was scanning the sky, watching the ragged shafts of red light that appeared in increasing numbers above the darkened horizon, gauging the moment for take-off.

'She's mad, sir,' said Smith more accurately. 'Being cooped up in this place, it's enough to drive anyone barmy.'

Poynter said nothing. Neither of them could understand the real depth of his hurt. It had been like biting into a pure, white peach and finding the stone melting into putrescence in your mouth. Now the poor girl was in her room again, Frau Mulder had taken to her bed and the missionary was spitting out dark threats that he was in no position to implement. There was certainly more than one reason to wish to be away from this place.

'Damn it,' said Cunningham, 'Did you ever know a dawn that took so long to break. Some devil's put a weight on the sun.'

'As long as he hasn't touched the aeroplane,' said Smith.

'You're a cheerful cove, aren't you, Smith? But you're right. We'll have to strip down to the barest essentials. Leave the rifles behind. Hide the ammunition. None of us must be a penny piece heavier than he needs be to appear decent in the King's uniform.'

'What about water?' said Smith.

Cunningham considered. 'We'll take a couple of bottles. With a bit of luck we'll be sitting down to lunch in the mess. What's today, Thursday? Should be curry, don't you think?'

Neither Poynter nor Smith responded. There was a forced edge of heartiness in Cunningham's voice that deceived nobody. In a few minutes they were going to try and take off in an overweight aeroplane that only one of them had the most rudimentary knowledge of how to fly. No matter what any of them said, he was thinking that these might be his last moments on earth.

Cunningham stooped, plucked some stalks of grass and held them aloft before letting them drop. There was a faint lateral movement as they fluttered to the ground. He repeated the movement and frowned. 'I'm not certain where the wind's coming from, what there is of it. Still, we don't want to leave anything to chance. Smith, shin up on the mission roof with a strip of material and do the necessary. We'll start the engine up when you get back.'

The first rays of the sun were playing on the sand-coloured fuselage of the Dove, and Cunningham ran his fingers along one of the dewy wings like a man comforting a favourite horse before mounting her. 'She's a beauty, isn't she?' he said.

Poynter tried to drag his thoughts from the girl. 'Yes.'

Cunningham hauled himself into the cockpit and Poynter heard the creak of his wicker chair. 'Pity we don't have any goggles.'

'At least we'll be flying away from the sun.'

A shot rang out from the direction of the mission and they saw Smith leaping from the roof and running towards them.

'Germans! Coming up from the desert.' They saw him stumble.

Poynter looked beyond him to the palm trees on the slope. There was no sign of the enemy.

'Propeller!' yelled Cunningham. 'Come on!'

Poynter rushed to the propeller and pushed it upright. He turned it twice before he felt resistance and shouted 'Contact!'

'Contact!' The reply came like an echo.

The propeller was wet with dew and his hands slipped the first time he tried to swing it. There was another shot and he glimpsed a man running across open ground near the mission. Smith was fifty yards away. Poynter wiped his hands on his shirt and wrenched the propeller as if he wished to tear it from its mooring. The engine coughed, shuddered, and then died. He wrenched again and sprang sideways as the blade cleaved the air inches from his head. The engine roar was sustained and he ducked under the wings-support girder and collided with a breathless Smith.

'Chocks away!' shouted Cunningham.

There was a rattle of rifle fire, and as Poynter kicked aside the stones he glimpsed a native soldier in a red fez kneeling to take aim from the top of the slope. A bullet tore a strip of fabric from the fuselage near his hand and the Dove lurched forward.

'Get in!' yelled Cunningham. 'Get in!'

Smith threw himself at the rear wing root and dragged himself forward so that he could raise a knee. Poynter started running. The Dove was beginning to bump over the ground, lurching because of Smith's weight. Poynter ran faster, seeing the machine drawing away. Then Smith hauled himself up and flopped into the observer's cockpit and Poynter could launch himself at the wing. Cunningham was directly above him, wrestling with the throttle and trying to pull him up by the scruff of the neck. He clung on and drew himself forward to the centre wing root and extended a hand to the edge of the cockpit. The engine roared in his ears and hot fuel stung his

87

face. If there were still shots, he could no longer hear them. He yearned to stay where he was but he knew that the Dove could never take off. With the roar building and the aeroplane gathering speed, he transferred his weight to the forward edge of Cunningham's cockpit so that he could swing out his legs and wedge in beside Smith.

'Tally-ho!' Cunningham shouted the words at the top of his voice and opened the throttle as far as it would go. The ground was racing past now as fast as he could remember it in his father's Bugatti. Despite the fear there was a stronger sensation: elation.

Cunningham loved speed for its own sake and he loved the beauty of things that could provide it, a horse, a motor car, and now a bird. And it *was* like a bird, this beautiful *Taube*, this Dove. He felt the wings quiver on either side of him and the stick tremble between his fingers. That throbbing bar of steel carried the power to lift them from the earth and turn them into different creatures. Dry-mouthed, he saw Poynter and Smith wedged before him and the grasslands swaying ahead like a great field of corn. The enemy had disappeared, he could not see or hear them. All that mattered was to choose the right moment, to harness the mounting engine roar to the power of the wind rushing against the reflexed wings and stabilizer. The stick was almost a live thing in his hand and he tightened his grip and drew it back towards him. The nose lifted and then dropped again. The pressure had been too tentative and the tyres screeched as they hit the earth. Cunningham took his courage in both hands and drew the stick back smoothly. There was a sensation like that of a yacht's sails catching the wind and, suddenly, magically, they were airborne and the ground was dropping away beneath them. Cunningham let out a great shout of joy and triumph.

By the Mission, Korpsgendarm Schutz squinted down the barrel of his Mauser rifle and gently squeezed the trigger.

SIXTEEN

It was Smith who first saw that Cunningham had been hit. Wedged uncomfortably against Poynter, he was forced to look back towards the pilot's cockpit and he saw the expression on Cunningham's face change from elation to agony as the bullet struck him. The craft's nose dipped alarmingly and for nightmare seconds it seemed that they must crash. Then Cunningham fought the pain, eased back the throttle and held the Dove level, four hundred feet above the swirling grass. Smith was transfixed by fear as the wind rushed past and he watched Cunningham's face contract in agony. 'I can't hold her!' Bitterness, rage and despair transfused his words accompanied by a terrible sadness. The aeroplane lived but he was dying. 'She's floating, dammit. She's floating!'

Poynter was beginning to breathe normally when he heard the shouts. He turned and tried to rise. Then he stopped himself. There was nothing he could do. No act of God was going to cast him in the role of a man who could extricate himself from one cockpit of a flying aeroplane and scramble into another; master the controls and fly the machine. Cunningham was the only man who could save them. If he could stay alive long enough. As Poynter watched in horror a spurt of blood flew from Cunningham's mouth and became a crimson wash against his cheek. A bullet must have penetrated his back and entered one of his lungs.

'Got to go down,' gritted Cunningham. 'Got to go down.' He was talking to himself, giving himself orders. 'Sorry, old girl. Nothing to do with you.'

The mission had now disappeared and the desert could only be seen as a distant band of yellow, fast mixing with the sky. It was impossible to know how fast they were going except that it was too fast. As the bracing wires hummed in the wind and the noise of the Daimler-Mercedes engine became a mere background noise, Poynter and Smith waited for Cunningham to keel forward over the controls and the machine to fall out of the sky and smash them to pieces.

But Cunningham clung on. His face was still racked with pain but there was tenacity in his eyes. He jerked his body sideways and tried to peer down through the gaps between the wing roots. 'What lies ahead? First bit of open ground you can see. Don't trust the grass, it could be covering an elephant.'

Poynter peered forward and screwed up his eyes against the wind. He found it easier to see if he squinted through his fingers.

A mile or so ahead the grassland gave way to what looked like a sandy plain punctuated with trees and sparse vegetation. Beyond that was a darker patch of green that swamped the horizon. This could be the beginning of the great rain forests that rolled down to the mangrove swamps and the sea. The nearest stretch of flat ground lay straight ahead, perhaps a little over a mile away. Poynter shouted the information to Cunningham.

Cunningham gripped the stick tightly and eased it forward. The movement was too jerky and the Dove bucked as if trying to shake him out of the cockpit. 'Sorry, old girl,' he gritted, 'Getting a bit clumsy.' He fought the pain that was pinching him like a crab and tried to repeat the manoeuvre more smoothly. This time the nose seemed to sink rather than drop and the horizon floated up like a blind. Cunningham cut back the throttle and then hastily let it out again. There were a series of violent oscillations as if the aeroplane had been racked by a spasm of coughing. Cunningham thought that his lungs were going to explode with the pain. Bracing himself, he struggled to keep the engine speed up and the stick moving forward, knowing that he could not afford to drop the revolutions too low before they were almost ready to

90

land. Now he could see over Poynter, Smith and the engine cylinders to what lay ahead. Like an admonishing finger, a strip of level, sandy ground lay directly ahead with some trees to the left of it. He must not let the trees affect his judgement. Nothing must affect his judgement. Damn this sawing, pinching, tearing crab that had got inside his body. Hold her steady, hold her steady! The land loomed up, closer, closer. The trees were nearer than he had thought. Don't look at the trees, don't think about the trees. Just a few hundred feet. Dammit! There were stones there. Not too fast. God, the pain! Pull her back a bit. Come on, my wondrous Dove. Cut the throttle. Pray.

The tail skid struck sparks from the ground, the wire wheels jolted down and the Dove skittered over the stony ground and came to a jolting halt a hundred yards from where it had first touched earth.

Cunningham was dead.

SEVENTEEN

'Animals,' said Mulder vehemently. 'Filthy animals!'

Von Graben nodded. At Frau Mulder's instigation he had glanced round the door of the girl's room. She had been lying on her back on a bed with a large wooden cross held tightly against her bosom. There had been a ghastly pallor to her face and she had been staring at the ceiling with wide open eyes. She might have been in a coma.

'Were they all involved in this attack?' asked von Graben.

'The lieutenant was the instigator,' said Mulder slowly.

Von Graben tried to form a picture of the man. Slight build, sandy hair, an awkward, boney countenance that gave the impression of being permanently ill at ease. Not a formidable opponent, nor, at face value, an obvious rapist. 'Surely, the Captain –' he began.

'He interceded,' said Mulder grudgingly.

Von Graben felt relieved. He even felt sympathy for Cunningham. In war one could not always choose the men one served with. It was strange that a man capable of such an act could achieve the rank of lieutenant in the British Army. He looked across the green sea. Perhaps they were all dead. The *Taube* had started to lose height dramatically after its hurried take-off and it was probable that it had come down only a kilometre or two into the grasslands. This was something he intended to find out, and soon. Ndinga Mountain could remain in the crabbed but capable hands of Major Herrmann. He would take whatever means necessary to preserve its secret.

But before he moved on there was another matter to attend to. Four men trembled on the precarious rail that surrounded the schoolroom. Their hands were tied behind their backs and lengths of rope stretched from their necks to one of the tie beams just below the thatched roof.

'You are sure that these are the men who revealed the whereabouts of the fuel?'

'Not only that. They helped the Engländer move it to the flying machine.' Mulder shook his head bitterly. 'It was a terrible betrayal after I had raised them up from their pitiful state and given them positions of trust.' He sensed that von Graben might be about to weaken. 'If they are allowed to remain alive their poison will spread through my whole flock.'

Von Graben said nothing. He found the whining pastor repugnant but the four men were clearly guilty of aiding the enemy. And there was no time to be lost. He nodded to Schutz and the Korpsgendarm walked behind the row of gibbering men and thrust them into kicking death with the point of a bayonet retrieved from the man with the bone through his nose. The whole structure shook and a cloud of dust, thatch and insects showered down on the jiggling bodies.

Von Graben turned away but Schutz and Mulder remained to watch with the men and the wailing women and children of the mission who had been specially assembled for the occasion. There was the outline of a white figure behind one set of louvred shutters and van Graben realized with distaste that the missionaries' daughter had put aside her cross and risen from her bed to watch.

EIGHTEEN

Poynter pulled his head away from the forward edge of the cockpit hardly able to believe that the motion had stopped and that they were still alive. He felt the sun beating down on the top of his head and heard the buzzing of flies. He opened his eyes. Beside him, Smith surfaced like a wary mole thrusting its nose above ground. They both turned.

Only the top of Cunningham's fair head was visible as he slumped forward with his chest against the wheel. Poynter struggled free from the cockpit to claw his way back. Blood spattered the fuselage and one side of Cunningham's fair moustache was soaked in crimson. His eyes were closed, not tightly, but like those of a man who is resting after hard labour. Already his skin was taking on the ghastly pallor of waxed fruit. In his young life, Poynter had seen enough dead men to know what they looked like. He dropped to the ground and his hands encircled his body, hugging in the pain and despair. Cunningham was gone. The event itself was terrible and it left him feeling totally exposed and vulnerable.

Smith edged along the wing roots until he could reach the fuel tank and locate the tap that turned it off. Carefully but firmly he pushed Cunningham's body back from the controls and examined the panel. The instruments made little sense to him apart from the compass, but there was a switch near a light that glowed and he judged it right to depress this. The light went out.

He looked down and saw Poynter. His first thought was that the lieutenant was injured and then he recognized the tremor passing through the head and shoulders. He scrambled down and stood in silence for a few moments before resting a hand on Poynter's arm. The lieutenant rose to his feet immediately and took a step away from the aeroplane.

'Right. We'll bury Captain Cunningham. Then we'll start walking.'

'We can't bury him,' said Smith patiently. 'The ground's hard as iron and we haven't got a shovel.'

'We'll cover him with stones.' Poynter cleared his throat. 'Come on. Let's get on with it.'

Painstakingly they clambered onto the Dove and dragged Cunningham's body from the cockpit. They manhandled him to a narrow fissure in the baked earth and went in search of stones. Already the heat was unbearable. As night drained away so the oven door opened. It had seemed less hot at the mission because there was some strange cooling agent in the presence of a human habitation. To pass under man-made shade gave the impression that there was always a retreat, a bolthole. Here there was nothing save the reminder that Africa was every inch the kingdom of the sun.

Cunningham's body disappeared until only his feet protruded and then they too were covered. The flies disappeared between the gaps in the stones.

Poynter wiped his forehead. 'I suppose we'd better burn her.' He lowered his voice as if the Dove might overhear him.

'We could start her,' said Smith.

'But we can't fly her, man. We'd never get off the ground. Look at those stones. It was a miracle we got down in one piece.'

'We don't have to fly her. We can run her along the ground. At least until the fuel runs out or the going gets too rough. It's better than walking.'

Poynter looked about him. The ground was stony but flat and although there were rock formations and clumps of stumpy trees they were isolated and could be avoided.

'I used to work in a metal shop in Kennington,' continued Smith. 'That's in south London,' he added as if he thought that Poynter might never have heard of it. 'One of the guv'nors had a motor car and we did some work on it. I'm not saying I could drive one but I understand the basics.'

'Why didn't you say so before?'

'Nobody asked. Captain Cunningham had everything in hand.'

'Yes.' Poynter turned away from the pile of stones.

'What we'd have to do is turn on the fuel and then the magneto,' said Smith firmly. 'The magneto makes the electricity that sparks the engine when you turn the propeller. I'm afraid you'd have to turn the propeller, sir. I wouldn't be able to reach it without standing on a wooden box.'

Poynter managed to grin. 'All right, Smith. Let's try it. But don't let her rip. I'm not up to another chase at the moment.'

The engine was still hot and started on the first pull as if the Dove too was anxious to be on the move again. The propeller whirled and a shimmering circle of light made the landscape seen through it look as if it was melting in the heat. Poynter ducked aside swiftly as the engine roared to life but Smith, almost invisible in the cockpit, held the craft in check until Poynter was in front of him in the observer's seat. He jerked his thumb in the air and they were off.

Smith bit his lip and nursed the throttle. The Dove ambled forward more like a farmyard duck than a graceful bird of flight. The wings shuddered and the warping wires rattled. Slowly at first but then with a slight increase in speed she bumped over the stones whilst the needles on the tachometer and compass quivered. As the distance grew and the pile of stones that marked Cunningham's grave disappeared into the haze, Smith began to feel more at ease. He had command of the engine and he could try and come to terms with some of the other controls. Keeping the engine revs low he pulled back the stick slightly and looked behind him. The warping wires to the stabilizer tightened and its aft end lifted into the air. When he pushed the stick forward the warping wires below the stabilizer came into action and the tail dipped gracefully.

Poynter looked back and saw what was happening. 'North,' he shouted.

Smith nodded. The wobbling compass needle showed that they were travelling west and he knew that the Dove had not changed direction since their take-off. Cunningham had been concentrating on getting her into the air and keeping her there. The additional complications of turning left or right could be left until later.

Smith looked along the trembling wings to the king posts and the sets of wires attached to the daintily reflexed wing tips. Obviously, raising or depressing these would effect the upwards or downwards motion of the plane when used in conjunction with the stabilizer. But supposing only *one* rear wing was warped? This would presumably have the effect of an oar stuck into the water. The craft would start to come round. There was also the polished wood-rimmed wheel with the chain like that of a bicycle descending to the floor. Careful experiment showed that by turning the wheel the warping wires that controlled the wing tips were brought into play and that the two pedals at foot level controlled the movement of the rudder to right or left. It was complicated but not unfathomable. Smith felt he could master it. He increased speed slightly and with astute use of the controls had the satisfaction of finding the Dove making a wide turn towards where he prayed Nigeria must lie.

'Jolly good,' shouted Poynter. He too was beginning to feel better.

After a spell of jolting progress, relief gave way to frustration. A steep ravine running towards the west barred their progress. It was not deep or wide but the Dove could not clear it without flying. They decided to follow the ravine and hope that it petered out. But the ravine did not peter out. It widened slightly and then debouched into a dried-up river bed whose steep sides were miniature cliffs. They stopped to stretch their legs and Poynter eased his pith helmet away from his sticky head and fanned himself vigorously. The country on the far side of the giant furrow did not invite walking. They could die there before nightfall.

'We'd better follow the line of the river,' he said. 'At least we can put some distance between ourselves and the Hun before the fuel runs out.'

Smith rose from beneath the fuselage. His face was grim. 'I'm worried about the wheels,' he said.

Poynter cursed. He had felt the shaking and rattling getting more and more pronounced as the rock-strewn ground took its toll. Any vehicle would have been hard pressed to remain unscathed in such conditions. He stooped beneath the fuselage and saw that the bedstead framework of the struts that held the sprung axle and wheels was beginning to buckle and the bolts at the joints were working loose. He ducked into the open and looked south. There was little change in the parched, brown landscape as it shimmered away into the haze. At some season of the year torrential rains must fall and sweep down towards the rain forests and the distant coast, but now there was no hint of water save where the smooth sand of the dry river bed had spawned a clump of spike grass and a few stunted, leafless shrubs.

Poynter followed the course of the sunken river bed. The smooth pathway of sand would form an ideal route for the Dove. If they could get down to it. He called to Smith.

It was not long before they found what they were looking for. A cliff fall had created a steep ramp of rocks and baked earth leading to the river bed. Like a giant flying ant with broken wings the Dove tilted over the edge and slithered down in a cloud of choking dust. The bracing girders scraped against the rocks and one of the petrol cans broke free and cartwheeled down the slope narrowly missing a boulder. Poynter waited for the impact, the spark and the explosion and closed his eyes. When he opened them the Dove's lower wing was pressed against the sand and the can lay a few yards away as if it had been washed up on a tropical beach.

With sweat running down their grimy faces they man-handled the Dove away from the subsidence and set off again. One mile, two miles. Slow laborious progress. Then the Dove started to wobble and within minutes there was the sound of snapping metal and she lurched to one side. Smith switched off the engine and they climbed down to examine the damage. One of the support struts had broken free from its mooring and caused a wheel to fold.

Poynter felt a great weight pressing down on his chest. 'We'll wait until dusk,' he said. 'Then we'll burn her and start walking.'

NINETEEN

Von Graben urged his mount forward and turned to see if Schutz was keeping pace with him. His feet scuffing the earth on either side of his sagging pony the Korpsgendarm was a load rather than a rider. His scarred face gleaming with sweat gave the impression of wax beginning to melt.

Von Graben frowned. The mount was not going to last much longer. None of them were.

There was a shout from a dried-up river bed on his right and he cantered forward to find Neecher and one of the Yaundes with an old man carrying a long spear. Around his neck was a garland of feathers and in one skeletal hand a small bush fowl with fresh blood dripping from its beak. In all respects he was like any other Baminiki hunter save for the scrap of clothing that swamped his narrow shoulders. It was the torn and bloody remnants of a British officer's shirt with three brass pips on each epaulette.

Von Graben leaned forward. 'Ask him where he got that shirt.'

The Yaunde spoke haltingly in a language that was strange to the old man and his face screwed up as he tried to understand. Eventually the story emerged. He had found the shirt on a blackened corpse that had been savaged by jackals. It was not far away. He could show them the place.

Von Graben reached out and the old man shook as the hand fell upon his collar. He had heard stories of the Germans. Von Graben twisted his head to read what was written on the slim, silk name-tape. "A. S. G. de P. Cunningham" in flowing italics.

Von Graben turned away feeling sadness and anger. Cunningham had been a reminder of happier, more civilized days. A man from his own background. Stalking each other across Africa they had been knights on a board littered with lesser pieces. Now the piquancy of the chase was gone. He was left with men inferior to himself, men like Schutz and the two Englishmen who had attempted to violate a missionary's daughter.

He thought of the body being abandoned to the ravages of birds of prey and wild animals and felt a new surge of anger. When he caught up with the two Englishmen they could expect no mercy. With Cunningham dead the rules of the game had changed.

His hand strayed to his chest and found his monocle. Suddenly it seemed a focus for his present discontent. It was a frivolous sop to poses that were no longer worth mocking. He snapped the cord that bound it to his neck and hurled it into the bush.

Schutz gazed at von Graben and wondered at the gesture. The hunter was still talking, saying that one of his tribe had seen a great wounded bird dragging itself across the plain. It must be the *Taube*.

Schutz waited for the fire to flare up in von Graben's eyes but again he was surprised. Von Graben merely nodded briskly and leaned forward in his saddle. 'We will find Captain Cunningham's remains and bury them,' he said.

Schutz waited for a further explanation but the Oxford man seemed to think that none was necessary.

TWENTY

Poynter sat under the shade of the Dove's wings, the sweat dripping from his forehead. They had drunk nearly all their water and the all too familiar pangs of thirst were beginning to rack his body. He thought of Cunningham's reference to a curry lunch in the mess and how easily it might have been a reality. No damn good dwelling on that.

He looked back along the river bed. The wobbling wheel tracks were clearly marked in the sand. Pursuit would be easy once anybody came across them. There was a clatter of movement and a vulture swooped down, touched the earth with its claws and then took off again. It had come to see if they were still alive.

Poynter shook himself fully awake and joined Smith as he knelt beside the wheel assembly. 'I think I could bind this up,' said the little man. 'Provisional like of course. We could use one of the wires on the wings. We've got a lot more than we need at the moment.'

Poynter was not impressed. 'How are we going to lift her so that one of us can tie the wire?' He placed his shoulder beneath one of the wing support girders and strained upwards. The steel bar cut into his flesh and after a few seconds he was forced to drop it.

Smith came to his side and together they manoeuvred the wing structure to a height six feet from the ground. Poynter braced himself under the wing support structure. Smith struggled to hold it above his shoulder. When he relinquished his hold, Poynter wavered, buckled, cursed and the wing came crashing down again with the lower king post burying itself in the sand.

'What a blooming nuisance,' said Smith. 'And I'm a genius at knots too.'

'Your nautical training of course,' said Poynter. He looked around trying to think of a way of solving the problem. Three feet from the collapsed wheel a boulder rose from the sand. Poynter looked at it and an idea began to form in his mind. He thought of experiments he had done at school. What he needed were some pieces of wood.

At first their proximity seemed as likely as that of a magic spring but he realized where he was: in a dried-up river bed which had once carried a mighty flood down from distant mountains. All manner of vegetation would have been carried with the torrent and amongst it surely some pieces of timber.

Ahead, the river's course had carried it to the right and the bend was sharp with a large boulder standing like a sentinel on the left. Poynter moved out into the blazing sun and almost at once found what he was looking for. Foliage had been trapped in an eddy against the boulder and remained there stranded as the waters fell. Two crippled branches bleached white as bones showed amongst the flotsam. Poynter pulled them clear of the debris. A large mottled lizard reared up, head arched, and then stamped away furiously, its tail curved forward over its body. Poynter examined his prizes with increasing disappointment. The wood was gnarled and tough, almost petrified in appearance, but neither piece was longer than four feet. There was no question of using them to prop up the wing as they were. He scouted the area of the boulder and looked ahead up the gully but, apart from the occasional large stone or stunted plant, there was nothing breaking the surface of the smooth sand.

His eyes screwed up against the glare and he returned to the Dove. Smith was crouched under the fuselage staring at the wheel assembly. He brightened when he saw the pieces of wood. 'What are we going to do? Tie them together to make a prop?'

'We want something that gives us more manoeuvrability,' said Poynter. 'Give me your knife.'

One piece of wood had a small V at the end of it where the branch had forked and Poynter cut an indentation in the other end like the notch behind the flight of an arrow. With Smith's help he lifted the wing and placed the notch beneath the wing-support girder so that the tilted aeroplane was resting on it. The other end of the branch rested in the sand near the stone. As Smith watched, intrigued, he used the knife to dig a hole on the far side of the stone and scooped out the sand and dirt. He rose, wiped the sweat from his forehead, rubbed his stinging eyes and rested the second branch on the stone so that its end extended down to fit in the inverted V of the branch that was supporting the wing. Smith understood what he was trying to do and the two men pressed down on the branch positioned against the stone. The straining wood settled into the slot and as more pressure was brought to bear, the prop and the wing it was supporting were levered into the air. Poynter pushed down with all his weight and held his breath. As the two pieces of wood trembled the prop started to slip. 'Stop!'

They lowered the prop to the ground and Poynter cut a slight indentation in the end of the lever so that it would serve as a buffer and prevent the prop slipping back when the lever was lifted above the horizontal. When he was satisfied, they moved the prop slightly and then repositioned the lever against the stone. More carefully applied pressure and the prop rose until the rear of the lever was resting in the hole that Poynter had dug.

'All right. Leave her to me.' Crouched low, Poynter took the weight and Smith set to with the warping wire. The strut that had worked itself loose was almost level with the wheel assembly and it was a simple matter for Poynter to adjust its position by raising or lowering the level as directed by Smith.

Smith spluttered and swore, chose one technique and then changed his mind and experimented with another. Poynter looked down into the hole and wondered if he was going to fill it with his sweat. At Smith's third attempt he began to get exasperated.

'I thought you were an expert in knots,' he gasped.

'That's the trouble,' said Smith. 'I know so many it's difficult to choose one.' His cackle of laughter sent a prying vulture scrabbling into the air and he continued to work unruffled. Poynter continued to sweat. His arms were ready to pop out of their sockets when Smith expressed himself as being satisfied. Thankfully, Poynter slowly relaxed the pressure and the support pole toppled to the sand. There was a strained squeaking noise from the wire and the wheel remained upright with only a slight deviation from the vertical.

'Well done.' Poynter straightened up and massaged his aching shoulders. He felt relieved but exhilarated.

'Well done yourself,' said Smith. 'That was a good idea.'

Poynter smiled. For the first time in their relationship he had done something to win Smith's admiration.

'We'll start her up,' he said. 'There'll be nothing but steam in the radiators if we stay here much longer.'

He primed the cylinders and the engine started on the first swing, sending a rasping, throat-clearing roar reverberating down the gully. Particles of sand danced in the haze and the Dove twitched and started to trundle forward. Poynter watched the wheel anxiously. It was scuffing one of its mountings but turning steadily. As long as they remained on the sandy river bed it should hold. The big problem now must be fuel. The Dove's thirst was far greater when she was running on the ground than when she was drifting gracefully through the air. Cunningham had gambled on their reaching the Nigerian border if they kept the craft's weight to the minimum so there had been no thought of carrying extra fuel. Soon the tank would be empty and they would have to wait for nightfall and start walking.

Poynter gazed back down the gully and his heart jumped. Four hundred yards away, seven figures on horseback emerged from the glare. They rode in line abreast and for a brief moment he thought that they were figments of his imagination. Then he heard the jingle of harness and cries of discovery and pursuit. Snatches of guttural German and the *'Hwei! Hwei! Hwei!'* of the Yaunde horsemen. They were coming for them out of the sun.

Poynter shouted at Smith and kicked up sand as he raced towards the Dove. He threw himself onto the wing and felt the structure sag beneath him as he scrambled into the forward cockpit. Already the Dove was picking up speed and the engine note rising to a screaming crescendo. For a moment Poynter thought that Smith was trying to take off, but then the Dove weaved sideways to avoid a boulder and the banshee wail faltered and changed key. Poynter clung to the sides of the cockpit and waited for the Dove to tip forward onto her nose and hurl him to the ground and break his neck. He looked behind and saw Smith hunched in his cockpit and the Germans seemed about three hundred yards away. They were keeping pace with the aeroplane but not gaining. If only he had a rifle, or a machine gun, he could have scattered them like ninepins. The engine choked and nearly stalled. Were they running out of fuel? He peered past the throbbing cylinders and through the swirling whirlpool of the propeller. The gully was widening, its sides falling away. There was open sun-baked ground with a litter of small stones and then Poynter blinked. The ground ahead appeared to come to an abrupt end. As if they were approaching the edge of a cliff – a waterfall. Hardly had the terrifying truth occurred to him than he glimpsed the baked furrows left by the separating waters and the glittering stone field that marked the edge of the abyss. The Dove shuddered and shook as if about to come apart and then hurled herself into the void.

TWENTY ONE

There are nightmares in which a man can hang in space and see the ground far beneath him. He knows he is going to be smashed to pieces against it and his heart lurches. The realization is there like a knife forced upwards beneath his rib cage. But he does not drop immediately. He hovers on wings borrowed from panic, explores the details of the emptiness about him and then, choking on fear, he begins to sink. This was how it was for Smith in the first seconds after they had shot into space. The engine screaming, the wind rushing round his head, tearing at his topi and threatening to strangle him with the chin strap. The ground far below them glimpsed as a great swathe of green, so different from the dusty plain that it added to the terrifying unexpectedness of what was happening.

Then there was a strange dreamlike time of repose when he sensed that the Dove was not going to fall out of the sky, that she was actually happy to have re-found her true environment and that her wing tips were braced against the heavens like the extended fingers of a dancer. The Dove was taking control, gently telling him that she could lie on the air, placid as a lily leaf on a pond. All he had to do was have faith. Cut back the failing engine and let her find her own wings.

But when he had done this and found that the sky was still above them and the ground below, the fear returned. They could not stay planing on the buoyant currents for ever. Already the massive face of the escarpment was hundreds of yards behind them and the lip of the parched waterfall above. They were descending and he was not in control. The Dove could not land herself, not in the great rain forest stretching away like the coat of some huge, shaggy animal. He pressed down with his right foot and the rudder began to bring them round in a wide circle. No point in looking down and inviting further panic. The engine faltered and he adjusted the throttle. The spluttering noise continued and the propeller was no longer a glimmering circle against the sky. Fighting to stay calm, he pulled the throttle out as far as it would go. The starved engine coughed as if sabotaged by an explosive charge and then cut out.

Their fuel was exhausted.

Smith sat transfixed, listening to the twang of the warping wires and the wind rushing past his head. The cliff loomed up before him and he could see clumps of vegetation clinging to the scarred brown rock. He kept his foot down on the pedal and instinctively turned the wheel to the right. The wing tip was plucked up like an aileron and the Dove banked gracefully and increased her angle of turn. Smith saw Poynter turning anxiously and raised his hand in an attempt at reassurance. Another cliff appeared and Smith looked about him uneasily. The jungle had vanished. He was surrounded by high cliffs littered with creepers and vegetation. Somehow he had become trapped in a series of deep valleys each one giving into the other. He must try and gain altitude. He pulled back the stick and the Dove's nose lifted slightly. A rising current of air bore them upwards for a dozen feet and then soughed away. The summit of the cliff was still above them shutting out the sun. Then Smith knew that without power the Dove was never going to escape by climbing above the valleys. He had to find a way through them or end up by crashing into one of the cliffs. With her forty-six foot wing span the Dove turned gracefully but laboriously. Without the use of her ninety horsepower engine there was no possibility of her being able to turn through a hundred and eighty degrees in the narrow valleys. It was difficult enough to manoeuvre through the gaps that separated one from the other. Provided that there were gaps. Sooner or later there was just going to be a wall of stone.

Smith pulled on the stick again and changed his pressure to the left rudder pedal. He must keep the Dove as far from the walls as possible. A snag of creeper swung out towards them like a pennant and flicked against a wing tip. The brutal vertical face loomed as if about to topple over on them. Then the Dove veered away and cruised on the still air.

Smith's eyes narrowed as he squinted ahead. With the dark towering cliffs and the shadows, it was not easy to see whether this valley led into another. He glanced behind him and saw to his horror that they seemed totally surrounded by cliffs. It was like a wasp trap he had once seen. One chamber led into another until suddenly there was no way out. Below, in shadow, the ground was stony and broken by small hillocks of rock. There was no chance of bringing the Dove down safely.

Comfort came from the Dove herself. She seemed unperturbed as she glided through air more suited to the passage of eagles. Smith watched the end of the valley approaching. There seemed no way out. Like a returning nightmare the mountainside rose sheer until it fragmented in the rays of the sun far above his head. He pulled on the stick but the Dove shuddered and a tremor ran through the wings as if to tell him that without power or wind he was asking the impossible.

Near the end of the valley a dark buttress of rock loomed, and beyond it a strange yellow light gleamed as if coming from a torch that had been shone downwards. Dry-mouthed, Smith peered into the gloom knowing that he had to make a life or death decision within seconds. The Dove would need time to turn and he would have to gamble on finding a gap. If there was no opening their course could not be changed again and the Dove would pile into the cliff-face. Smith hesitated and then pressed down the pedal. He felt the wire tighten and heard the wind smack against the rudder assembly as it changed direction and the Dove began to make a wide turn that took her to the very edge of the valley before she swung round. An expanse of green and brown swam

107

before Smith's eyes and then the cliff was behind him and he was desperately peering across the valley.

At first there seemed to be no gap in the wall of stone. Then, as the Dove swung through her arc, he saw that there was an opening with blue sky beyond. But it was narrow. Narrow as a gap in a row of clenched teeth. It seemed impossible that the wingspan of the Dove could pass through without striking the sides. Poynter saw where they were aiming and turned again, his face white. This time there was no wave of reassurance from Smith.

Smith eased his foot off the pedal to keep the turn wide and was relieved to find that the distance between the two pinnacles expanded slightly. At its widest point it might be forty feet. The wingspan of the Dove was over forty-six feet. His heart pounded but the craft that carried his body lay soft on the air. The personality of the Dove seemed to flow into his own. He remembered the banking motion that he had induced when first approaching the cliff face. If he reproduced this and tilted the Dove then there might be a chance. He turned the wheel and the panorama before him lurched as one wing rose and the other dropped. Quickly he corrected the movement. When he banked, the Dove's turn became tighter and more precipitous. He must try and hold his course in level flight and then bank at the last minute. The cliff loomed up ahead and he began to talk to the Dove as Cunningham had done. 'Come on, my beauty. Come on, come on. Hold her there . . . steady.'

The Dove replied by a rustle of the wings. The bows of bamboo and ash flexed and the cloth between measured itself against the challenge of the wind. Where the still air of the hidden valley met the currents rushing in between the peaks there was turbulence and the Dove lifted and shook. Smith could feel the temperature of the air change against his face and felt powerless as the Dove fought her own private battle for survival. Then the shuddering stopped and he was still on course with the rudder responding to the pressure on the pedal and the wheel firm between his hands.

108

The peaks came nearer, one side in shadow, one in sun. Steep-faced rocks grooved vertically. They were coming up so fast. Great stone axe heads poised to fall and smash the flimsy Dove from the sky. Smith glimpsed walls of brown rock and turned the wheel further than he had ever dared turn it before. The Dove tilted and for an instant he thought he was going to be tipped into space. He slid against the side of the cockpit. A wall of cliff filled his vision and he shut his eyes. Then, miraculously there was a confident ripple from the wings as if the Dove was inviting him to look about him.

Smith peered through half-opened eyes and saw a great expanse of blue. He corrected the wheel and the Dove levelled out and floated majestically with the escarpment behind her and the gap through which she had passed barely visible.

Poynter turned and shouted, laughing, almost hysterical with relief. 'You're a genius, Smith. A downright thundering genius!'

Smith said nothing. He was still barely able to believe that he was alive. He pushed the stick forward and the craft obediently began to descend as the stabilizer warping wires tightened beneath the tail assembly.

A dark shape hurtled from the sky behind Smith's head. He raised a hand to protect himself and felt something sharp tear at his flesh. An eagle, larger than any bird he had ever seen, had taken exception to the intruder in its kingdom. As Smith struck out in desperation the great wings buckled and buffeted as the hooked beak and talons lunged for his face. He felt the Dove's nose dropping dangerously and pulled the stick back as he fended off his attacker. The eagle broke off its challenge, made one more threatening sortie and then swept upwards as if honour had been satisfied. Soon it was one of two specks circling far above them near the twin peaks.

Smith controlled his breathing and looked for somewhere to land. Seen from the air, the forest did not stop abruptly when it came to the escarpment but petered out in patches of grassland surrounding isolated islands of jungle like a yellow sea. It might be possible to bring the Dove down here but it would depend upon the height of the grass. Cunningham had said that it could be tall enough to hide an elephant. He strained his eyes ahead and saw what at first he thought were wisps of low cloud. Then he realized what he was looking at. Smoke. And coming from more than one place.

They passed over an isolated hut near some cultivated ground and a track running like a parting through the grass. They were approaching civilization. More huts and buildings with corrugated iron roofs that flashed messages came up to them. Several had blackened walls and one was burning brightly with flames coming out of the windows.

Poynter looked down to see people running for shelter as the shadow passed over them. His stomach tensed. Had the British and German forces clashed here? Supposing the Germans had been the victors? If the Dove set down in one piece, they would be taken prisoner. But there was no alternative. It would be suicide to try and glide over the jungle.

The smoke was now at the level of the wing tips and a patch of ground opened up ahead. Smith glimpsed a railway line stretching away into the jungle and dense black smoke billowing up from a building with a tin roof the size of a tennis court. He caught his breath as some trees loomed up beneath them and pulled the stick back so that the Dove hopped in the air before continuing her gentle descent. Like a field of burnt stubble, the ground opened up before them and Smith pressed down with both feet to hold the rudder steady. The black earth rushed up and before he could brace himself the wheels jarred and there was the noise of the stricken props collapsing as the warping wire tore free. The Dove lurched to one side and almost immediately settled and skidded across the smoking earth with the wheel assembly disintegrating beneath her. Smith clung to the cockpit and waited for the impact.

The headlong pace slowly slackened and the Dove slewed to a halt. Spirals of smoke drifted up about them as if they had landed on the floor of Hades. The air was full of particles of black ash. Poynter sat silently waiting, unable to believe that they were actually alive. Then he raised his head. 'God bless you, Fräulein,' he said quietly.

TWENTY TWO

Poynter climbed down from the wing. Around them the grass fire had burnt itself out but there were still clouds of sparks and tiny dancing flames eager to ignite the touch papers of creeper that dangled from the nearest trees. It was hot but with a different kind of heat to that of the desert. Here it was clammy with a sweet, sickly smell of rotting vegetation. The air was heavy. Even standing still the sweat began to trickle down from his armpits.

He looked towards the plume of thick black smoke and the smoke trails of other fires. Their arrival must have been seen from the ground but there was no rush to greet them. Any observing eyes were remaining hidden. The natives would surely not have seen an aeroplane before and the arrival of a great bird-like monster from the sky would inspire terror rather than excitement.

Poynter puzzled over where they might be. He had seen maps of the country but could not remember them in detail. The journey to Ndinga Mountain had been made via the Niger and the Benue rivers and he had not been to Douala since his arrival in West Africa. But he knew that a railway ran inland from Douala and had glimpsed a track as they came in to land. If this was the main railway and not a branch line, then their route to the South and the British lines might be assured. It would no longer be necessary to try and trek through the dense rain forests to the Nigerian border. They could change direction and head south along the railway line. He knew that this part of the country was a 'no man's land' and control of the railway line of vital strategic importance to both sides. Either would prefer to see it destroyed rather than fall into the other's hands. Poynter wondered if this could have happened here. After the battle, the victors had burnt the installations and pursued the enemy into the jungle.

He gazed back to Smith who was squatting to examine the tangled mass of metal that was the remains of the bedstead landing gear. 'Poor old love,' he said in genuine regret. 'She's a gonner now and no mistake.'

'We'll strike a medal for her when we get home,' said Poynter forcing himself to sound cheerful. 'She may have been made in Austria but her soul was English.'

'She had a soul all of her own,' said Smith. He straightened up and turned away. 'What now?'

'You saw the railway line when we came down. If I'm right it ends up in Douala. It's our pathway through the jungle. Maybe we'll find a train going south, maybe we'll have to walk.'

Smith took a last regretful look at the Dove and shook his head. 'Shanks's pony,' he said resignedly.

Poynter tried to get his bearings. Seen from the air the railhead and the surrounding township had seemed to straggle over a wide area. Now there was no trace of a building and the jungle closed in about them, the smoke from the grassland mingling with the strange wisps of mist that clung eerily to the tops of the closely packed trees. There appeared to be a path leading back towards the railhead. He wiped the sweat from his eyebrows and started to trudge over the blackened earth.

Poynter had disliked the forest on his way up the coast and as the huge trees closed in above his head all his old uneasiness returned. This was only a thicket by comparison with what he knew lay between them and Douala but already the sky was blotted out and the sun reduced to dusty shafts of light that broke through the thick foliage like lance thrusts. There was a perpetual, unnatural gloom. The sharp piercing cry of unseen birds, the rasping of cicadas. Always the ear was waiting for the snapping of a twig, the sound that would announce danger. In that strange green light the huge buttress roots of the trees broke the ground like writhing sea monsters and there was hardly a trunk that was not encircled by a serpent of creeper struggling to reach the sun and survival. Other slim shoots rose directly upwards for a hundred feet as if performing a version of the Indian rope trick and the thick spongy earth threw up a myriad fresh, green saplings waiting their chance to shake free of the leaf mould and soar towards the sun. How ironic. A few minutes before they had been soaring above this dark chaos. Now they were picking their way through its roots like insects.

'Hope we find some water soon,' said Smith. 'Think we can eat these?' He gestured towards a starburst of succulent green leaves.

'Hang on until we get to the village,' said Poynter. He remembered a carrier on the way up from the coast who had nearly died after chewing a similar plant.

'Didn't see a river –' Smith broke off and the two men looked at each other. An unmistakable tinkling sound cut across the drone of the insects.

The stream was shallow and meandered amongst the tree roots. The water was clear and in places the bottom sandy. The musical note they had heard was caused by the stream-let dropping over a small waterfall. Poynter dropped to his knees and drank greedily before splashing water over his face. When he looked up Smith was already naked except for his boots and losing no time in removing these. He waded into the shallow water and sat down with his back against the waterfall so that it cascaded over his skinny shoulders. '*Oh, I do like to be beside the seaside* –!' He sang lustily and grinned up at the lieutenant. 'Come on in, sir. The water's fine.'

Feeling slightly self-conscious, Poynter stripped off his clothes and obeyed. The sensation of well-being was ecstatic. As if the water was entering his parched body through his pores. He luxuriated and watched Smith splashing water against his sprouting beard. His fingers rose to his own chin.

'Hardly a whisker,' observed Smith.

'You look like Rip Van Winkle,' said Poynter. 'I ought to put you on a charge.'

'Matelot's privilege,' said Smith chirpily. 'I could grow a beard down to my waist if I wanted to.'

'And practise your knots on it.' Poynter stood up. 'Time we were moving.'

Smith kicked at the water. 'Shame we can't sail down this to Douala.'

In the forest there was one permanent source of visual relief amongst the gloom. Butterflies. As he buttoned his shirt, Poynter watched a cloud of them, small and bright blue, dancing like confetti above the sap that oozed from a snapped trunk. Twisting and turning, jostling in the air, their wings quivering, they settled for a few instants before shooting up as if on a jet of water. The sight reminded him of the Common Blues he had seen on the hills at home and with it came a rush of memories: childhood rambles, picnics, his mother and father. He turned away from the butterflies, almost wishing he had never seen them.

The path wound on and, looking ahead, he could see where the sunlight was breaking through in a diffusion of gold and the trees coming to an end. A fallen tree lay across the track ahead and hovering beyond it was another cloud of butterflies, this time white. Even smaller and more numerous than the blues, they soared upwards and then fell, spiralling downwards like tiny aeroplanes out of control. They were beautiful with the sunlight glowing behind them and Poynter approached the trunk to see what they were feeding on.

A dead German soldier sprawled on his chest with his rifle a few inches away from his extended arm and a patch of sodden scarlet in the middle of his back. This scarlet was ringed by a circle of butterflies so that they seemed like a moving wreath. A column of ants disappeared into the man's sleeve. He had not been dead long because his flesh was not swollen and only the corners of his eyes were flyblown.

The face that Poynter could see pressed against the leaf mould seemed scarcely older than his own. He gazed down at the blond hair protruding from the helmet and for a nightmarish moment felt that he was looking at himself.

Smith dropped to his knees and quickly relieved the dead German of his rifle and ammunition pouches. 'Shall I keep this?' he said.

'Yes, yes. Yes, keep it.'

Poynter hurried along the track. He must concentrate on what lay ahead. If the young German had been shot fleeing into the jungle then perhaps the British had been victorious.

The sunlight hit him like a blow and he shaded his eyes. Before him there was a field of cassava and some date palms. There was a rustle of movement to the left and he turned to see two men peering at him round the great red earth bulwark of a termite mound. They were smaller than the men of the grasslands and ducked away as Smith appeared carrying the rifle, the curiosity on their faces replaced by fear.

Poynter started across the field towards the smoke. The sun had disappeared behind a bank of clouds but the heat was still unbearable. A rivulet of sweat ran down his body and his shirt clung uncomfortably. Ahead was a fence of pickets interwoven with palm fronds and beyond it a clump of bamboo. With Smith at his heels Poynter forced his way through the fence and penetrated the bamboo.

The black smoke was pouring from the gutted remains of what once must have been an engine shed. The corrugated iron sides were buckled and twisted like wood shavings and a stubby locomotive blazed like a blackened tea kettle. Some trucks and a tender were also burning, but less fiercely, and a column of sparks and cinders swarmed in the air. They looked on the scene with sinking heart. The engine was burning. Neither side would ever use it and its blackened remains would rest here until the jungle vines encircled it and cane rats chased each other round the inside of its rusty boiler.

Poynter moved uneasily towards the first of the sheds. After the discovery of the dead German he had expected to come into contact with soldiers of one side or the other. But save for a skinny cur that slunk between two huts with something in its mouth, there was nothing. Only the stench of human excrement and a thin pall of smoke that drifted from an untended fire. No companions of the two men glimpsed by the termite mound. Either the aeroplane had terrified them into flight or they already had sufficient cause to remain hidden at the approach of strangers.

The huts were of a prefabricated design and must have been brought up by train from the coast. Poynter tried the door of one and his hand came away sticky with oil. As he looked about him he saw that oil had been splashed over the wooden slatted walls and that a trail of it led away to the next hut. Somebody had intended to burn not only the engine but all the buildings in the area. He pushed open the door and found himself in a storeroom that must house parts for the blazing locomotive. There were piston rods, crankpins, wheels and even a spare boiler and welding equipment, piles of tin boxes and trays of nuts and bolts. Whoever had tried to burn down the building must have left in a hurry. It was another cause for unease.

'Look at this.' Smith was calling from the doorway of a nearby hut. The word 'Sir' seemed to be disappearing from his vocabulary. Poynter was untroubled. Smith was peering through the doorway into the dark interior that reeked of fuel. 'It's a wireless set. One of ours. I think it's all right.'

Poynter pushed forward eagerly. If he could make contact with Douala – or, more realistically, some British unit in the jungle – then the secret of Ndinga Mountain could be relayed to the coast and their mission would be accomplished. There would be no need to continue the journey. They could join up with the first Allied unit they met. He screwed up his nostrils against the smell of fuel. It was indeed a British set.

He recognized the bulky casing mounted on blocks with the leads still attached to batteries. Poynter held his breath and depressed a switch. Thank God! The machine was working. He gazed at it for a few seconds, unable to believe their good fortune.

'Yes, seems all right.' Poynter hesitated before picking up the speaker. 'I just hope they've been operating on the same frequency as we were.' He depressed the button and tried to speak calmly and clearly. 'Hello, any station. Please acknowledge. Over.' He relaxed the pressure and waited agonizing seconds listening to the unbroken crackle of the static.

Smith looked from him to the set and back again. 'Perhaps they only come up on the hour.'

Poynter looked at his watch. 'Another ten minutes. Have a scout around and see what you can see. I'll keep on trying to make contact.'

'I'd like to see Newington Butts on a Sunday,' said Smith wistfully. 'Just before opening time.'

He went out clutching his rifle and Poynter returned to the set. It was too dark to see the dials closely so he threw the door wide open and seized upon a candlestick and matches that lay upon a crude wooden table. Shielding the flame against the draught he lit the candle at the second attempt and made a note of the wavelength. Now he could experiment with other settings. He did so but only once was there a broken pattern of human speech, so distant as to make even the nationality of the speaker indistinguishable. Carefully, he reset the original wavelength and looked at his watch. There were two minutes to the hour and it was quite likely that the British army signallers would only turn on their sets for a few minutes at every hour in order to conserve battery life.

Poynter waited another minute and repeated his message. Again there was no reply. His hopes began to fade. Not only was he unable to raise another station, there was no sound of anyone else on the air. Perhaps it was something to do with the presence of the escarpment or the thickness of the jungle.

Possibly the wireless had been brought up by rail before anybody discovered this. He repeated his message once more. 'Hello, any station. If you receive me, please report signal strength and position. Over.'

To his amazement and jubilation there was a dip in the static almost immediately and a voice spoke clearly. 'Receive you medium strength. Our position Bassi. Report your position. Over.'

Poynter nearly shouted in triumph. Bassi was on the way to Douala and might even be in wireless contact with it. 'Fetch Sunray,' he almost bellowed into the speaker. 'Have message of utmost importance – repeat – utmost importance. Over.'

'Wilco.' The signaller seemed unperturbed but his signal was clear. He was going to fetch his commanding officer.

Poynter listened to the static and saw that his hand was trembling. Only a few seconds more and a mission that had seemed increasingly doomed to failure would be crowned with unexpected and certain success. Poynter drew closer to the receiver as if the few inches gained brought him nearer to the voice he wished so desperately to hear.

Seconds passed and he began to regret not having blurted out his message immediately. The static soared and crackled in his ears as if a great fire was raging through the forests that separated him from Bassi. He heard something behind him and started to turn. At the same instant there was a dip in the static and a voice spoke out weaker than before but discernible above the crackle of atmospherics. 'Bassi to unknown station, Sunray speaking. Over.'

Exultant, Poynter spun round expecting to find Smith behind him. What he saw was the silver glint of a Luger pistol pointing at his heart. A figure stood in the doorway gripping the weapon. Instinctively Poynter dived to one side knocking the candle over. A shot crashed out.

'Blast it!' said a female voice with a slight Irish accent. And then: 'Don't move. *Nicht* move. Do you speak English?'

Relief and anger swelled up inside Poynter. 'Of course I

speak English!' he shouted. 'I *am* English! What the devil do you think you're doing!'

Poynter had never raised his voice to a woman in his whole life. Now he felt that he could cheerfully have strangled the newcomer wearing the uniform of a British nursing sister.

'I didn't mean to shoot you,' she said without undue remorse. 'The pistol went off.'

Poynter did not reply but launched himself at the wireless set and snatched up the receiver. To his horror there was no sound. He glanced to see that the battery leads were still connected and felt urgently for the wavelength control. His finger tips met rough metal. The bullet from the Luger had shattered the calibrated dial and buried itself in the set. Poynter bellowed in anguish and exasperation.

'What's the matter?' said the woman.

'I had a life and death message to pass to Douala,' said Poynter, trying to keep his voice under control.

'I'm sorry,' said the Sister. 'I thought one of the Germans had come back. My name's Regan O'Donnell by the way.'

Poynter was no more used to young women introducing themselves than he was to them taking pot shots at him, and as she moved towards the door he studied the newcomer with wary interest. Her hair was a deep copper colour that was almost red and was held down by her nursing bonnet only with difficulty. She was tall, as tall as he, and her features were proud and angular. She had high, pronounced cheek-bones, deep-set eyes the colour of cornflowers and a mouth that was sensual, almost over-generous. Her jaw line was firm and lent her an aggressive air reinforced by her athletic, Junoesque body with prominent breasts and long legs that her bodice and skirt could not conceal. The whiteness of her face was relieved by a dusting of freckles around her nostrils that gave her an appealing tomboy quality. Poynter saw that he was looking into a face of no little beauty and considerable character.

'Lieutenant Poynter,' he said. And then, after a pause, 'John Poynter.'

To his surprise, Regan held out a hand and he found himself shaking it. She handed him the pistol. 'Thank God I missed you. I'd be a fool to be making more work for myself.'

'What happened here?' asked Poynter.

'Everything, and too much of it,' said Regan taking off her bonnet so that her lustrous hair fell in coils about her shoulders. 'I don't know if you know where you are, but this is Ndala. The Germans held it and then the British. That's when I came up on the railway. Then the Germans counter-attacked and held the town for a while. That's when they set fire to the locomotive. They were going to destroy everything but the British regrouped in the jungle and Captain Somebody marched from Somewhere to reinforce them. It was a very brave affair. The long and the short of it is that they've re-taken the town and chased the Germans into the jungle. I'm left here with a couple of orderlies to minister to the sick and wounded. They're in one of the huts near here.'

Poynter nodded. Now he could understand why there had been so little sign of activity when they had entered the town. And why there was evidence of fuel having been splashed everywhere. Quickly he told her about their mission and the Dove.

Regan laughed. 'And that's what made me think you must be Germans. The local natives were told all about it by the Germans when it came in on the train. It made quite an impression.'

She broke off as Smith reappeared in the company of a grizzled native wearing nothing but a long pair of khaki shorts several sizes too large for him. He smelt of antiseptic and there was blood on his forearms. Poynter introduced Smith and told him of the fate of the wireless.

Smith accepted the news phlegmatically. 'So we're back to walking down the line,' he said. 'At least we're in better shape to do it than some of the poor devils back there.' He nodded over his shoulder towards one of the huts and looked at Regan. 'I wouldn't fancy your job, Miss.'

Regan looked at him levelly. 'I wouldn't fancy yours.'

'Is there anything we can do for you before we move on?' Poynter asked.

Regan pushed her hair back under her bonnet in a businesslike gesture. 'Not unless you're a priest or a grave digger. We have precious few medicaments and there's little enough I can do to be sure except hold hands and mop brows.'

'There's Germans there as well,' said Smith. 'Two of them. I think they're both gonners. They wouldn't speak. Turned their heads away.'

'They were civilians working on the railway,' said Regan. 'They feel bitter and you can't blame them.' She began to walk towards the adjoining huts and Poynter fell in beside her. Although the metal path through the forest was there, enclosed by two steel lines, he felt no immediate desire to be on it.

'You'll stay here?' he said.

She seemed surprised by his question. 'Of course. Are you planning to walk to the coast?'

'We have to get the information back somehow. When our men return, pass on what I've told you. They may be able to get the wireless working again.'

'*If* our men return. It may be the Germans I see first. It's happened before.'

Poynter looked up at the daunting mass of the escarpment and Regan followed his eyes. 'It's two hours from top to bottom. A detachment spent the night up there.'

'Then we don't have too much time.' His nostrils pricked with the odour of death and disinfectant and he knew that he was standing outside the sick bay. 'I don't like having to leave you here.'

In his youthful eagerness to please, Poynter expected Regan to be receptive to his words. She was not. Her expression hardened. 'Then you're a poor soldier. The sooner somebody wins the war, the sooner it'll be over.' She opened the door and he caught a glimpse of rows of litters with rush matting between them resting on earth. There was a pile of bloody waste in the foreground crawling with flies and a stench such as he had never smelt before. His eyes flew to one or two white limbs, the rest were black. There was no way of telling for which side any of them had fought. Regan stepped across the threshold.

'If you want to hear treason then here it is: I don't give a tinker's cuss which side wins. I just want it to finish.' She moved to shut the door in his face but Poynter stopped her.

'Then why did you point that pistol at me when you thought I was a German?'

She paused for a moment and then blushed so that her freckles became pinpoints of flame.

'Because I'm a damn' fool woman.' She closed the door in his face and Poynter walked away feeling certain that if he lived to be a thousand, he would never understand any woman.

TWENTY THREE

'Do we scupper her?' said Smith. He was standing beside Poynter looking down the line towards the forbidding wall of trees and creepers that marked the edge of the forest. Already fresh shoots of grass were springing up between the rails and a coil of wire bisected the rusty steel.

'What?' Poynter knew what Smith was talking about but half of his mind was still with Regan, the other loath to contemplate the destruction of something that had saved their lives.

'If the Germans come back they could repair her. There's all the stuff they need in that shed back there. It wouldn't need much to burn off some grass and clear a few trees to make a proper landing strip neither.'

'Are you thinking that we could do it ourselves?'

'I reckon I could handle the welding job – I told you I used to work in a metal shop. What we'd need is fuel. There's enough of it seems to have been splashed about. We should be able to lay our hands on some.'

'Then we have to level a proper landing field and get the Dove over those trees.' Poynter's head tilted back as he gazed up at the awesome tangle of greenery. 'It was a miracle that we got down. Are you seriously suggesting that we could take off again without killing ourselves? God-dammit, Cunningham had flown before. He'd some idea what he was doing. And there was nothing but space back there at the mission. Here we're totally hemmed in.'

Smith sighed. 'So I suppose it's walking.' He kicked the rail. 'Pity we haven't got a locomotive. Always wanted to be an engine driver when I was a nipper.'

'We'd better burn her,' said Poynter, thinking out loud. 'We haven't got much time whatever we do. You heard what Regan – I mean, Sister O'Donnell – said.'

Smith smiled. He had noticed how Poynter's now sunburnt cheeks seemed to turn a deeper red whenever he addressed the girl. In another man this might have been construed as an unspoken declaration of incipient love but Smith suspected otherwise. The events of the mission had left their mark.

A siding branched off from the main line and curved in the direction they had taken when coming from the Dove. The rusty rails disappeared into the sun-browned elephant grass as into a dark tunnel. 'This'll take us some of the way back,' said Poynter. 'We'll collect some kindling on the way.'

They walked in silence for a hundred yards with grasshoppers like small, blinded birds blundering against their chests and an unearthly screech of cicadas reverberating on all sides. In places the track was obscured by giant cobwebs and a thick dust of grass seed settled on their shoulders.

Where the grass pressed in so that it touched across the track they came upon a low trolley, its balks rotten and eaten away by termites. Poynter thrust at it with his foot and the rusty wheels shrieked in protest as giant black centipedes dropped to the ground and scuttled away into the grass roots. Poynter brushed the grass away from his face and walked on a few paces before stopping.

'Dammit,' he said.

'What?'

Poynter did not reply but turned back to the trolley and dropped to his knees beside it. 'Probably used to bring produce in from the fields, wouldn't you say? Light but pretty strong. How badly is the metalwork rusted?' He rose up and stamped down so that more of the rotten boards disintegrated and one of the axles was exposed.

Smith produced his knife and scraped away at the rust. 'It's not too bad. Needs to be rubbed down and oiled.' He paused and looked up. 'What are you thinking?'

'Your desire to become an engine driver. We may be able to do something about it.'

Light began to dawn on Smith's face. 'Blimey,' he said. 'I see what you mean. Fit these wheels on the Dove . . .'

'. . . and we can drive her down the line to Douala,' said Poynter.

TWENTY FOUR

Max von Graben frowned as he looked down. For the first time since they had started to descend the escarpment he could see the tin roofs of buildings glinting in the sunshine far below and the pencil line of the railway stretching away into the forest.

But the railhead must still be at least another hour away and he was worried about Unteroffizier Neecher. The corporal had tried to ride his horse down a steep section of the mountain and the beast had collapsed on top of him breaking its leg in the process. The injuries to Neecher were not established but it seemed that he had either broken or dislocated his hip. He was in considerable pain and his horse had been shot. With every groan and exclamation of pain von Graben felt more bitter and his bitterness found an outlet in the two Englishmen who had deserted their leader and led him on this ridiculous and increasingly arduous chase. He was eager to catch up with them – dead or alive.

Von Graben was also conscious that with every step he was moving further out on a limb. Despite the magnitude of the secret that the two renegade Englishmen carried, he had no authorization to make their pursuit his personal grail. Though it mattered little to him, he knew that he should have waited for the Ndala patrol at the mission and handed the responsibility over to them. At this very moment Major Herrmann would be pacing the ramparts at Ndinga and wondering why there was no word from him.

Another cry from Neecher and Schutz steered his over-worked mount to his captain's side. He nodded towards the Unteroffizier propped uncomfortably on the horse he shared with a Yaunde and spoke softly, the words spilling out clumsily from his twisted mouth. 'We should leave him.' Von Graben tightened his grip on his reins but said nothing. 'He is interfering with our progress. We can leave him some food and pick him up on our way back.'

'You think we should leave him some food?' asked von Graben. Schutz seemed puzzled by the question. He considered and nodded.

Von Graben stared into Schutz's face as if looking into an empty space. 'He will continue to ride with us.'

'But –'

'You will return to your position.'

Schutz hesitated and then wrenched his mount's head round and dug his heels into its sides. He rode away.

TWENTY FIVE

Regan O'Donnell gazed down at the small German and marvelled at the obstinacy with which he clung to life. He had not eaten for several days and his stomach wounds were such that he would never eat again. All that one could offer him was a place to await death, where there were not too many flies and where a crude system of fans operated by orderlies could do something to dissipate the embalming heat. His flesh had already taken on the colour of death, but his eyes missed nothing. He had not spoken a word since being admitted. When somebody mopped his brow or wiped his lips there was no sign of gratitude. But he did not refuse their ministrations. He seemed to be biding his time. Clinging to life for some purpose that she could not divine.

She turned away from the bedside and walked down the row of wounded men. Two more had died during the night and she was fearful for three others. They needed more specialized attention than she could give them and they could only get that at the coast. Here sick men seemed to rot away before her eyes. Already undermined by malaria and dengue fever the smallest wound seemed to let death into their bodies as a flood might breach a tiny hole in a dyke.

She stepped out into the heavy air and was relieved to escape for a few moments. How she yearned for the touch of cool water against her skin. Even out here in the open there was still the omnipresent stench of decay, the jungle feeding on itself in order to renew. Those plants that did not reach the sun dying in brown, putrefying coils, like the flesh that rotted beneath her eyes. And they were so young, some of them. Against the train of her thoughts she smiled. She was seeing Poynter and Smith setting off down the line in their aeroplane. The young lieutenant so serious in the front seat but continuously darting glances in her direction. The little sailor barely protruding from the cockpit behind him. He was like a small dog ever bustling protectively at his master's heels.

'Missee! Missee!' Regan turned as Peter, one of her orderlies, ran towards her across the clearing. She knew what he was going to say before he opened his mouth. 'Germans come!' Her heart fell and she felt a surge of anger. Once again her work was in danger of being interrupted.

When the Germans had retaken the town she had refused to leave her patients and so she expected to recognize the officer who appeared round the corner of the hut leading a horse with another man slumped against its neck. But she did not. The newcomer was tall and slim and carried himself very erect. He wore baggy riding breeches with puttees wound up to his knees and a solar topi which he doffed respectfully. He had blond hair cut close to the head, luminous blue eyes and fine, proud features. She had to concede that he was handsome. His eyes fixed hers and did not waiver. 'Fräulein,' he said, clicking his heels and inclining his head politely. 'I understand that you are in charge of the hospital here. I have a patient for you.'

Regan was surprised. Had it not been for the 'Fräulein' and the insignia on the tunic she would have thought that she was addressing an English officer. The man's accent was impeccable. Better than her own, she thought, suppressing a smile. Coming from County Antrim in the North of Ireland she was aware that her slight brogue had set her apart from the other nurses she had trained with.

'Then you'd best let me have a look at him.' She took a step forward and caught her breath. Schutz had appeared. He slid from the back of his slavering mount and stood staring at her as if she was on the platform at a slave market. It was not the disfiguration of his face that disturbed her, she had seen many mutilated men; it was the inner evil, the malevolence that transmitted itself through his small, pig eyes.

Two of the Yaundes carried Neecher into the hospital and von Graben instructed the others to stay on guard. Regan noted how soft the voice of the Captain sounded in comparison with the guttural bark of his sergeant major. She felt his eyes searching her face as she cut the clothing from the injured man and tried to determine the extent of his injuries.

'How serious is it?'

'Can he understand English?' Von Graben shook his head.

'Very serious. I think his hip is broken. He needs specialist attention before gangrene sets in.' She smiled down at the man and mopped his sodden brow with a sponge dipped in cool water.

'You have no doctor here?'

'Not any more. He was killed.'

Von Graben looked along the lines of wounded men. 'What is happening here? The natives we have seen speak only of fighting.'

Regan took a sheet and draped it over the corporal. He smiled up at her. A smile with a wince in it as even the effort of contracting his cheek muscles caused pain.

'The natives are right. That is all there is: fighting. Somewhere in the forests. I only see the result.'

'And have you seen an aeroplane?'

'An aeroplane?' Regan repeated the word as if totally bemused by it.

Von Graben did not waver. 'Yes, an aeroplane.' His eyes continued to search her face.

Regan hesitated uneasily and looked away to see that the brutish sergeant major who had been striding up and down the rows of beds was now in conversation with the surviving German.

'I must ask your men to wait outside,' she said, firmly. 'Many of my patients are very sick. They must not be disturbed.'

Before von Graben could reply, the sergeant major approached and unleashed a stream of German. Regan was unable to understand everything he said but with a start of alarm she recognized certain words: 'Flugzeug' and 'Lokomotive'. She realized now why the little German had fought so desperately to stay alive: he had heard the orderlies chattering about the great bird that was going to fly along the railway line with the Englishmen in it.

'I must repeat –' she began, but von Graben cut her short and beckoned his sergeant major from the room. Thoughtfully she walked down the line of beds to the little German. 'You can sleep now,' she said, but his eyes were closed and before she sought his pulse she knew that he was dead.

Time elapsed and then she was startled to hear an unexpected noise: the impatient wheeze and snort of a steam locomotive. The sound puzzled her. She had seen the locomotive burning in the engine shed and knew that no amount of German ingenuity could have brought it back to life in so short a time. Uneasy, she opened the door. The Yaunde guards had gone. A child ran past and was scooped up by its mother. Suddenly, the space in front of the hospital was empty. Regan hesitated and told the orderlies to remain where they were. Had another train come up from the south? Would it be German or English? Keeping to the shadow of the huts she ran towards the line. The huffing sound grew louder and she peered from the gap between two huts to see a rusty brown locomotive chugging from one of the sidings that led into the elephant grass. It was covered in a cocoon of branches and creepers. Camouflage. Regan thought again of her dead German patient who had worked on the railway. He had probably been responsible for hiding the locomotive.

Now the Dove's chances of reaching Douala seemed to have disappeared. A locomotive behind her would run her down in no time. The wheels ground to a halt and angel-puffs of steam spurted from between the spokes. Schutz stood on the foot-plate and bellowed orders at a group of natives who were pushing an open wagon behind the locomotive. He looked at her and she turned away quickly. She had taken half a dozen steps against the building tide of onlookers when she felt a hand touch her arm. Frightened, she turned quickly. It was the German captain.

He nodded brusquely. 'Excuse me, Fräulein. We will be leaving shortly. Please prepare Unteroffizier Neecher for travelling.'

Regan flushed angrily. 'That's ridiculous. The man is in no condition to travel. He needs specialist attention.'

'He will receive it,' said the captain calmly. 'You will be coming with us.'

'What! I can't leave my patients. It would be murder.'

'I hope you exaggerate,' said the captain. 'I regret this course of action, but I have no alternative. I am certain that the two English soldiers confided their secret to you and I cannot afford to let it go further.' He produced a thin gold watch from the breast pocket of his tunic. 'I would be grateful if you could collect your things and be ready to move in ten minutes.'

Regan stood her ground. 'And if I refuse to accompany you?'

The captain tilted his head towards the sergeant major. 'Then I will send Schutz to fetch you. Incidentally, my name is von Graben. Maximilian von Graben.'

Regan said nothing but turned on her heel and walked back towards the hospital.

Von Graben looked after her thoughtfully before going on his way. One of the Yaundes had come across a wireless telegraph in a hut at the edge of the village and he was eager to see if he could make contact with a German garrison further down the line.

TWENTY SIX

The Dove clattered down the track and Poynter listened to Smith's unmelodious singing voice competing with the shrieking cacophony from the treetops. It was almost agreeable, this journey through the jungle. He had no idea exactly how fast they were going but from the tachometer he judged it to be around fifteen miles an hour. They could go faster but it would be risky. Already they had been forced to stop and move two vine-strangled saplings that had collapsed across the track and to clear away vegetation that threatened the passage of the wings. The forward edges of these were green with grass stains and the wires from the king posts encumbered with vines and creepers so that they seemed to have been decorated. The once beautiful Dove was showing signs of what she had endured. There were fresh tears in her fuselage covering made by the natives who had manhandled her onto the truck and her tail assembly was bent. Wires that had once been tight as bow strings now sagged and she creaked like an old sofa as she trundled down the rails.

At least the Dove was back in the environment of her conception. Poynter remembered Cunningham telling him that a German doctor of science had got the idea for the design when watching a strangely shaped vine seed drift towards the earth in a Javanese rain forest. How strange, and how ironic that it should be a German who was helping them now.

To increase stability, Smith sat astride the rear of the longerons near the rudder and gave added weight to the tail. Poynter got to grips with the controls.

Only once had they seen signs of life, apart from a tribe of baboons who had stormed across the track with the females

131

carrying their young on their backs: two spindly native hunters, naked except for brightly coloured woollen caps, who had taken one look at the strange apparition heading towards them and disappeared quickly and silently into the forest.

It was late afternoon and already one of the four cans of fuel they'd secured to the fuselage had been used up. Poynter wiped the sweat from his forehead. The sun was no longer overhead and the huge trees provided welcome shade, but it was still infernally hot, especially with the roaring engine spitting oil and fuel in his face and the propeller spinning so that he saw the world through a haze that matched the fever-induced turmoil inside his head. He changed position. Despite its wicker seat the cockpit of the Dove was no Pullman car.

The curved forward spar of one of the wings struck a tree and the Dove shook with the blow. How much more could they ask her to take? The sky, the desert, and now this. If the forest pressed in much closer about the track they would have to try and fold the wings up above the fuselage. At the moment they were fully extended in order to try and gain the maximum stability.

Poynter screwed up his eyes and peered ahead. The track curved away to the right. He eased back the throttle and nursed the Dove round the bend. There was little play in the wheels transferred from the trolley. He was checking the tachometer when a shout from Smith made him look up. What he saw terrified him. Four hundred yards away a locomotive was coming down the line towards them. A flag bearing the Imperial Eagle was draped across the boiler and there was no mistaking its nationality: German.

In his panic, Poynter throttled back so hard that he nearly stalled the engine. He heard Smith cursing as he scrambled to the ground and glimpsed the little man running beside him.

'What are we going to do?'

The question reached his ears above the roar of the

revving engine. Before he could reply a shot rang out and he saw that there was a catwalk constructed round the sides of the approaching locomotive and that men with rifles were scrambling round to its front. A bullet screamed off the propeller and another punctured the oil tank above his head. Smith asked no further questions but launched himself at the wing like a man eager to seek shelter from a hail-storm. As he dived head first into the observer's cockpit, Poynter opened the throttle and the Dove began to pick up speed. What made him choose a collision course with a mass of reinforced steel several tons in weight was a question that he would have been unable to answer. What was apparent was the speed with which the two objects were converging. The tail of the Dove started to judder and then jumped the rails so that the rudder assembly shook from side to side, rattling and bumping over the cross ties. The warping wires were jangling and the whole craft reverberated as if about to burst apart before it even made contact with the approaching train. Poynter felt the speed building up and saw the catwalk before him empty as the marksman took one look at what was hurtling towards them and scurried back to the comparative safety of the cab. He boosted his courage with a blood-curdling yell and pulled out the throttle to its fullest extent. There was an additional surge of power and he felt the tail starting to lift from the ground. Now the Imperial Eagle was before him like the centre of a target and he could see its baneful, haughty eye as if held up in a mirror before his face. As one spread claw stabbed at air he jerked back the stick and the Dove rose and soared above the train, its wheels inches from making contact with the belching funnel. For an instant a whiff of smoke passed beneath Poynter's nostrils and then he was only aware of the terrifying avenue of green on either side. He felt as if he was being fired down the barrel of a gun. He thrust the stick forward and the Dove's nose dropped towards the track. Two lines of grey looked up and a flurry of stones struck the undercarriage. A jolt ran through the whole structure and for a second he thought that she was going to tip forward on her nose. Then the wheels took the strain, the back came down and they were thudding across the sleepers. They had leap-frogged the locomotive.

Any elation Poynter felt was short-lived. The Dove's wheels were no longer on the rails and with every second he expected her to veer to one side and crash into the forest. As the aeroplane rattled from side to side and the wheels clattered against the rails he cut back the engine until the Dove trembled and shuddered to a halt. Smith's head rose from the observation cockpit and he looked about him as if surprised to find that he was still alive.

Poynter looked back down the track. The German locomotive was four hundred yards away and he could hear it squealing to a halt, see the angry steam puffing from its sides. Soon it would be back. There was a blunt, square tender, ideal for smashing them to pieces. Poynter's first impulse was to dash towards the forest. Then he saw a dull gleam of metal. A length of rusting rail curving away from the main track almost invisible in the undergrowth. It was a siding onto which trains could be shunted so that they could pass. There was a lever beside the track that controlled the points. He scrambled from the cockpit shouting at Smith to bring a can of fuel. Tearing down armfuls of creepers, he began to spread them across the track.

Three hundred yards away, men dropped to the track and bullets began to whistle overhead. Poynter seized the fuel can and splashed petrol over the foliage yelling at Smith to collect more. He seized an armful of grass and razor sharp blades slashed his palms. Down the track he could hear the 'Whoomph! whoomph!' as the locomotive began to build up steam and trundle towards them. A bullet splintered a cross-tie near his foot. Fumbling desperately, he retrieved a box of wax matches and fought to light one as they crumbled beneath his scrabbling fingers. One spluttered to life and he threw it on the pile of foliage. A flame leapt high and then a pall of smoke surged up as the green, sappy vegetation smouldered across the track. Poynter threw another armful

134

of creepers onto the building smokescreen. Dropping to one knee he wrestled with the lever that controlled the points. It had rusted solid. Smith ran to his side and together they tore at the bar of metal until a section of rail grudgingly swung over with a grinding rasp. The locomotive was gathering speed and reversing fast. They could hear the eager thumping of the pistons and feel the vibration in the rails at their feet. Poynter fired two shots from Regan's Luger and ran back down the track to the Dove. Her wheels straddled one of the rails and with Smith at his shoulder he seized one of the wing-stiffening girders at a point near the fuselage and strove to lift the craft back onto the rails. The locomotive was a hundred yards away. Poynter glimpsed the outline of the tender going through the smoke and prayed that the rusty point would do its work. There was a piercing whistle and suddenly the thunderous vibration was beside them. And then past them. The locomotive had veered onto the siding.

Poynter glimpsed startled faces looking down and heard shouts of alarm and a squeal of brakes. There was a mighty shower of sparks and a deafening splintering sound as the heavy object crashed through wood. The locomotive disappeared into the trees and then the earth shook. A tremor ran back up the rail and a sound like a landslide lasted for several seconds before culminating in a terrible hiss and the screams of men in pain. The train had been derailed.

For a second the terrible sounds of destruction transfixed the Englishmen. Then they began to thrust with all their force and the Dove's wheels brushed the track and dropped between the rails. Poynter straightened up and stumbled towards the tail plane. A figure appeared through the smoke. Poynter drew his Luger, fired twice, and the man dropped. Others turned and ran for the forest. Smith seized the tail assembly and dragged the welded wheels into position on the track. Poynter glanced at the forest and heard the crackling of flames. The screaming had stopped but there was still an unnerving hissing noise.

The Dove was ready and Poynter ran to the propeller. The

engine was still hot and started on the first pull as Smith scrambled into the cockpit. The aeroplane started to move forward, nearly decapitating Poynter as he ducked and stumbled backwards. He caught his foot on a cross-tie and sprawled full length as the Dove passed over him, the wheel-bar just clearing his nose. Twisting quickly, he rolled from the track as the rear wheels brushed his fingers. A German officer appeared from the siding brandishing a pistol and fired. Poynter scrambled to his feet and ran after the Dove. He managed to drape himself across the rear of the fuselage against the horizontal stabilizer. The Dove picked up speed and the distance between her and the Germans lengthened until they were swallowed up by the jungle.

TWENTY SEVEN

Regan wiped Neecher's forehead carefully and listened to the rain beating down on the tarpaulin above her head. It had started an hour before and fallen at the same steady rate without any variation ever since. This was the beginning of the rainy season and she knew what to expect. A downpour that could last for twenty-four hours with only an hour's respite at dawn and dusk. The temperature falling, the sun melting from the sky, the ground turning to mud. Everything dripping, leaves, eaves, noses. A damp that entered into the bones. A time of rotting, of fever, of pneumonia. Debilitated men who were already sick or wounded, or both, caught a chill and died overnight. Small pot-bellied piccaninnies, the children of malnutrition, huddled under the dripping palms with ribbons of mucus stretching around their grossly inflated umbilici. Vapours and mists clung to tree and shrub like ghosts of the departed or those who still waited to be ensnared. It was a terrible place but if you were born in it, there was at least some understanding of the perimeters of your life. You knew nothing else, so nothing could be better. To the men who came from afar to fight here, anything could be better.

Regan looked down at the man by her side. He was trembling with the vibration of the wagon but his eyes were closed. He was either asleep or in a coma. Regan guessed that he was dying. He must have internal injuries as well as his broken hip. He could keep nothing down. Liquid spilled out of his mouth as soon as he closed his lips. His skin had the feel of freshly-worked clay. At least he did not scream. He was brave and he seemed resigned. That was something about the jungle. It ate the heart of men slowly, undermined them so that their fibre turned to water.

There was a wild screech of brakes and she threw out her arms to prevent herself from falling on top of the corporal. He woke up with a scream and his eyes flew open in terror as he started to slide towards the side of the wagon. Regan held him as gently as she could and tried to reassure him. From the cab she could hear raucous German shouts with Schutz's voice in the ascendant.

The locomotive ground to a halt and Regan squeezed the corporal's hand and rose to her feet. The two Yaundes who were working in tandem with their comrades on the foot-plate were already draped over the side peering into the murk. Night came down fast in the Cameroons and in the forest it was always half night.

A man with a groundsheet over his head against the rain was talking urgently in German to von Graben and two other white soldiers hovered in the background with half a dozen blacks. She could see a body lying under the trees and with a start of fear she immediately thought of the young lieutenant and his companion. She tried to look beyond the locomotive but could see nothing.

Seconds passed and von Graben descended from the cab and approached her. His face was grave as he reached up and slid back the bolts that held the side panel of the wagon.

137

'We are going to need your assistance again, *Fräulein*. There has been an accident.' He smiled bitterly. 'Perhaps "accident" is the wrong word.' The panel crashed down and he extended his hand. She smelt the familiar smell of rank vegetation and stepped down to the sodden black earth already strewn with puddles. Looking ahead she could see no more than twenty yards before the mist came down like a wall. To her relief there was no sign of the flying machine.

One glance at the man beneath the trees was enough to prove that he was dead. A blow of considerable force had shattered his temple. She looked up towards von Graben who directed her towards a length of railway track that led into the undergrowth. 'Your companions succeeded in derailing a train,' he said coolly. 'There is a man trapped beneath it.'

She walked along the track and the forest closed in about her. Bright green ferns sprouted from the tree trunks and there were strange fungoid growths like layers of twisted mouths. She looked at them and felt Schutz's eyes boring into her as she picked her way through the puddles.

After a few yards the line buckled and disappeared and she was looking down a steep hillside where trees had been snapped off to leave exposed white teeth of fractured timbers illuminating the gloom. At the bottom of the slope a mass of black metal lay on its side glistening in the rain. Spouts of steam rose from the boiler and it was enmeshed in creepers. The sides of the slope were churned where men had scrambled to and fro between the stricken locomotive and the rail and she could see a huddle of moving bodies on its far side. It was a grim scene and made more so by the rivulets of water running down the scraped banks. Even as she looked the rain came down more heavily with an insistent drumming on the shiny leaves and her feet began to sink into the mud. Creepers had been plaited together to form a rope and this trailed down the hillside providing a handhold to the locomotive. Regan looked into von Graben's face. For the first time that she could remember, the impassive mask had been broken. He was a man under strain. For a reason that she could not fully understand, she found the sight of his distress reassuring.

'I will go first.' He picked up the rope and began to lower himself into the abyss.

Regan's cumbersome skirt was already soaked to the knees and she hitched it up and handed the case of medical instruments that she had inherited from the deceased doctor to one of the German native soldiers. Waiting until von Graben had reached the locomotive, she took the slippery rope in her hands and began to slither down the hillside, her skirt snagging on the razed vegetation, her buttocks rubbing against the muddy earth.

When she reached the bottom of the hollow, she saw what the cluster of men were trying to do. A man lay trapped beneath the footplate with its steel edge forcing down on the small of his back like a blunt knife blade. His face was pressed into the mud and his comrades were desperately trying to construct a barrier that would stop him from drowning in the water that was rushing down the hillside and splashing about their ankles. Their attempts to arrange stones and pieces of bark were coming to nothing. The water found a way through or seeped up through the mud. Now they were bailing with their bare hands, but the water could only be cleared for the fraction of a second before more came rushing in. The very agitation of their kneeling bodies churned up mud and broke down the slender barriers they had erected. The man tried to raise his head and his eyeballs showed white in terror. Regan was transfixed by anguish and pity. The man's injuries were horrible enough without him having to endure this.

'*Gott hilfe dem armen Kerl.*'

She heard von Graben breathe the words beside her without knowing what they meant. What could she do? She had no divine power to lift the locomotive or stop the flood. She could only wish that the man's agony be over as quickly as possible.

There was a crack, and the locomotive shifted as if it were about to slide again. The soldiers near it sprang back and scrambled for their lives. There was a shout of warning and alarm and somewhere in the chaos and confusion a last despairing cry. When the locomotive did not topple and the men returned, their comrade was lying still, with only the back of his head visible above the black bubbling tide. They pulled him up again but his eyes and mouth were wide open and he was dead.

Regan turned away and von Graben steadied her with his arm. For a second she hoped that he was going to speak. Then he stepped back and began to shout orders up the hillside.

TWENTY EIGHT

'*Dammit!*'

Cunningham's favourite expletive spat from Poynter's lips and Smith smiled.

The propeller juddered to a halt and the sound gave way to the steady drumming of the rain that had been falling for the last two hours. Poynter took off his solar topi and beat it savagely against his arm, the sound reverberating around the hillside.

Before them, totally blocking the track, was a giant tree trunk that had slid down the hillside in a fall of mud. It was one of the many piled untidily beside the rails. The churned earth and the neatly severed stumps revealed that they had come upon a logging camp. The slope on one side of the track had been cleared and there were coils of steel cable and the remains of half a dozen ramshackle huts which had once sheltered the woodmen. Now the site was mournful in its emptiness. The war had driven everyone away and what looked as if it had been a flourishing enterprise was reverting to jungle. Already tentacles of creeper and vine were reaching out to shackle the resting logs and snake-tongues of green reared from the butchered stumps.

Poynter climbed from the cockpit and pressed his shoulder against the glistening trunk. He might have been pushing against a stone wall.

Smith helped him. But it was to no avail. He shook his head and brushed the rain from his eyebrows.

Poynter dug his toe into the track. What an end to their journey. This desolate slope with the mist closing in and the rain thudding against the earth. With the Dove silent his sense of desperation returned. In full voice she helped to drown fear. She was the comforting sound of a kettle bubbling on the hob, the crackle of a friendly fire. Now, motionless against the smoking hillside the fast approaching darkness seemed to be drawing her inexorably into the landscape.

Poynter pulled his hands from the slippery wood. 'We'll have to walk. Follow the line. I suggest we start tomorrow.' He found himself waiting for Smith's confirmation.

'Fine,' said the little man. 'We can't have anybody breathing down our necks and I don't fancy stepping out in the dark.' He looked up at the gaunt shape of the Dove. 'Maybe we'd better cover up the engine. We might think of a way of lifting her round in the morning.'

Poynter agreed half-heartedly. The slope below the track was steep, the ground slippery. There was no hope of their being able to support the weight of the Dove. Above the track, a mass of felled trees was held in place only by the one that had fallen. There was no possibility of manoeuvring the Dove round them.

Bitter and depressed, Poynter skirted the logs and trudged towards what seemed the most habitable of the moss-strewn huts. The gloom matched his spirits and the mist was closing in. Behind him, the tattered Dove looked as if she had crashed into the obstruction. When the thick foliage crowded in upon the track they had been forced to break the wings at the king pins and fold them above the fuselage where they had been lashed with vines.

Poynter kicked the door open and peered inside. Spiders' webs choked the interior and he took Smith's rifle and swung it until the weapon looked like a silken club. There were strips of rotting hessian tacked to the collapsing bunks and Smith took these to drape over the Dove. The one heart-warming sight in the dismal dwelling was a pile of dry logs, and Poynter dodged the fleeing spiders and built a fire in the doorway. It was hard to believe that any German patrols would be out on such a night.

Without the continuous excitement of movement he realized how hungry he was and it was a relief when Smith returned with some yams he'd found in an abandoned native garden. They scraped off the earth and baked them in the fire until they were black. The texture was sinewy, the taste unappetizing. After three mouthfuls, Smith spat his meal into the night.

The rain slackened whilst they were eating and when the moon came up it stopped altogether. They listened to the water dripping from the eaves and the strange plink-plonk counterpoint of the frogs. The cicadas were silent.

Poynter stretched out his arms towards the fire and felt the warmth basting his bones. His whole body ached but the most acute pain came from his toes. They felt as if they were on fire. Self-consciously he removed his boots and peeled off the remains of his socks.

'Taters', said Smith. He saw that Poynter had no idea what he was talking about. 'Potatoes: holes in your socks.'

Poynter nodded and extended his foot towards the fire. By its light he could detect a yellow discoloration beneath the nail of his big toe with a faint black mark in its centre. A thorn, he told himself, somehow my toes have become peppered with thorns. Feeling in the flap of his shirt pocket he withdrew a pin and held it in a flame to sterilize it until the point glowed red. He let it cool and then leant forward bracing his foot against his knee. Carefully he positioned the pin and slid it down into the soft flesh beside the black spot. To his horror a maggot popped out of his toe. Speechless he watched it writhing in a blob of pus, the black spot marking its head. He squeezed again and two more appeared.

Smith leant forward to observe the spectacle and scratched his ear. 'Jiggers,' he said matter of factly. 'Horrible little devils, aren't they?' He read the expression on Poynter's face. 'Haven't you had them before? They burrow under your toes to lay their eggs. You should see some of the native fellows. They've got toes like frayed ropes.'

'I thought they were thorns,' said Poynter weakly.

'You'll have a few more then,' said Smith. 'Best to check regular. They can cripple you if they get a hold. Pity we don't have that Sister O'Donnell here with some disinfectant.'

Poynter was silent. He felt total revulsion as he looked down at the writhing mass on his toe; the thought that they were actually feeding on his own flesh, that he carried them with him everywhere he went. The image of maggots in a dead creature was repellent enough. He probed each toe and found that the soft flesh just beneath the nail was the favourite point of entry. Sometimes there was actually a cavity full of pus that he had to scrape out, spewing forth several of the plump, wriggling parasites.

'Cheer up,' said Smith. 'Worse things happen at sea.' He laughed. 'You need to scour them wounds, though. Maybe petrol will do the trick.' He took a brand from the fire and started back towards the Dove without another word.

Poynter watched the wavering flame grow fainter and felt a new intense fear. What would he do if anything happened to Smith?

In the jungle, Poynter's imagination was a dangerous force, capable of destroying him. He saw phantoms in mists and the maggots were not only physical horrors but symbols of mental disintegration. The further they plunged into the labyrinthine maze of all-enclosing trees, the more he felt his spirit trapped and imprisoned.

Poynter stared through the flickering flames of the fire and

143

eventually the Will-o'-the-wisp light bobbed towards him. Smith materialized staggering under the weight of an almost full petrol can. He put it down and felt in one of the pockets of his voluminous shorts.

'You may need this.' He withdrew a slim silver flask and handed it to Poynter. It was engraved with an intertwining set of initials, the most prominent of which was 'C'. 'I took this off Captain Cunningham before we buried him. Didn't seem no point in leaving it. I imagine he was saving it for something important.'

Poynter sniffed the brandy and remembered. 'Yes,' he said.

'Better take a swig,' said Smith. 'This could hurt.' He produced a strip of cotton waste and moved away from the fire to soak it in petrol. Poynter did as he was told and the spirit seemed to explode inside his mouth, scalding his throat. He passed over the flask and extended his foot. Smith drank and smacked his lips. 'Right, let's get down to it.' He began to dab with the cotton waste and Poynter hissed through his clenched teeth. The pain was excruciating.

Smith suppressed a chuckle and calmly demanded the other foot. 'I was thinking,' he said. 'It's like the Bible, isn't it. Didn't the disciples anoint Christ's feet? Don't reckon Christ would have fancied this lot much.'

Poynter stretched out his hand for the flask. 'Where did you learn that?'

'At Sunday School. My old mum was very keen on my having a good religious education. 'Fraid I was a disappointment to her. I used to nip off with the lads most of the time when I should have been learning my Catechism. I never was one for schooling. That's why I went into the metal shop – as an apprentice. My mum wasn't happy about that neither. She'd have preferred me to be a clerk. Posher somehow, you didn't come home with oil and muck all over you. But I liked it well enough until the war came along. Then I saw a chance to get out of the back yard I'd been in all my life.'

'Do you know,' he laughed again, 'I joined the Navy because I didn't fancy marching. Just shows you, doesn't it?' He stepped back and threw the rag on the fire where it was engulfed in a column of flame that for a second illuminated the stark hillside like a starburst. Smith dropped down on his haunches and held his hands out towards the fire. His head turned towards Poynter. 'What about you?'

Poynter hesitated. 'Well,' he began. 'My father was – still is – a country solicitor. I went to boarding school not far from home and joined up because it seemed the thing to do. I didn't have time to think about a profession but I'd probably have become a lawyer like my father. I was in my local county regiment but I had an uncle who'd served in the West African Frontier Force during the Ashanti wars. He made it seem like a splendid life and, like you, I wanted to see something of the world, so I asked for a transfer.'

Smith accepted the flask and took a generous swig. 'And now we're stuck here.' He wiped his mouth with the back of his hand.

Poynter hiccupped and found that his hand had automatically reached out to retrieve the flask. A warmth was spreading through him that did not come from the fire. He had forgotten his toes. 'What about your father?' he asked.

'Oh, he walked out when I was a nipper. Just went off one morning and never came back. That's why I felt bad about leaving my mum, but I couldn't stay there for ever.'

Smith turned away and looked into the night. He sniffed twice. 'Funny. There was a fellow who used to sell hot pies on the corner of our street. Every Saturday he used to be there. I smelt those pies just then, clear as if I had one under my nose.'

Poynter sniffed, but all he could smell was the heavy scent of some night-blooming shrub mingled with the aroma of the burning wood.

The little man turned to him again. 'How much further have we got to go?'

'Two hundred miles at a guess.'

Smith whistled through his teeth. 'That's quite a hike. What'll it be like?'

'Forests. Perhaps some mountains. Very much up and down I'd say. I believe Douala is in a mangrove swamp. I've never seen it.'

'And we've no idea who'll be waiting for us along the way. That German train must have come from somewhere.'

Poynter started to pull on his socks and boots. 'I think they were out looking for us. That means that the Hun must have reached Ndala and got the wireless working.'

'So all the Germans down the coast will have been alerted.'

'Those who are in wireless or telegraph communication.'

Smith thought. 'Maybe we'd be better off leaving the railway line. Maybe there's some big rivers here, like the ones we came up on the Nigerian side.'

Poynter nodded. 'It's possible. There must be some rivers that drain into the swampland around Douala. At daybreak we'll climb as high as we can and spy out the land.' He raised the flask to his lips and found it was empty. Perhaps that was why he felt so light-headed.

Smith rose unsteadily and tossed some more logs on the fire. 'At least we don't have to worry about what's behind us.' He rubbed his hands together and then threw back his head and began to sing in a high, cracked voice:

> 'When I went for a soldier,
> Mother she got drunk, father did a bunk,
> And the Old Dun Cow caught fire.

You must know that one.'

Poynter shook his head. ' 'Fraid I don't.'

'How about "It's a long way to Douala"?'

Poynter was puzzled for a moment and then laughed and clapped Smith on the shoulder. 'Of course!'

Floating on brandy he began to sing and Smith picked up the refrain. The sound soared up with a mounting gusto that

drove away demons and drowned out all the other noises of
the night:

> '*It's a long way to Douala,*
> *It's a long way to go,*
> *It's a long way to Douala,*
> *To the sweetest girl I know!*
> *Goodbye Piccadilly,*
> *Farewell Leicester Square,*
> *It's a long long long long way to Douala,*
> *But we're going right there!*'

TWENTY NINE

Regan shivered against the cold and listened to the rain
dripping from the trees. The tarpaulin about her head had
filled with water and now bulged down in two smooth curves
like a woman's breasts. She was alone in the wagon save for
the wounded corporal and had been provided with a small
lamp which had attracted a bustling crowd of moths and a
predatory bat which was profiting from this unexpected
flying larder. Around her, finding what shelter they could
beneath the trees, slept the Germans and their native soldiers. It had been decided that they would move again at
daybreak, there being too great a danger of a subsidence or a
fallen tree brought down by the heavy rains to risk travelling
at night. After witnessing the horrors of the derailment a
mood of sober caution prevailed, laced with bitterness and a
desire for revenge.

Regan gingerly moved the lamp to floor level. She had no
liking for bats and remembered how her grandmother in
County Antrim had told terrifying tales of them becoming
lodged in young girls' hair. Sometimes the natives caught

flying foxes which carried such virulent fleas that the creatures were speared and roasted alive to prevent the parasites transferring themselves to their captors. Their screams of agony were so horrible that she could never see a bat without hearing them.

She knelt and rummaged in her bag seeking articles of dry clothing. Her skirt was caked with mud and her blouse damp against her breasts. She found a clean blouse, skirt and under-clothing and laid them out on the blanket. There was great comfort in clean linen, a boost to the morale. She shook the raindrops from the shawl her mother had woven and laid it tenderly beside the clothing that she was going to put on. Rising, she pulled off her bonnet so that her hair fell about her shoulders. The sides of the wagon rose to the level of her forehead so she had no fear of prying eyes. She swiftly undid the buttons of her blouse and slipped it from her shoulders before wriggling out of her under-vest. Now her breasts were exposed and on an impulse she glanced down at the wounded corporal propped against the side of the wagon. So near was he to death that she had almost ceased to think of him as still in this world. When she had last ministered to him, his eyes had been closed in a coma. Now they were staring up at her. Her first reaction was an instinctive one of modesty. Her hands moved across her breasts. Then she read the expression on the man's face. It was not one of lust but rather of innocence, a look of child-like wonder, as if the man was already slipping away and seeing in a dream some vision of beauty that reassured and enchanted him. A feeling of great tenderness overwhelmed her. She dropped to her knees and gently leant forward so that her arms could encircle the man's head and she could draw him to her breasts. She held him there, feeling his sweat like tears against her flesh, until the cold crept across his skin and his sinews stiffened and she knew that he was dead. Still she did not move but squeezed him even tighter for several moments like a lover, while her own tears fell and she wept for all the men who had died and all the men who were going to die.

148

There was a noise behind her and she immediately thought of the bat swooping down on the lamp. Afraid, she turned and saw a hand grasping the edge of the wagon. Schutz's gargoyle face stared down at her and with the lamp beneath it took on the hideous appearance of a Hallowe'en mask lit by a cruel interior light. A glimmering bar of silver hinted at the position of the twisted mouth. She cried out and the face disappeared so fast that for seconds she wondered if she had really seen it. She listened, tense, for the noise of footsteps stealing away but as the minutes passed there was no sound apart from that of water falling on leaves. It had started to rain again.

THIRTY

Poynter awoke cold and stiff and savagely bitten by vermin that he imagined had not had a good meal since the departure of the last inhabitants of the hut. No cheerful refrain lingered from the previous night. Only a dull ache behind the temples that he knew was a hangover. He carefully pocketed Cunningham's silver flask and scratched himself as he peered out of the doorway. It had stopped raining and a mist clung to the grey slopes. The fire was out and the temperature glacial. Uncertain whether his shivering was caused by the cold or a fever, he splashed some water on to his face from a nearby puddle and awoke Smith who had been curled up in a ball beside him. Smith groaned and then cursed as he found that his body too was a mass of angry red blotches. He struggled to his feet and began to shrug off his clothing and search for something on which to reap his vengeance.

Poynter examined his watch. It was six o'clock. They might as well start doing something positive before the rains come.

'I was thinking,' said Smith between curses. 'Maybe we could hop over that tree like we did with the train. Take a run at it. I don't mind having a go.' He scratched himself again. 'With all these blooming fleas on me I reckon I could hop over anything.'

'We'll never be able to get the wings straight,' said Poynter. 'Certainly not rigid enough for take off. There are too many wires loose. And there's the hillside. It's too steep for us to extend both wings fully. We wouldn't be able to get into the air.' He took a few steps down the slope and gazed at one of the great abandoned spools of steel wire. If only they could tie that to the timber and pull it out of the way.

'I'll be sorry to leave her,' said Smith following his gaze.

'Let's take a look up the hillside,' said Poynter quickly. He turned his back on the outline of the Dove glistening with dew and spiders' webs and led the way up the slope until wisps of mist drifted above their heads like low-flying clouds and they could see patches of grey sky lightening into blue. The ground was littered with huge brown slugs and he noticed with distaste that where one had been crushed, the others clustered in to feed upon its body. Sticking wet creepers entrammelled their legs until they came to the jungle proper where a stockade of trees crowded in on the cleared land. Heads bent they forced their way upwards, shoulders brushing against the saplings, the wet foliage soaking them to the skin. Every few yards they looked up, hoping for a sign that they had reached the top of the hill but with every curve they came to another rise and still the forest crowded in. It was only when they were on the brink of turning back that the trees suddenly became more sparse and there was a prospect of blue sky above them. A clearing opened up and they could see what lay on three sides.

First impressions were not cheering. The mist still gathered in the valleys, giving them the appearance of silken lakes and a succession of rugged mountains covered with thick jungle stretched away towards the west as far as the eye could see. There was no hint of human habitation nor of any road nor track. If there were rivers, then there was no inkling where they lay. There were so many complex folds and valleys that they might have held a multitude of streams. All that was apparent was the perfect uniformity of the landscape in the direction that they had to travel. The only variation came in the shades of green that streaked the vertiginous slopes so packed with vegetation that they seemed about to burst open and spew forth in a viridescent tide. Poynter looked down and his spirits tumbled into the bottom of the smoking valleys. How could they ever walk out of this place except along a railway line?

Behind them was the same view, seemingly unending jungle-clad hills thrown into greater relief by the clear sky that had appeared above them. Lakes of low-lying mist were being sucked into the air even as he looked. On the horizon a phalanx of dark clouds gathered like the black sails of galleons running before the wind but directly below them the sun was gleaming on the trees and in the far distance they could see the railway line where it ran straight as a die, before being swallowed up by the jungle.

Poynter looked and looked again. Like a creature emerging from its hole something had appeared on the railway line and was coming towards them. The distance was more than five miles but there was no mistaking what he was seeing.

'It can't be!' Smith was shading his eyes with both hands. 'A train.'

Poynter's mind began to whirl. The locomotive seemed to be hardly moving but it would be at the barrier within fifteen minutes. They could take to the jungle immediately; they had their weapons. But the water bottles were at the hut. Finding water, however, was not going to be a great problem in the present conditions. Around them the forest was as thick as the fur on a cat's back. They would be lost in no time. Better to retrace their steps, flee along the railway line and be ready to plunge into the forest at any moment. The locomotive would probably be able to pull the tree away but at least they would have a start.

Suddenly an idea struck him. 'Come on!' He started to plunge down the hillside impervious to the vines and the prickly creepers slapping against his face. Twice he fell and once the Luger escaped from his grasp and slithered away into the undergrowth. He had the same mad demon goading him as when he had leap-frogged the German locomotive. Puffing and panting he half fell down the steep slope until he burst from the trees and saw the clearing and the Dove below him. Fighting for breath he stumbled on until he reached the first spool of wire and started to push it upright. Smith fell in beside him, his rifle garlanded with creepers.

'No time to explain. Just do as I tell you. Hang on to this.' Poynter thrust an end of the thick wire into Smith's hands and heaved the giant bobbin round until it was pointing down the slope. A kick and it started to trundle towards the line. Smith was nearly dragged with it and dug in his heels. The wire played out and Poynter ran alongside it, trying to keep the spool upright. The reel reached the line and he thrust his shoulder against the wood and forced it across the rails to where the ground fell away sharply. A final shove and it careered down the hill spilling wire until suddenly there was none left and the bobbin crashed away amongst the trees, leaving the wire to spring back in a series of untidy coils. Poynter yelled at Smith to secure his end to the log nearest the downhill slope and started to descend below the track, gathering in the wire as he did so. It was heavy and thick with grease and a coil soon snagged on a tree root. He tugged in vain and was forced to scramble down and disengage it with his hands. With every second the train was drawing nearer. Dragging the wire after him, he staggered along the embankment until he came to a tall tree directly below where the log was blocking the line. Smith had secured his end of the wire and Poynter shouted at him to prepare the Dove to move. Smith stared down at him as if he was mad and then disappeared. Poynter took the wire round the tree twelve feet below the track and scrambled along the hillside parallel with the line. There was another large tree thirty yards before him with the circumference of a lighthouse. Gasping and spluttering he ran towards it, his heart hammering. Stones skittered down the slippery hillside and his ears strained for the sound of the approaching locomotive. It must be less than a mile away.

He reached the tree and stretched the wire round its jagged bark before making a turn of ninety degrees and driving his aching legs up the slope. He crossed the line and doubled back to force the wire into an untidy slipknot that resembled a giant hangman's noose. The splayed fibres at its end scored his forearm. Shaking, he gazed down the line in the direction the train would come from. There was nothing. Fear snapping at his heels, he ran down the line to where Smith was sitting in the pilot's cockpit of the Dove. A thumbs up signal and he hurled himself at the propeller. Checking that there was a piece of wood against the wheels, he primed the pots and pulled down with all his force. There was a thump and a cough but nothing happened. He tried again. Still nothing. Rain had got into the cylinders. Beneath him he could feel the rails beginning to tremble. The train was coming. Rubbing his oily hands against his shirt he reached up and grasped the propeller. 'Come on, my beauty! Come on! Don't let us down now.' He closed his eyes and wrenched. There was a whirl of air beside his cheek and the engine roared into life.

Now, back down the track to the noose; feet kicking up clinker, expecting at each second to see the train appearing round the bend; snatch up the wire and plunge full length into the ground ivy beside the rail.

Slowly, he raised his head until one eye could see above the bitter-smelling leaves. A parrot flew away with a wild shriek and the locomotive appeared round the bend in the track. It was dirty brown and smoke belched from its funnel. He tightened his grip on the steel noose.

The locomotive bore down and a man leant out from the footplate, then another. They had seen the Dove. Poynter slid his hands along the wire and strained to make out the exact arrangement of the buffers. Now he could smell the engine grease and the aromatic odour of the wood she was burning. There was no sound of brakes being applied but rather an increase in the threshing of the pistons as if the pursuers, having caught a glimpse of their prey at rest, were determined that she should not elude them. The thumping note of the engine became deafening and the great mass of metal roared closer, flattening the vegetation by the side of the track. Fifty yards, forty, thirty. . . . He sprang to his feet and thrust the wire noose out before him like a hoop. The brown wall of the boiler loomed above him and he concentrated on the two protruding buffers and the coupling hook that bisected them. There was a shout and a buffer snatched the wire. He heard the screech of the loop sliding tight and then the rasp as the continuing movement of the locomotive started to pull the wire round the first tree, cutting into the porous bark. He sprinted across the track and plunged down the steep embankment. Smoke and flames were pouring from a deepening groove in the wood as the wire bit deep; the locomotive slammed on her brakes. There was an ear-splitting grating sound and a shower of sparks and then the noise he had been waiting to hear: the heavy log that had barred the Dove being dragged across the track by the weight of the pursuing train. He kept his head down and ran towards the Dove.

THIRTY ONE

Regan was on the footplate when the locomotive caught up with the Dove. Bathed in currents of warm air from the furnace she was almost asleep, hypnotized by the flickering needles of the steam pressure dials. She heard a shout and glimpsed a man running past beside the track. The brake lever jerked back and she was hurled forward as the furnace door swung open and blazing logs spilled at her feet. She screamed and von Graben snatched her to him and kicked out at the logs. The driver fell cursing and one of the native stokers threw himself from the footplate to avoid the flames.

Regan's first thought was that they had been attacked. It did not matter by whom. An English bullet could kill as easily as a German one. The brakes squealed on interminably and she saw the quivering wire gouging flame from the tree. Von Graben kicked the furnace door shut and seized the rail at the side of the foot-plate. Ahead, the huge log pulled by the wire began to move. As it slithered across the track so the buttress against the rest of the logs was removed. The jam began to tremble.

Von Graben shouted at the driver and the locked pistons thrashed into action jarring the locomotive into pursuit. Regan glimpsed a man scrambling along the embankment beneath her. Poynter. The Dove jerked forward and the first logs of the disrupted jam began to slither towards her. Von Graben tore out his pistol and Schutz leapt from the truck onto the footplate, a Mauser in his hand. The log torn by the wire disappeared down the hillside and others brushed the tail of the fleeing Dove before sealing off the track behind her. As von Graben fired, the locomotive piled into the mass of logs with a loud splintering noise. Bodies flew with the impact and a log thrust into the cabin nearly decapitating the driver. Steam hissed from half a dozen points on the control panel and the needles danced.

Regan picked herself up and scrambled to the side of the cab. Her temple ached where she had cracked it against the tender. Men were running along the track and scrambling over the pile of logs that blocked their way but the Dove was now drawing away and seemingly impervious to the bullets that whistled after her. Regan glimpsed two heads protruding from the cockpits and let out a shout of encouragement.

A violent blow struck her on the side of her head and she reeled back to see Schutz's furious face coming at her again.

He thrust his rifle against her chest and pushed back with the force of a maddened bull. Regan was knocked from the cab and glimpsed the sky cartwheeling above her head before the wind was driven from her body. She slithered down the steep embankment and came to rest as Schutz launched himself after her. She saw the soles of his boots in mid air and felt the small avalanche as he crashed down the slope towards her. He towered above her and his boot rose.

'Halt!'

The voice was von Graben's but Regan's eyes remained tightly closed, her body braced. Seconds passed and she withdrew her hands from around her head and looked up. The butt of Schutz's rifle trembled above her.

Regan's fear turned to anger. Her mother had told her she was descended from the kings of Ireland but now her impulses were more like those of a drunken tinker. All her Celtic fury boiled in her veins as she scrambled to her feet. '*Brute!*' she screamed. '*Cowardly brute!*' Her foot drew back and she kicked Schutz in the shin with all her force.

'Genug!' Von Graben read the expression in Schutz's hate-filled eyes. 'That's enough, Korpsgendarm. Start getting those logs out of the way. *Schnell!*'

Schutz hesitated and then pulled his rifle close to his body. For a second he stayed motionless and menacing. Then he spun on his heel and started to lumber up the embankment.

Von Graben watched him until he was out of sight before turning to Regan. 'You chose a bad audience for your display of enthusiasm.'

Regan shrugged. She wanted to express her thanks but found it impossible to form the words. 'He's an animal,' she said.

Von Graben's voice was calm. 'Every army has its Schutzes and for the conceivable future you are going to have to live with this one. Try to keep your wild Irish temper under control. You're supposed to be an angel of mercy, are you not?'

'I'm a nurse, not a nun,' said Regan fiercely.

156

For the first time that she could remember, von Graben smiled. 'Nevertheless, take my advice and step warily. Schutz does not like you.' His finger reached out and brushed against her temple. 'And now you'd better go and practice some medicine on yourself. That's a nasty bruise.' He bowed and climbed to join the men toiling amongst the logs.

Regan looked after him and raised her hand to her temple before quickly snatching it away.

THIRTY TWO

Poynter licked his lips and carefully folded the palm leaf into an elongated cone which he inserted into the mouth of the fuel tank. Beside him, Smith perched uncomfortably under the arched wings, petrol can at the ready. Poynter steadied the makeshift funnel and the precious amber liquid began to flow. There was one more can left. Enough fuel in total for another fifty miles. Both men were tense. The temporary exhilaration of the escape from the logging camp had disappeared.

'Watch it!' Poynter spoke sharply. Smith's eyes had been wandering towards the steaming jungle.

Smith concentrated on the can again. 'Don't want them to catch us on the hop.'

Poynter looked up. 'Like at Ndinga.'

Smith seemed genuinely puzzled. 'I didn't mean that.'

'Sorry. Sore point. You're right, of course. We must bump into some Hun sooner or later.'

Smith jerked his head over his shoulder. 'What about the lot behind? They'll be unloading those logs faster than lascars on piece rate.'

'It's not worth trying to make another barrier. They'd

clear it in no time. We'd need to blow up the track.'

'And we've nothing to do it with.' Smith shook the last drop of fuel from the can and tossed it into the bush. 'What wouldn't I give for a slice of fresh bread and butter.'

'Try a plantain,' said Poynter. He felt no hunger. A diet of fear and tension soon took the place of food and drink and filled a belly just as easily. The mist drifted across the face of the jungle and he glimpsed something that made him crane forward. A pole rose vertically and from it stretched a length of wire following the line of the track. A telegraph wire.

'Dammit!' he said. 'We should have had that down.'

'Never too late,' said Smith.

'I hope not.' Poynter jumped down and had taken two steps towards the trees when he realized that he had left his pistol in the cockpit. The Luger was large and cumbersome and fitted uncomfortably in his waistband. He cursed and hauled himself into the cockpit to retrieve it.

By the time he was on the ground again, Smith had disappeared. Poynter waited and then shouted his name. There was only the sound of some parakeets squabbling unseen amongst the treetops and the steadily pouring rain pattering against the leaves. Poynter looked up and down the track. Nothing. Puzzled, he moved towards the telegraph pole and called again. A maypole tangle of creepers encircled the wood and the first tiny shoots were reaching for the wires like splayed fingers. Cutting the telegraph wire had suddenly ceased to be the first priority. Poynter's ears strained, trying to pick out any unusual sound. Perhaps Smith had called out and he had failed to hear him. Where could he have gone?

Standing back from the track a dead tree tilted forward under an untidy weight of lianas. Its roots had torn free from the soft jungle bed and the thick, serpentine coils of creeper passed temptingly close to the sagging telegraph wires. It would be the obvious tree to climb if one was going to cut them. The spot Smith would have headed for.

Tense, Poynter pushed the wet foliage aside and left the track. It was like stepping into a darkened room with a thick carpet underfoot. Young saplings rose between the tall trees but there was a way through the leaves that might have been a man-made path or an animal run.

'Smith!' The trees crowded in bludgeoning the sound to nothing. Poynter stepped forward and then stopped. The ground before him sagged and a severed length of sapling rose at an odd angle. There was a cavity. A trap! A hole had been covered with foliage and then a camouflage of mud and leaves. Poynter dropped to his hands and knees and edged forward. He looked down through the broken fronds. A shape showed up against the darkness. 'Smith!' There was no reply. Poynter clenched his fists. Sometimes the natives placed sharpened stakes at the bottom of their traps.

He stood up and tucked his pistol into his waistband. Stay calm. What would the natives use, ropes? A tangled curtain of creepers hung from a nearby tree. Almost hidden by it was a crude ladder formed by lashing cross pieces to a length of trimmed sapling. Poynter tore it free and dragged it to the pit. Removing part of the covering he lowered the ladder into the darkness. Now he could make out Smith lying face downwards and seemingly surrounded by gleaming white bones. Poynter started to scramble down and felt the ladder sinking into the mud beneath his weight. Roots clawed at his face and the smell was awful, animal and vegetable decay. He dropped into the mulch and hung his pistol on one of the cross pieces of the ladder to make bending easier.

He had taken a step towards Smith when he heard something move behind him. As he spun round, the floor rose up and the darkness came alive. Thick coils twisted round his legs and brought him crashing down into the slime. One arm remained free but the other was pinioned to his side by a force capable of shattering his rib cage. A python had been tempted into the trap by the prey it contained and had fallen asleep after consuming it. Now it was very much awake. The knots tightened and Poynter threshed and lashed out with his free arm. If he could reach the pistol. His hand brushed against the inert Smith and then closed about a piece of bone.

The python was not only crushing the life from him but trying to suffocate him by thrusting him deep into the mud. It was like a giant fist squeezing, squeezing. Its heavy coils pressing down, pinning his voice at the back of his throat. It was going to stave him in like a bird cage. A coil twisted round his thigh and Poynter jerked his head from the foul-smelling mud. The sky was a tattered square above his head. The snake's head reared before him and its mouth opened wide, the tongue flickering against his cheek. Poynter twisted again and thrust out with his free hand. Still grasping the bone he rammed it into the creature's lunging mouth and down its throat as far as his arm would go. He felt the hard, serrated lip rasping the flesh from his forearm and twisted the sharp bone from side to side. The pressure on his ribs tightened. One more turn of the vice and he would be done for. Fight! He turned the bone again and saw the tiny, red eyes glowing inches from his own. His foot struck the ladder. The dangling pistol twitched and started to swing. He kicked again and the ladder shifted, the pistol started to slide off the rung.

Fight! Poynter tried to breathe but his lungs were sealed. The strength was leaving his limbs as if a marionette's strings were being cut one by one. He tried to twist the bone but the python's throat contracted, seeming to set about his arm like plaster. Still its eyes were there before him gleaming with deadly purpose. Fight! He thrust again and was rewarded by a minute relaxation of pressure. He kicked out and the pistol dropped into the mud near his feet. If only he could work his left arm free. There was a groan behind him. Smith was coming round. Distracted, the python opened its mouth, and Poynter struggled. As the mouth snapped shut the coils relaxed to take up a new position. Poynter plucked free his left arm and stretched out. He felt calm. He knew exactly what he had to do. His fingers slid into the slime and he searched about him. As the coils tightened again he found the pistol. Clumsily he drew it up and levelled it with the python's eye. The bullet would have to pass within a centi-

160

metre of his own arm. He tightened his grip on the trigger. Hold yourself steady, man! He fired. There was a raw, red mess on his arm and a scalding sensation across his flesh. Fragments of gristle stung his face. The coils slowly relaxed and turned to heavy rubber. Poynter began to wriggle free.

By the time he had slung Smith across his shoulders and hauled them both to the rim of the pit the rain was coming down in earnest. He propped the little man up against a tree and watched the downpour washing the mud from his face.

Smith's eyes opened and he blinked up. 'What happened?'

'You had a nasty fall,' said Poynter.

THIRTY THREE

Unteroffizier Blum slaughtered his fifty-second mosquito of the day and studied the piece of paper that had been placed before him. 'Destroy the bridge?' he said incredulously.

The signaller nodded. 'That was the message.'

'Why?'

'There was no explanation given. The line went dead immediately after the message came through.'

Blum stared at the piece of paper as if he expected words containing additional facts and reassurances to magically appear on it. When his commanding officer had departed up the line with the locomotive, Blum had been left in charge of the post and had relished his situation as long as there were no important decisions to be made. When it was merely a question of brow-beating Schranz or shouting at the native labour he was happy. But blowing up a bridge? The repercussions of such an action would be far-reaching. How was the locomotive going to get back across the ravine? Supposing, terrible thought, that Schranz had misunderstood the message and that he, Unteroffizier Blum, blew up the bridge when he was not supposed to. He would be shot and it would be no consolation that Schranz was standing beside him waiting for painful death at the hands of the native levies whose aim was terrible. 'Try the line again,' he said. 'Ask for confirmation of the message.'

Five minutes later Schranz returned and Blum had been so preoccupied that he had not killed a single mosquito. 'Well?' he said.

Schranz shook his head in a gesture of defeat. 'I cannot make contact. I think the line is down.'

Blum groaned. The line was always being broken; occasionally by enemy action but mainly by elephants, falling trees, and natives who used sections of it for making decorations and animal traps. It was necessary to hang them sometimes to underline the point that this was undesirable behaviour.

'I'm certain that the message said to destroy the bridge,' said Schranz.

Blum scowled at him. It was typical of Schranz to be certain when he did not have the responsibility of blowing up the bridge. Schranz was normally never certain of anything.

'Be silent!' he snapped. He gazed out of the square block-house window and tried to see through the wisps of mist drifting above the ravine to some resolution of his problems. To blow up the bridge would be precipitous. He could not imagine walking out of the door and attaching the sticks of dynamite to the piles and lighting the fuse without some more exalted embodiment of the Kaiser's will being present and actually issuing the order that would sanctify the act. On the other hand, not to blow up the bridge might be an equally self-destructive decision. What he needed was some kind of compromise. He thought again. If he attached explosives to the bridge it would only require the application of a match to a fuse and the passage of a few seconds before the structure toppled into the ravine as apparently demanded by the wireless message that Schranz said he had received. But what would have precipitated this order? Only the arrival of the enemy. Blum peered at the steep sides of the gorge. How many directions were there from which they could come? The railway line was obviously a possibility with choices of a westerly or easterly approach. Hostile forces might arrive by the river but this was extremely unlikely as with the beginning of the rainy season the bottom of the ravine resembled a millrace running over rocks. There was a hunters' track leading to the hills behind the native village but apart from that, just precipitous forest and a few paths known only to the villagers. The directions from which the enemy might approach in force could be narrowed down to three or four at the most. If he stationed look-outs at strategic points he could be advised of any enemy advance and blow up the bridge if he thought it necessary.

Of course, it would be better if the Sons of the Fatherland were manning these important positions but, apart from Schranz who must stay with the telegraph and himself who must stay at the helm, the only other two Germans on the strength were men so racked with fever that they were stretched out on their beds barely able to distinguish night from day. The native levies would have to be pressed into action.

Unteroffizier Blum removed his extended fingers from the sides of his nostrils and was glad to see Schranz tilt his long neck forward and pay him the respect of rapt attention. 'Right,' he said firmly. 'This is the plan.'

THIRTY FOUR

The drizzle increased to a steady downpour and Gefreiter Ngi drew his rifle closer to his chest and stepped back under the unsubstantial shelter of a poinciana tree. He was used to the rain but he would rather have been watching it from the shelter of his hut. Not a hut in the nearby village but one a hundred miles to the west and not far from the border with Nigeria. He had been born in Nigeria but shortly after his birth the British rulers had decreed that a tax would be levied on every dwelling. Outraged, the locals had rebelled and in reprisal the British had killed several of them (including Ngi's father), and in a brilliant stroke burnt down all the houses, thus setting themselves the problem of having to find something else to tax.

Homeless and husbandless, Ngi's mother had taken her infant child and fled across the border into the Cameroons where, being a handsome woman, she soon came to the notice of a local Chief who took her as one of his wives. Ngi's new tribe was not vastly different in language or culture to his old one across the border and the rest of his life might have passed on the fringes of the white man's society had not the Great War turned the world into a battlefield.

German soldiers had come to Ngi's village and told the gathered inhabitants that in return for the unspecified advantages of being colonized, they must defend their country against the British, who would not hesitate to take all their wives, cattle and crops and burn the place to the ground. Having heard his mother's stories Ngi could imagine that this was true. In order to combat the British, all able-bodied men would be enrolled in the Imperial German Army of the Kamerun and be issued with a scarlet cap, a tunic with five brass buttons on its front and one on each shoulder, trousers and puttees. Also, a belt with a large metal buckle and two cartridge pouches. A native soldier was paraded wearing this garb and the crowd was impressed. It was only later that Ngi thought to enquire if there would be anything to go in the cartridge pouches or any possibility of being issued with a weapon such as he saw the white soldiers carrying. He was told to concentrate on his drill and that weapons were on the way. This to an extent was true but they often arrived as unannounced bequests from the fingers of dead men and even in those circumstances there were never enough to go round. The weapon he was clutching at the moment was a British Lee-Enfield rifle which had fallen into German hands during a skirmish in the jungle thirty miles to the East and he also had a clip of five .303 bullets which on pain of death he had been ordered to keep separate from his weapon in case of accidental discharge or over-developed hunting instinct. A rogue elephant that was terrorizing villages to the south had had its temper exacerbated by a bullet fired by a reckless and now well-flogged recruit to Four Company.

Ngi shivered and stepped forward so that he could get a clear view of the railway line. From his position on the ridge he could see the track for about three hundred yards before it began to curve round another ridge and make its laborious approach to the bridge up a steepish gradient. By running straight down the hillside he could be at the bridge within seconds and had been told to do so should he see anything moving. Unteroffizier Blum had made this instruction abundantly clear by frequent repetition.

Ngi peered down into the valley and then peered again, wiping the raindrops from his eyebrows. He was not quite certain that he believed what he saw. He hesitated and then started to run down the steep hill almost immediately bumping into a sweating Blum who had decided to break the monotony by making a tour of the nearest look-out posts. Ngi's relief at completing his mission in so short a time was transparent. 'Masta! Masta!' he cried. 'Something comes!'

'What?' breathed Blum feeling his heart jolt.

'A bird.'

'A bird!? What are you talking about, dummkopf?'

'It has a big tail and I think its wings are broken.'

Blum pushed Ngi aside and scrambled the last painful feet up the hill. The poor dolt had clearly taken his instructions too literally. 'Anything that moved' was clearly not intended to refer to birds. He swore under his breath. How was one supposed to deal with these people? The inmates of a kindergarten would make better soldiers. He reached the

165

summit of the ridge and glanced about him cursorily before peering down at the track. His expression changed.

'You see, masta. It is a bird.'

Blum said nothing but snatched up the binoculars he had removed from the Feldwebel's office. He had never seen a flying machine before and with the wings folded in the middle it was not immediately easy to discern the faint black crosses on the dirty mottled greyish-brown balloon cloth. He directed his attention at the two men partially obscured by the wings bent up above the fuselage. They were both white and one was wearing a pith helmet. He recognized neither of them. 'Destroy the bridge,' he said almost to himself.

THIRTY FIVE

Poynter looked up at the tall crags that crowded in from all sides and wondered how there could be a way through. But there had to be a way through. This was a railway line. A spout of water gushed from the hillside and a stream cascaded down, glimpsed as fragments of white against the greenery. The stream must flow into a river and where the line crossed the river there must surely be a village.

The line started to curve and Poynter craned forward. For some reason he felt uneasy. Round the bend and three hundred yards ahead lay a high-sided iron bridge approached between towering cliffs. Beyond it could be glimpsed a wall of green embroidered with huts and a square stone building like a fort. One dark window looked across the bridge like a gun barrel.

Poynter searched for signs of movement but his field of view was limited by the steep sides of the ravine. His flesh prickled. There was no sign of a human being, not one child peering from behind a tree, not even a dog. The bridge loomed nearer and he saw how narrow its metal framework was. Even with its wings folded up above its fuselage it was doubtful if the Dove could pass. They ought to stop. But Poynter was not going to stop. His eye had been trapped by the black square on the far side of the bridge. There was something there.

Smith began to slow down and Poynter yelled at him to keep going. As his voice echoed off the rocks there was another shout and a flicker of movement at the dark window. A bullet screamed overhead and ricochetted down the gully. Puffs of smoke appeared against the darkness. Smith opened the throttle and the Dove surged forward against the bullets.

THIRTY SIX

Blum shouted the order to fire when the fuse would not light. There was no fault with the matches, he had struck several of them and almost succeeded in igniting his fingers. The fuse must be damp. He swore and tried again as the rain splashed down on his shoulders. Above him the painted girders rose at angles of forty-five degrees to make contact with the underside of the bridge. Six sticks of dynamite were attached to one of them where it met the rock and a length of fuse hung down like a rat's tail. He struck another match and the fuse swayed away caught by the wind. He snatched at it with his free hand but the match went out. Now there was a fusillade of shots above his head and he prayed that the marksmanship was better than usual. He pressed forward against the rock and struck a match so that it ignited against the very tip of the fuse. The flame was snatched away but a red glow remained and began to splutter. Blum caught a whiff of saltpetre as he turned and ran for his life.

THIRTY SEVEN

Poynter hunched in his seat and heard a bullet scream off the side span of the bridge. The ironwork loomed and the folded wings of the Dove smashed against it with a sickening crunch. There was the sound of shattering wooden spars and grating metal and the wings were reduced to matchstick stumps, the tangled wires flailing against the latticework of iron. Jarred sideways by the shock he looked down to glimpse black, slippery rocks and a raging torrent thundering between vertical cliffs. All around was uproar as the Dove's engine railed above the rattle of small arms fire.

A man in khaki scrambled up the steep slope that led to the fort and then was snatched away in a vivid explosion of yellow and scarlet. The Dove jolted into the air and a fireball engulfed Poynter, singeing his eyebrows, making him choke for breath. Buffeted by the blast, he heard the despairing groan of the structure as it began to drop. This was what he had been waiting for, the moment of ghastly, unspeakable death. At any second he knew that the metalwork would disappear beneath him and the Dove plunge with it to the bottom of the ravine. There was a ferocious grinding noise and the structure lurched to rest against a cornice of protruding rock. The rails tore free and trembled in the air with a few sleepers still attached. It was on this precarious platform, scarcely stronger than a primitive suspension bridge, that the Dove wavered with the world a pendulum, the whole structure threatening to drop into the void.

Poynter saw the far side of the ravine twenty feet away and heard a buzzing that was not just the aftermath of the blast. It was the sound of a trapped insect determined to escape. Once again he had the strange but vivid impression that the

Dove was a living creature and that harnessed to their faith she could carry them through when all else had failed. The hopeful note of the engine swelled and as the rails trembled the Dove found the far side and once more had solid track beneath her wheels. No sooner had her mangled wings ceased grating against the metal than there was a noise like cannon fire and the whole structure of the bridge disappeared into the ravine. Poynter glimpsed black faces and heard guttural shouts. There was a volley of shots from the hillside and then the line swung away to follow the course of the river and the cliff shut out what lay behind.

THIRTY EIGHT

Von Graben gazed down at the white water swirling around the remains of the bridge and his jaw set firm. He had the feeling of a man who has plunged into the sea to recover a toy and suddenly finds a powerful current plucking at his body. But there would be no turning back. He would swim the Hellespont if necessary. To Maximilian von Graben, adversity was the seasoning that gave the bland taste of life a little flavour. He savoured the challenge.

His thoughts turned to the two men who were now two-thirds of the way to Douala with a secret that could change the course of the war. Once he had hated them as straw men pinned to Cunningham's coat-tails, even responsible for his death. But now his contempt had been forced to change to a grudging respect. They had been resourceful and courageous. He wanted nothing more than to see them dead but he would salute their graves.

Ropes had been passed across the ravine and a crude suspension bridge was being hauled into position. It was identical to the one which had been the only means of

169

crossing the river before the white man came. Schutz was in his element bellowing orders and spreading terror amongst the natives. Von Graben looked about him for Regan and thought for an uneasy moment that she had slipped away. Then he saw her sitting calmly on a rock beneath the shelter of the cliff. On an impulse he strolled to where she was fanning herself, one long leg crossed over the other and her skirt falling gracefully to her ankle. She smiled up at him, shading her eyes against the sun. 'The end of the line.' She read his face. 'Perhaps that's an unfortunate remark.'

'It might offend some.' Von Graben observed her calmly as she brushed her hair back over her shoulders. Striking red tresses the colour of maple leaves in autumn. He thought of the darting tongues of flame in the forests of the family estate at Malchin.

'I assume that I will be able to return to the hospital now?'

Von Graben shook his head. 'I regret that will not be possible. You will be continuing with us.'

'What!' Regan stood up. 'That's ridiculous. I've come quite far enough. I must go back. My patients need me.'

'There are German soldiers to look after. You can still exercise your function as a nurse. I have already explained to you why you must come with us.'

Regan let her anger abate and sat down. 'You think they're going to escape, don't you?'

He hesitated. 'No. But that does not mean I can allow you to fall into British hands.'

Regan enjoyed his discomfort. 'I think you're worried. They'll be back in England by the time you've repaired that bridge.'

'We are not going to repair the bridge. We will be proceeding by boat.'

'By boat?' Regan's face fell.

'Just below this point the river becomes navigable until the Malguri Falls. Leutnant Zimmerman has gone to fetch a boat.'

Regan struggled to regain her composure. 'Faith, and how

can a stupid boat bring you closer to the flying machine? They'll be miles ahead of you.'

'Quite the reverse.' If von Graben was enjoying a small triumph there was no trace of it in his well-modulated voice. 'The railway line makes a long detour to avoid the mountains. It eventually crosses the river again at the Malguri Rapids. The river follows an almost straight line to the rapids and with the current that is now running we will have no difficulty in being there before them.' He watched the hope draining from Regan's face. 'Their adventure is almost over.'

THIRTY NINE

'Poor old girl,' said Smith.

Poynter said nothing. It was true. The Dove was barely a shadow of her once beautiful self. The graceful wings looked as if they had been pinioned with a blunt hatchet and were reduced to jagged stumps trailing a medusa of tangled wires. The horizontal stabilizer flopped like a wet peacock's tail, the rudder lurched to one side and the fuselage covering was freshly ripped by bullets and brushes with jungle foliage. One of the bolts on the engine mounting had sheared loose and the welding of the wheels was a constant worry. Smith lifted down the last can of fuel. 'I wonder if she'll see this out.'

'She'll do her best or bust in the attempt.' Poynter addressed the Daimler-Mercedes engine sternly.

'I don't like the way we're heading,' said Smith. 'We seem to be turning back on ourselves.'

Poynter had noticed the same thing but deemed it best not to admit it. 'We'll head west soon,' he reassured. 'We've got to skirt those mountains, that's all.'

'It seems a blooming big "that's all",' Smith started to

pour in the fuel. 'If only the Dove still had her wings, we could be right up above this lot.'

He began to sing in his high quavering voice. '*Oh, for the wings, for the wings of a dove, soaring, soaring, high up above.*' He broke off into a cackle of laughter and the sound rolled off the hillside sending a flock of parakeets screeching in search of a new feeding ground.

Poynter groaned. 'Spare me your serenading, for pity's sake. Save it for the Hun when we run out of ammunition.' He released the makeshift funnel for a second to scratch his chin.

'Your beard's getting longer,' said Smith. 'It's put on a bit of a spurt recently.'

'I can hardly see your face,' said Poynter. 'You look as if you're peering over a bush – hold the can steady, man! She needs every drop of nourishment she can get.'

'She's not the only one,' said Smith. 'My stomach's so empty I could dine off a ship's biscuit.'

Poynter nodded. He knew that they could not go on much longer with only the occasional root or handful of berries for sustenance. They were both pitifully thin. He now found it an effort to haul himself in and out of the cockpit. His concentration was beginning to wander and he knew that his lack of appetite was a bad sign.

'There's got to be a village round here where we can get something,' Smith's eyes roamed the jungle-clad slopes. 'What's that?'

Poynter followed his gaze. Plumes of mist hung over the trees and at a casual glance it would have been easy to confuse them with the column of smoke rising steadily a quarter of a mile away. Poynter measured the distance and looked along the edge of the forest near the track. There was an opening between the trees that might be the beginnings of a path. 'It could be a German patrol,' he said.

'They wouldn't be up there. They'd be walking along the track. It must be a native village.' Smith turned. 'What do you think? We can't have anyone on our heels.'

172

'I don't like leaving the Dove.'

'You stay here then. I'll go and have a look.'

Poynter was shocked at how terrible that suggestion seemed to him. To be left alone? 'All right,' he said. 'We'll take a look together. But we must be quick.'

'As lightning,' said Smith. He finished emptying the can and shook the last drops from the palm leaf funnel. 'In and out.'

They crossed the track to the forest and at Poynter's instigation took the empty fuel can with them. He knew the natives treasured any receptacle that would hold liquids. The can might provide a useful instrument of barter.

There was a path at the edge of the railway line. Exposed roots had been polished slippery by the passage of naked feet and the ground worn bare of vegetation. The way mounted steeply, zig-zagging from side to side, and occasional footprints could be seen in the mud. Giant ferns glistened and twitched under the rain and the moss-covered trunks crowded in menacingly.

Poynter waited to see a habitation or a human being. When the sun went in all his old fears of the claustrophobic forest returned. The idea that people could make their lives here depressed him utterly. He would have to rebel, break out and find the sky; breathe air that had not been filtered through a billion leaves straining for their own survival; see further than a few gloomy yards before his face. At least on the railway line there was some space. There were two rails beneath your feet that had been forged by men and laid by men as proof that *homo* could be *sapiens* and impose his will on unruly nature. Here he felt that he was slipping back into the savage state.

Smith accidentally struck the petrol can against a tree and the sound rang out like a gong. Poynter seized his hand and they waited. The reverberation trembled away to nothing and there was no sound save that of raindrops splashing onto thick, rubbery leaves plangent as drum skins.

The path rose even more steeply and Poynter felt his

strength ebbing. How long could their bodies stand this punishment? He drove himself forward and at last the wall of a brown, thatched hut marked a plateau in the forest. Mist hung round it and to his disquiet there was no sign of human life. No children running away up the track to announce their coming, no wide-eyed suspicious faces peering from behind crude window openings. It was like the bridge. Behind the first hut was another and quickly they fell upon the village, spread out but still following the line of the widening path. There was a crude drain in the middle of the way choked with maize husks around which the water ran as if skirting a dam. The flattened earth glistened and be-draggled palm fronds shrank around the unsubstantial frameworks of the huts. There was a smell of human effluent that no rain could wash away. But there was no sign of a human being.

'I don't like this place,' said Poynter. 'I think we should go back.'

Smith had unslung his rifle at the entrance to the village. His shrewd eyes darted warily. 'Let's go on to the end of the village.'

'Why're there no people?'

Smith ducked down and tried to peer in to the interior of one of the huts. The doorways were knee high to the sodden earth. 'Perhaps they're frightened.'

Poynter said nothing.

The path twisted to the left and came to a piece of open ground flanked by thatched buildings. One was low and long and like a Chief's house or a dormitory for his wives. A carved stool rested outside the hut and there were fresh wood shavings before it as if someone had been whittling and left hurriedly. A fire smouldered in the middle of the clearing and the carcass of a small animal lay above it impaled on a wooden spit resting between two blackened posts. In its skinned nakedness it resembled a human foetus.

'Ahoy there,' shouted Smith. 'Anyone aboard?' His voice rose into the trees and echoed away amongst the sodden foliage of the huts but there was no answer. The rain continued to fall and the mist hung low above their heads.

'Dash them the tin and we'll take the meat,' said Poynter. 'They must be hiding in the bush.' He made no effort to hide the anxiety in his voice. He wanted to be away from this place and he was beginning to worry about the Dove. They should never have left her. As Smith placed the petrol can on the stool, he approached the smoking fire and stretched his hand out for the spit. There was a strange creaking noise as the wind stirred through a passage between the huts and his eyes rose to look through the smoke.

Two bodies were hanging from one rope, their black heads pressed together as if in some obscene parody of the final notes of a stage duet. Their feet were barely above the earth and as the wind blew, so the tree they were hanging from creaked and their dangling, rag-doll bodies began to twist in a laborious dance.

Poynter froze, his hand still reaching out for the meat.

There was something so calculatedly cruel and contemptuous about the form of execution. He heard Smith's intake of breath and withdrew his hand. Now the meat seemed contaminated, as did everything else in this terrible place. He could understand the fear that had built inside him ever since they had left the track. The village was cursed.

Poynter started back and heard the hissing noise as something thudded into the side of his pith helmet. At the edge of the clearing a figure squatted gripping a long tube with both hands. A blow pipe. Shadows turned into men and the air was full of hissing darts as Smith fired and started to run back the way they had come. The skies opened and rain fell in a torrential downpour. Not so much water as sharpened knives. It splashed up above their knees and formed an opaque wall. Poynter ran through the murk seeing only Smith before him. Two silhouettes crouched with bows bent and an arrow sped past his nose. He could hear shrill, yapping cries above the thunder of the rain. Terror drove his feet.

Smith fell cursing and rolled twice before dragging himself up still clutching the Mauser. As he staggered on, Poynter turned and fired his pistol. The sound was snatched away by the downpour. More figures materialized like dark smudges against the grey and a spear snaked down the rain-lashed slope. Poynter ran on until the trees loomed up and he could see the path zigzagging away into the gloom. He plunged down the hillside and snagged his ankle. He fell full length and struck his shoulder against a protruding root. As he struggled upright he saw a man dropping to one knee further up the slope. The bow twanged and an arrow thumped into the bark beside his head. Now there were a line of figures appearing through the mist and in their midst a man who had materialized like a genie. His head was shaven and painted red with black chevrons on his forehead. He was naked save for a loin cloth and broad bands of white ran vertically and horizontally across his body. As he advanced with arms outstretched he resembled a human cross or an aeroplane.

Poynter plunged on, slipping and slithering using the great trees as buffers to slow his descent. Twice he crossed the path which was now more like a mountain stream in spate and then found that there were only trees about him with great creepers hanging down like bell ropes and the squelching leaves rising up above his calves. There was no sign of Smith and he feared that he was blundering deeper and deeper into the forest. He threw himself against a tree and listened. At first there was only the dripping of the rain. Then a strange sing-song cry that was growing louder. It throbbed and echoed away amongst the trees, more chilling than a single shout.

Poynter thought of the painted man, the Witch Doctor, and his fingers dug into the palm of his hand. Now the sound seemed to be coming from all round him. With a strange clarity that mocked place and time he remembered his hunting days in England. Now, he was the fox waiting in the covert, listening to the sounds of the huntsmen drawing nearer. The mist had been beaten down to ground level and he ran on through patches of it with a pain like a sharp object lodged inside his chest. His head swirled with the grey wraiths around him. He heard a sharp cry which seemed to come from his left and a babble of excited speech. Small, stooping figures were flitting through the trees. An arrow hummed past him. Suddenly he came upon a path. He had no idea in which direction he was travelling. He heard a step behind him and he spun round and almost fired at Smith. Figures threaded through the trees with the Witch Doctor capering at their head and the sing-song chant gave way to frenzied whooping. Poynter and Smith splashed on across puddles like miniature lakes. Ahead, the rails gleamed through an opening in the trees. Poynter burst onto the track and looked to right and left. The Dove waited fifty yards away seemingly intact.

He started to run towards it and then stopped. There was no hope of getting the engine started before their attackers were upon them. He turned and raised his pistol as the first men broke from the trees, the Witch Doctor in front. Faced by two white men with the Dove behind them the Witch Doctor paused. His followers crouched and rattled their weapons. Awed in the presence of the flying machine they wavered and looked towards their leader. Undaunted he took a firm step forward and threw his arms wide. His ochred head went back and he howled to the heavens until his chest muscles quivered. One arm started to swing faster and faster and Poynter suddenly realized what he was doing: the man was trying to turn himself into a flying machine to challenge the Dove. The natives had been watching as the Dove penetrated their kingdom. The shout stopped abruptly and the Witch Doctor's red head jerked forward. He began to run towards them, his arms spread wide again, the villagers screeching at his elbow. Poynter stood firm and with both hands swung up his pistol. He fired and the painted figure crashed to the ground. The attackers slithered to a halt, their screams locked in their throats. The only sounds came from the rain and the rattle in the throat of the dying man.

Smith turned and ran for the Dove, Poynter at his heels. He tossed his rifle into the cockpit and scrambled after it. Poynter thrust the Luger under his belt and grabbed the propeller. An arrow glanced off the engine cowling. First wrench and the engine roared into life. He ducked and ran as the Dove began to surge past him. More dark shadows poured from the trees. The concerted hallooing had given way to staccato shouts of rage and despair. The Witch Doctor flooded the ground with his blood. No man dared advance beyond him.

Poynter threw himself at the wing and clung on waiting for the fatal arrow. The fuselage shuddered as if about to disintegrate and the Dove roared down the line. Within seconds the shouts were snatched away and all he could hear was the doughty triumphant growl of her indefatigable engine.

FORTY

When she first clapped eyes on the *Kaiser Wilhelm* it had struck Regan that the owner of that illustrious name would not have been flattered to find it inscribed in peeling letters along the side of a fifty-foot launch that closely resembled a tug which had been squeezed in a vice until it took on the shape of a primitive flat iron, with a funnel and wheelhouse protruding from the place where the handle ought to be. Everything about the vessel suggested that none of its innumerable trips up and down the river had been without incident. Whether scraping through shoals in the dry season or being driven ashore when the rains swelled the course into a moving lake, colliding with sunken logs or resisting the challenge of islands of floating foliage, the *Kaiser Wilhelm* bore the marks of her diurnal battle with the river on every inch of her hull and superstructure.

If her colour was rusty brown, it was because the vessel herself seemed to be made of rust, with the exception of the funnel that did have a band of fading black around its jagged top. Everything above deck level tilted as if trying to avoid some hazard. At aft and stern, her hull was dented like a pie crust and her fenders had been chafed away to shreds of coconut matting, leaving the sides deeply scored as if the vengeful hands of some ferocious river god had attempted to seize her and drag her to the bottom. If the wheelhouse had ever possessed windows these had long since disappeared and even the wheel had two broken spokes. Behind it, stood the grizzled skipper, whose face seemed to have contracted in the vertical plane whilst his boat was expanding in the horizontal. He spoke only to his spluttering engine and that in truncated German curses that spurted from a volcano of frustration, threatening to erupt with each groan, shudder and judder of the decrepit craft. Even with all stores and ballast removed to make room for von Graben's party, the gunwale was still only a precarious couple of inches above the water line.

Regan stood before the wheelhouse and looked at the wild water. Pecked by a million drops of rain it rushed past in a thick brown torrent, sometimes carved by crests of white foam. The *Kaiser Wilhelm* was racing the current in order to keep some measure of control over it and the water slurped over the distant banks, hissing as its curling lip sped away to become lost in the bobbing and swaying of the overhanging foliage.

Regan gazed down and watched a spreading column of alluvial black insinuate itself in the brown and then succumb to it as if stirred into a can of paint. How different to the streams of home where the water ran crystal clear amongst the rocks and you could see each grain of sand and the quiver of a trout's gills; where the fields ran clear to the horizon like slabs of green and brown polished by a buffing cloth. Here, with the huge trees closing in eternally, one seemed to be below the earth with the thick brown flood, like some kind of visceral fluid, churning life out of darkness.

The *Kaiser Wilhelm* came to a wide bend in the river and the muttering captain escaped from the main race and sought the shelter of the shore. Nearer the bank there were still sullen eddies and circling patches of greenery but the course of the river was much slower. Regan heard the shrill, repetitive shriek of a bird and searched the treetops. It was a strange interlude, this blustering down the swirling river. After being confined in the train it was almost agreeable.

There was a shout from one of the Yaundes and she followed his pointing finger to the bank. A horse appeared to be entering the water and then she recognized the bulging eyes and the squat calf's head grafted to the thick body like a huge potato. It was a pygmy hippopotamus hurrying to take shelter. As it sank below the water, Schutz threw up his Mauser and took aim. There was a crack and a spurt of water where the animal's head had been. In the wheelhouse the captain turned and swore angrily. Schutz fired again and the captain stepped towards him bellowing. Regan felt the vessel veer sharply and heard another shout. As she turned, water surged over the gunwale and she heard a great crack as the *Kaiser Wilhelm* smashed against the foliage of a submerged tree. Branches soared above the water and then there was a solid thump as the launch butted the trunk head-on and her prow lifted towards the sky. Regan was hurled backwards against the wheelhouse and then into the water. There was a numbing pain at the back of her head and the brown tide washed over her, chilling her to the bone and turning her clothing into a leaden straitjacket. She swallowed a mouthful of water and panicked even before colliding with the branches of the submerged tree. Like the bars of a grille they thrust against her body and she only broke free as her lungs were bursting. Gasping for air, she swallowed another mouthful of water and saw to her horror that the launch was thirty yards away and veering out into the open stream.

Either they had not seen her fall in or they did not care. She tried to call out but could only choke. Her head sank below the water and in her pain and horror she realized she was drowning.

Something closed about her jaw and panic surged. Then she recognized a human form swimming beside her and realized that a hand was striving to support her above the water. 'Lie still!' The voice was firm. It was a tone she would have used herself when dealing with a difficult patient. She fought to obey it and felt herself being drawn through the water across the current. Strong fingers still held her jaw tightly and she began to sense the rhythmic movement of the muscular arm that was powering them through the water. With every stroke her panic lessened and her belief in her own survival increased. Her sodden skirt, instead of being an instrument of destruction, now seemed to be buoying her through the water. The pressure on her jaw relaxed slightly and she sensed that the pull of the water was far less strong. She cleared her throat and opened her eyes.

Above her was the sky, grey and lowering but now as beautiful as any, blue and cloud-flecked, that she had seen in County Antrim. Her feet touched the bottom and strong arms drew her from the water and half carried her to a bank beneath overhanging trees. She turned her head and saw von Graben on his knees gasping, his hair plastered across his head, his cheeks hollow, his eyes red with exhaustion. Slowly, he raised his head to look at her and then rose unsteadily. Taking one step towards her he stretched out his hand. She took it and allowed herself to be drawn to her feet. Now they were face to face and his eyes looked at her as no man's had done before. For a terrible moment she thought that he was going to kiss her; then, in a moment even more terrible, she realized that she wanted him to.

FORTY ONE

Poynter listened to the sounds of the night. It was now that the forest came awake. Rustles and squeaks from the grass near the track, the demented shriek of cicadas, the sound of animals shaking ripe fruit from the branches, strange cries that might have come from animals or birds and been formulated in pain or passion; armies of toads and frogs vying to outdo each other's arpeggios; croaking, whistling, sighing, hiccuping, flying foxes yawling, bats flickering through the air with the sound of pages turning, silver moths, mosquitoes armed with lances attacking in their thousands.

Smith was sleeping beside Poynter and the two men were beneath the Dove, the rails hemming them in like the bars of a crude bunk. It had stopped raining but the air was heavy with dew. The mist coiled through the trees like a giant snake. It was cold. Poynter was preparing to settle down when he paused. There was a noise he had not heard before. A shrill trumpeting sound. He looked along the track and immediately began to shake Smith awake. A large black shape was etched against the night sky. It was moving towards them. A low whinny and an answering call, shrill again but this time cut off at its highest point. There was pain in that sound, pain and anger. Other shapes were advancing down the track, three of them in a line so that there might have been an invisible yoke across their shoulders. Elephants. How silently they moved, hardly making an impression on the noises of the night. A crunch of stones, a swish of foliage.

Poynter felt Smith reaching for his rifle and held his arm tightly. In the sound of the shrill trumpeting was a note of malice searching for an outlet. Beside them, the first elephant paused and its huge, swept-back ears twitched so that they crackled like sails in a squall. Its head bent and its trunk ran along the fuselage of the Dove as if testing it for possible consumption. Poynter watched the great foot within crushing distance of his head and held his breath. The elephant shifted its position and stationed its bulk against one of the shattered wings. It began to sway from side to side and the Dove creaked and lifted in the air. The elephant was using the aeroplane as a back scratcher.

'Blimey', breathed Smith.

Another angry trumpet jerked Poynter's head back down the line. There were dark shadows everywhere and it was impossible to see how many elephants there were in the herd. Of the three advancing abreast, two were trying to support the one in the middle. With a bellow of pain it collapsed on one heavy knee and the others closed in sweeping their trunks across the ground as if urging it upright. They pressed their weight against its flanks and bore it with them refusing to leave it behind. The wounded elephant shuddered and threw back its head to emit a long defiant trumpet, a rallying cry against death. A message of courage and hope to any creature that heard it.

The three elephants pressed forward and brushed against the one that was scratching itself as if telling it to move on. With one final nudge at the wing the animal folded its trunk in the air and slowly faded into the shadows. The sounds of the night again took over.

Poynter sank down beside Smith. His heart was pounding, it was not fear he felt but elation. He could still hear that triumphant, jubilant sound. Smith's arm stretched out and he felt the pressure of the firm hand against his back and the solid warmth of the body against his. It lent additional reassurance as it was meant to do and soon both men fell asleep.

FORTY TWO

Regan heard something slither across the floor and raised herself on one elbow. It was night and she was in the hold of the *Kaiser Wilhelm* with the hatch half open above her head and rain and spray splashing down on her face. She listened intently but heard nothing above the sound of the water and the occasional "craw, craw, craw" of a bird in the jungle. It had probably been one of her shoes stirring with the motion of the boat, or perhaps a rat wondering where the stores had gone to. Regan had seen enough rats on her father's farm not to be frightened of them.

She was alone in the hold which formed not only a damp and smelly dormitory but a prison. Still muttering and cursing, the captain had brought the *Kaiser Wilhelm* charging into the bank above the Malguri Rapids. Here there had been no shortage of volunteers to hurl themselves gratefully onto dry land and throw ropes round the first tree strong enough to bring her to a grudging halt, her bows twitching angrily like a dog with its lead between its teeth. Had Regan been able to understand more German, she would have heard the skipper say that because of the rains the river would soon be un-navigable and that anybody who expected him to make another trip up-stream could go to hell on a tsetse fly's back. He was going to retire to the office of the Kamerun Trading Company with a bottle of schnapps and wait for the Kaiser, the British, or the dry season, whichever came first.

He had made fast and stumped off and von Graben had quickly assembled Schutz and the Yaundes and headed for the railway line. Not where it crossed the swollen river by means of a steel suspension bridge now barely two feet above the rising water, but where it followed the curve of a steep escarpment dropping down to the river. It was from this small mountain that the line made its laborious descent to the bridge.

Regan had seen that the native soldiers were carrying picks and shovels and had started to follow them, but von Graben had immediately ordered her to stay where she was and assigned a Yaunde to guard her. Common sense told her that they were going to disrupt the line and lay an ambush for the Dove. Regan swung her feet to the floor. She must do something. Try and warn them. The timbers creaked as she felt for her shoes, tapping the heels soundlessly on the floor in case uninvited guests with a propensity to bite or sting had secreted themselves inside the toes. She rose, put on her shoes, and felt her way to the half open hatch. It had stopped raining and a watery moon showed itself behind broken cloud. There were no steps but the roof of the hold brushed the top of her head and it was easy to find a foothold on the edge of a bunk and raise herself up so that she could peer across the deck. There was no sign of life save for the wheel, stirring as if steered by an invisible hand. Keeping her head low, she hauled herself up on her elbows and squirmed across the damp planks until she could peer towards the bank. Her heart sank. The mooring ropes had been lengthened and the *Kaiser Wilhelm* now stood off the shore with twenty feet of angry water between her and dry land. Facing her the Yaunde sat with a camp fire between him and the launch, toasting his hands and clearly very much awake.

Regan sank below the shallow gunwale. She would have to take to the water again. If she worked her way round to the stern she could drop into the river and let the current take her downstream to within striking distance of the land. It was risky with the rapids so near, and in the dark the river seemed doubly terrifying. But there was no other way.

She started to move and her long skirt tugged at her legs. Best to take it off. She unbuttoned her bodice and wriggled until she could raise her hips and twist sideways to pull the garment from her legs. Turning on her stomach she rolled

185

her dress into a ball and held it before her as she crawled past the wheelhouse towards the stern. From the bank she could hear the splutter of the fire and the monotone humming of the Yaunde. He would not be the only guard. She had watched attentively as von Graben deployed his men on previous nights.

At the stern the wheelhouse reared between her and the Yaunde, its outline silhouetted by the glow of the fire. Below, the water swept past at a speed that she hoped was exaggerated by fear and the launch bucked and quivered. Ahead, the crest of a long white wave refused to break and she guessed that it must mark either a sand bank or a submerged log. Either might save her from being swept away down the rapids.

She wriggled to the side of the stern nearest the bank and swung her legs over the side. How cold it was and how fast the current moved. She hesitated but knew there was no turning back. Taking a deep breath she released the gunwale and thrust towards the shore, trying to cling onto her dress.

Immediately she realized that she had underestimated the speed of the current. The dress was torn away and the dark bank flashed by. Her body hardly seemed to break the surface. Two scrabbling strokes and she was already at the obstruction. As it thumped against her ribs it felt like a living creature. Yielding, slippery, heavy. It began to swing and for a terrifying second she thought that it was going to take her with it down the rapids. Then it steadied and she felt the bottom beneath her feet; she had arrived against a submerged tree trunk. Straining against the flood she pulled herself up and hauled herself towards the shallows, constantly battling against being sucked beneath the trunk.

At last she was able to break the grip of the current and collapse shaking against the sloping bank. As her heart beat returned to normal she heard the tuneless chanting of the Yaunde mingled with the sound of rushing water. He had heard nothing. Waiting long, patient minutes to regain her strength she slowly raised herself above the level of the sedge

186

and peered back towards the camp fire. The Yaunde was not alone. She could see the dark shadows of half a dozen sleeping men.

Regan rose carefully and worked her way down river to the edge of the clearing. Her shoes had been carried away by the river and her shift clung uncomfortably.

After a hundred yards of following the trees a white band glowed in the moonlight. It was the path that led to the railway line. Regan waited and watched, listening to the sounds of the night and the hum of marauding insects. This was where she would expect a sentry to be posted. Minutes passed and she edged forward again. If she followed the railway line it would be easier than trying to make her way through the jungle. Von Graben and his ambush party would be facing the other way and with any luck she could make her way round them.

She tugged her shift down about her knees and brushed her tangled hair from her eyes. There was still no false note in the relentless clamour of the jungle night. She advanced warily to the railway line and began to follow its slow rise, keeping as near to the trees as she could. Ahead, the escarpment showed up as a great black shape against the night sky and the summit of railway line as a notch cut into its steep side. On the upper slope there was thick vegetation but below the track the ground fell away with a few scattered shrubs so that it was almost a cliff dropping directly into the river. Something stirred near Regan's foot and she stepped forward quickly dislodging a flurry of stones. The noise seemed like that of a small avalanche and she stooped low and strained her ears. Somewhere near her a cicada shrieked as if in its death agony and she hurried on again, eager to leave the sound behind. Her eyes were always on the rails, knowing that where they had been disturbed, this would be a sign that the ambush party was waiting. As she approached the place where the track curved round the hillside she stopped. There was a faint glow rising like a candle flame from further down the slope. She pressed back into the shadows and waited. After a few seconds there was the rasping sound of a human throat being cleared. They were waiting on the bend.

Schutz squatted before the fire and brooded. The *Engländer* were not likely to travel at night and therefore nothing would happen until after first light. That left six hours to kill. A Yaunde dampened down the smouldering fire and he watched von Graben turn in his sleep and pull his blanket over his shoulder. Schutz's face hardened.

A rattle of stones from up the hill made him turn his head. Some night animal closing with its prey. A snake. He listened but there was no further sound. Some smoke from the smothered fire wafted into his face and he brushed it aside wishing that it had a human form on which he could wreak his frustration. He stood up and buckled the strap of his pistol before starting up the hill.

Regan shrank to the side of the hill and craned her neck into the darkness. Two piles of earth and the glint of twin bands of steel showed where a section of the track had been separated from the rest. With the enemy below she would have to make a detour through the forest. Turning to the bank she reached up and seized a protruding root. As her grip tightened there was a sound from the hillside beneath the track. Fighting her panic she struggled to haul herself up. Stones fell and her shift snagged on a branch. She tore it free and thrust into the bush.

Schutz emerged onto the track and controlled his breathing so that he could listen. Further up the track there was the unmistakable noise of something pressing through the undergrowth. Or someone. His eyes roamed the thickly jungled hillside and the sounds grew fainter. Quickly he moved along the railway track. A hunters' trail rose at right angles to the line and he thrust his shoulders into the narrow passage. His palms were sweating.

188

Regan felt as if she was forcing her way through the bristles of a broom. Twigs and branches scratched her face and creepers clung to her ankles as if imbued with human life. A sharp pain in the small of her back stung like the jab of a goad. Her bare feet were being torn to pieces. Was the noise all of her own making or was there something else? She paused and looked about her desperately. The chirruping of the insects had stopped. Only when the moon came out could she see through the foliage to a mottled chiaroscuro that represented the heavens. Her head jerked. On the left. A sound of movement. Something pushing warily through the bush. Imagination. God say it was her imagination.

She turned again like a trapped animal, her will oozing away into the ground. She was hypnotized; the rabbit waiting at the end of the tunnel, seeing the red eyes of the stoat draw closer and closer. She turned and nearly blundered into a tree fungus. Its ghastly, luminous whiteness made her think of Schutz as he had appeared over the side of the wagon. She bit back a scream.

Totally panic-stricken, she threw herself forward, the branches scourging her and a thousand fingers of foliage trying to hold her back. She had lost all sense of direction. All she wanted to do was escape from this terrible place.

The wall disappeared and she fell. A path. Panting and sobbing she pulled herself up and began to run. What a relief when there was some space and a corridor of light above your head. And then the hand came out.

Regan felt thick fingers close about her mouth and wrench her backwards as if trying to tear her head from her shoulders. Her body hit the ground and through the pain, Schutz's hideous face leered down at her. Now hatred and lust were allied with triumph.

She tried to scream and bit his fingers but he jerked her head up and pounded it against the ground so that a fresh agony of pain leapt between her eyes. His spittle leaked onto her face and his knee bore down between her thighs. One

189

hand was still across her mouth and she felt the other fumbling beneath her shift. She clawed at his face but he shook her aside as if brushing away an insect. Now his fingers had closed over the rim of her underclothing. A whiplash of pain and the garment was ripped from her body.

Schutz was happy. Happy and excited. His troll-like face glistened with sweat and desire. His head loomed towards her and she felt his foul mouth sliding across her flesh in the mockery of a kiss. The rank odour of his body filled her nostrils. A second knee thrust down between her legs and something slapped against the side of her thigh. A holster. Regan screwed her head sideways and stretched out her arm. She could just touch the hard leather.

Above her, Schutz was fumbling with his belt. His legs kneed hers apart and he thrust at the tight passage she had shared with no man. Regan fought pain and terror. *The pistol, she must think only of the pistol.* As Schutz grunted and bore into her she stretched out her arm again and plucked at the holster flap. Her fingers brushed against the cold metal. Schutz was thrusting and growling, thriving on her pain, penetrating her as with a bayonet.

Slowly, inch by inch, she began to ease the pistol from the holster until her hand could close about it. She could feel Schutz beginning to tremble against her as her forefinger slipped inside the trigger guard. She thrust the muzzle against his side. Schutz turned. His hand lunged out. Too late.

Schutz's body jerked in the air with the shot and he screamed in pain and anger. His hands fled to his side and then to the pistol as Regan rolled sideways. He knocked it from her grasp and fell back cursing. By the time he had scrambled to his knees and retrieved the weapon, Regan had disappeared.

Von Graben was first upon the scene. He found a dishevelled Schutz fumbling with his belt, pistol in hand. A dark stain coloured one side of his tunic.

'What happened?'

'The girl shot me.'

'*Shot you!*' Von Graben grappled with the statement.

'With a pistol. She must have had it concealed. I challenged her and she came towards me. She suddenly swung out her arm and shot me from point blank range. I was careless. I am sorry, Herr Hauptmann.'

Von Graben looked at Schutz. There were blades of grass and twigs clinging to the front of his uniform. Some of the buttons were undone. His face bore the marks of scratches.

Schutz followed the Hauptmann's eyes. 'I tried to follow her into the bush but she got away.'

Von Graben said nothing but bent to examine Schutz's wound. A bullet appeared to have torn through the rolls of flesh that encircled the Korpsgendarm's waist like swaddling. If the bleeding could be stopped and the wound resisted infection his life would not be in danger.

'What you have told me is the truth?'

'Yes, Excellency.' Schutz's tone suggested that he had received a second wound.

'Very well. We will attend to your wound and send two of the Yaundes after the girl at first light. She will not get far.'

'I would like to find the girl,' said Schutz.

'I do not doubt it.' Von Graben's voice was a rapier drawn from ice. 'But you will stay with me. Very close.'

FORTY THREE

Poynter watched the compass needle quivering towards west and began to feel more cheerful. At least they were now heading in the right direction. Sooner or later they had to leave the forest and descend to the coastal swamps that would signal the approach to Douala and the British garrison. If only there was more fuel. The contents of their last can were filtering away from the fuel tank above his head. Whenever the Dove's engine changed key he waited for the telltale splutter and the death-roll of its pistons choking into silence.

Smith shouted and pointed and Poynter strained forward to hear his words. The track had been climbing for some time and now the jungle was falling away on their right. The line was levelling out and there was a prospect of open sky which suggested that they had reached the summit of a pass. The lieutenant followed Smith's arm and saw what he had waited to see for so long: the hills disappearing and an area of flat land stretching away to a horizon lost in mist. There was even a river lying in coils like a huge silver serpent slumbering on a cloth of green. A river which must go down to the sea.

Smith gave a 'thumbs up' sign and Poynter raised his topi in salute. On their right the ground disappeared and the track shrunk to a narrow pathway running along the edge of a steep escarpment. They were beginning to descend. A new day was beginning and the end of their journey was in sight.

Smith's voice could be heard rising above the roar of the engine: *'It's a long way to Douala, It's a long way to go –'*

Poynter threw back his head and bawled the refrain.

FORTY FOUR

The baying of the dogs started at daybreak. Regan heard it first with alarm and then in mounting terror as the sound grew closer. She remembered the half-starved hounds kept by the hunters at Ndala, so vicious that they would turn on each other if denied another prey.

Regan searched the steep slopes. The Germans must have commandeered the dogs from the local village. She imagined

Schutz at their heels and shuddered. After her escape she had been too exhausted to go far and had found a hiding place near the railway. The jungle was so thick that a man could have passed within a foot and not seen her. But a dog. There was no stream she could wade through to throw them off the scent. Even if she could find a tree to climb, they would be scratching and whining at the bottom of it.

The frenzied barking drew nearer and she looked across the steep ravine. There was a flicker of movement amongst the trees and a flight of cockatoos lifted into the air. They must have her scent. Within minutes they would be on her.

She started to hobble down the slope. Her feet were torn and swollen, her head swimming; she could feel the welts of insect bites against her shift. Maybe she could reach the river.

Two faltering steps and she stopped and listened. She could still hear the dogs but there was something else. Something faint and far away. So distant that it might have been a product of her fevered imagination. The drone of an engine.

The baying of the dogs drowned all other noise and she launched herself down the hillside.

FORTY FIVE

Poynter glanced down and his stomach contracted. A hundred feet below, foaming white water rushed between steep cliffs. The way ahead was a notch blasted out of solid rock, barely wide enough to take the track. A shattered wing grated against the cliff face and he winced. One nudge from a protruding rock and they could jump the rails. He could feel the space below drawing him as if he was poised on the brink of a mighty waterfall. He eased back the throttle still further and forced himself to look ahead. They were approaching a bend.

As he measured the distance, a figure tumbled from the thick undergrowth on the hillside and began to run towards them. It was a woman, white, naked except for the remnants of a torn shift. Her hair streamed behind her. Red hair. Regan! She was running like a deer and waving frantically.

She was forty yards from the Dove when two black dogs spilled from the hillside and skidded almost to the brink of the precipice before racing in pursuit. Low and sinewy, their bodies flowed over the ground, narrowing the distance fast.

Poynter's head jerked up as a bullet whined off one of the radiators. They had come under fire from an outcrop of rock that dominated the line ahead. He hunched in his seat and opened the throttle. Smith returned fire and the Dove surged forward, one pinioned wing tearing at the hillside. Regan's terrified face loomed up and she ducked as the shattered wing swept towards her. Leaping for her back, the first dog caught the buckled wing support bar flush across the side of the head and went down kicking with its neck broken. Regan threw herself at the tail assembly and tried to haul herself to safety as she clung to the rudder control wires. The second dog skidded beneath her feet scrabbling and returned to the attack. Its yellow teeth snapped inches from her trailing foot and Poynter lunged out to fire at the beast. His third shot sent it cartwheeling into space.

Regan was screaming something that he could not hear. He fought the controls and reeled as a body crashed onto his shoulder. One of the Yaundes had launched himself from the hillside. Six inches of steel wavered before his eyes and he struggled to hold the knife arm away from his throat. There was a resounding 'thwack' and the pressure slackened. Smith had swung his rifle butt against the man's head. Another blow sent the Yaunde spinning onto the track.

Regan hung on desperately, her body barely supported by the sagging rudder wires. Poynter stretched out his arm and closed his fingers about her wrist. She was still trying to tell him something as he began to draw her towards him.

Poised in the observation cockpit, Smith saw the man on the rock disappear as the bend loomed up. A splutter of fire came from the steep hillside. There were puffs of smoke but no clear target. Bullets whistled above his head but the demonic wail of the spitting engine inches before his face drowned all other sounds. A wall of rock lunged in from the left and a shattered wing stump grated against granite. On the right was a void and the glimpse of a bridge far below.

Smith froze. A section of the line had been moved just after the bend. The warning shout from behind came too late. The Dove tripped and was suddenly thudding towards the edge of the precipice. Smith was thrown forward as the nose tilted and then he felt the ground disappearing below the wheels. All round him was air. He could hear it screaming through the flailing wires and blustering at the shattered wing ribs.

Poynter saw the water rushing up and braced himself. Regan was wedged against him and his stomach seemed to be tearing itself free from the rest of his body. His head crashed against the side of the cockpit as they hit the water. He felt himself being dragged below the surface and then suddenly released like a fish that had shaken free of a hook. The engine, already half-severed from its mooring between the longerons, had broken free on impact with the water and sunk to the bottom. Now the Dove was little more than a birch bark canoe, the rubberized cloth stretched across her ash frame affording lightness, the spread of her wide tail, equilibrium.

The span of the suspension bridge was snatched away inches above his head and Poynter felt the first rush of angry white water. The Dove scraped against a rock and then twisted through three hundred and sixty degrees before resuming her course. A wing reared up like a crippled arm and was torn from the fuselage. Senses reeling, he hugged Regan to him and braced his knees against the inside of the cockpit. Another rock loomed up and a narrow passage of

195

mad water that seemed to swallow the Dove before spitting her into the maelstrom of foam. A crushing force of water broke over his head and he struggled to suck in mouthfuls of air through the spray. The roar of the cataract was deafening. Bucking and tilting, the Dove surged on with the tide.

Then, quite suddenly, as if the raging waters had lost interest in them, the current slackened and the white water lost itself in choppy brown. The borders of the river were no longer steep and crowding in, but mud banks adorned with white egrets, stepping stones to clumps of thinning vegetation where the tall trees rose singly beneath their garlands of lianas. On this expanding waterway the Dove's progress slowed to the pace of a drifting leaf. Small spouts of water spurted through the tears in her fuselage covering, but her remaining wing and tail lay flat and graceful against the surface.

Poynter slowly relaxed his hold on Regan and looked forward to the observation cockpit. To his anguish he saw that it was empty.

FORTY SIX

Max von Graben gazed down upon the brown waters as they swirled under the bridge. In his mind he could still see the flying machine as it had shot into space and descended like a dart. He could register the spot where the fuselage had creased the surface shooting a spurt of white spray into the air.

As strong as his vision of the incident, was his recall of the emotion that had accompanied it: despair. He had seen Regan O'Donnell half trapped beneath the waters and he knew at that moment with a terrible certainty that he loved her and that he would never forgive himself for having been the instrument of her death. As much as for what he had done he cursed himself for what he had not done. Never had he given her one intimation of his feelings, save perhaps when he had dragged her from the river and conquered the impulse to take her in his arms and tell her that he loved her. It was something that he regretted as he had never regretted anything in his life.

Schutz appeared beside him clutching a pistol. On his face too was a kind of disappointment. 'Dead.'

'Almost certainly.' Von Graben looked down to the wild water disappearing amongst the trees beyond the bridge. 'Nevertheless –'

Schutz finished the sentence for him. 'We must confirm.'

Von Graben hesitated. Schutz had tried to exert pressure on him before. But there were other reasons than Regan O'Donnell for continuing the pursuit to the bitter end. His mission would not be accomplished until he was certain that the two Englishmen were dead. He stepped back and turned to Schutz. 'Fall in the men. We will work our way down the bank and search for their bodies at the foot of the rapids.' And if we find Regan, he told himself, I will be able to look upon her again before we bury her.

FORTY SEVEN

Poynter smeared another mosquito and looked about him wondering at how quickly the landscape had changed. Once there had only been tall trees but now there were banks of reeds, feather-topped grasses and wild sorghum, convolutions of tubers and bright green water grasses. A few trees had managed to seed themselves but they were mostly dead, embalmed in funeral weeds of vine like the husks of dead crows on a gamekeeper's line.

The pace had gone from the river. It meandered in great serpentine coils, the bends sprinkled with islands of cane-grass bristling like sheaves of corn, so many that the course of the river could only be followed by keeping in contact with the sluggish current. What was most apparent was the odour of decay. It rose from the mud banks and from the streams of bubbles that punctured the dark brown surface. The debris of the forests and highlands washed down to form an apron of half-submerged swamp where the sea had once held sway.

The dismal landscape mirrored Poynter's spirits. Cunningham and now Smith. With the little man's death he had felt numbed and impoverished. But not beaten. He was going to get to Douala. Country, Regan, absent friends; there were enough incentives. Not least the spirit of the crippled Dove twitching beneath him like a dying dragon fly. Dying but not dead.

Regan rested her driftwood paddle. Poynter and she were perched on the fuselage with their feet propped against the remaining wing. They had tried to plug the gap left by the engine but the river had quickly breached the crude weed caulking. Water swished inside the fuselage.

'We're sinking.'

'She won't sink.' Poynter seemed to treat the statement with contempt.

'You're sure or you hope?'

'I know.'

Regan tried to equate the man beside her to the diffident youth who had arrived at Ndala. Now the hard eyes were sunken, the mouth tight, the skin clinging to the bone. One preoccupation ruled the face: stay alive.

Ahead, the broad river divided into channels some sprouting a spring wheat of sedge and wild grasses. Poynter stopped paddling and the searing white flowers of giant lilies waited patiently for his judgement.

'We'll take the middle channel.'

Ten minutes later he knew that he had made the wrong choice. The channel had divided and divided again. They were now in a series of shallow lagoons where water fowl rose in clouds and the water was speckled with a mosaic of bright green weed. Paddling, which had always been difficult, became nearly impossible as the trailing wires of the shattered Dove snared underwater tubers. Mosquitoes formed a grille before their faces and the rain stopped to give way to a greasy sun that made the marsh steam and the odours of decay even more pungent.

Poynter was wondering whether to turn back and start again when there came a strange rustling noise as if a great creature was running through the reeds. Ahead, the tops of the grasses began to joggle and dance and the crackling noise grew louder. Poynter expected to feel a gust of wind beating against his face but there was nothing. The undulation swept nearer and the reeds went crazy. With a hissing roar, a wave of water broke from the reeds and surged towards them across the whole width of the lagoon. The Dove rose into the air and Regan clung to the cockpit. Water swished against the side of the lagoon and the wave crashed on to disappear as suddenly as it had appeared. Within seconds there was hardly a tremor to disturb the emerald green surface of the water.

Regan gasped and looked at Poynter. 'Blessed Mary! What was that, a boat?'

Poynter shook his head. 'No boat could have raised a wave like that, not up here. Anyway, we'd have heard it. It must have been a bore.' There was no comprehension in Regan's face. 'When the mouth of a river is wide and it narrows sharply, a high tide funnels into it until it starts climbing over itself. It rushes up river in a huge wave.'

Regan looked apprehensive. 'Faith, I wouldn't like to be near the neck of the funnel if that's what it does up here.'

'At least it's shown us the direction of the main stream. We've got to go down it, that's certain.'

'And what happens when we meet another of your unpleasant bores?'

'There won't be another one for several hours, maybe twelve.'

'And we're approaching a full moon too. Doesn't that have some effect on the tides?'

'It makes them higher.'

Regan gave a snort of laughter. 'I'm glad I asked.'

Poynter started to slide into the water. 'We're not getting anywhere by paddling. I'll have to pull her.'

Regan was beside him before his feet had started to sink into the slime. '*We'll* pull her.'

Poynter smiled grimly. 'Good.' He pulled up one of the trailing wires and pressed it into her hands. 'I'll go on the other side.' The brown water rose above their waists and turned to black. Streams of bubbles released the nauseous smell of rotting marigolds.

Step by clinging step they dragged the Dove across the lagoon and found another channel almost choked by reeds that led towards the source of the wave. As they struggled through the rank marsh grasses, insects dropped down their backs and cane leaves slashed them like cut-throat razors. A stinging pollen filled the air that lodged in nostrils, armpits and groins like a million needle points. Washed by their sweat it turned into an angry smarting rash that became even more agonizing if touched.

Eventually the channel opened up into another lagoon and a lone stork took off and flapped laboriously towards the west. Doggedly they waded on as the sun slid behind dark clouds and an ominous wind sprang up to agitate the grass tops. On the horizon the sky was black. A storm was coming in from the sea.

They were in the middle of the lagoon before a gap became visible in the reeds ahead. Through it something glistened like the back of a basking whale. A mud bank. Poynter's spirits lifted. This could be the main channel of the river. A few feet away the green mosaic pattern of the water was being disturbed. A thin disruptive line parted the bright confetti as trails of bubbles rose to pock the surface. But they did not come from escaping marsh gas. Something was gliding towards them. A tiny bow wave ruckled the iridescence and Poynter filled his lungs.

'Crocodile!'

Snatching the makeshift paddle from the wing he lunged forward and struck down into the water as Regan launched herself at the fuselage. There was a flash of white belly and jaws opened wide as a sprung trap. The wood hit what seemed like a log. Teeth like jagged glass on a wall snapped and the brute's tail broke the water and slammed against the side of the fuselage. Poynter lashed out again and his feet sank in the mud. Black water swirled about him and he took a blow from the crocodile's tail before twisting away through the tentacles of trailing wire and grasping a shattered wing tip. He hauled himself up and the crocodile's head shot up beside him. For an instant he could smell its foul breath as if a coffin lid had been wrenched open before his face. Then the jaws slammed shut and the creature fell back with a great splash.

Poynter scrambled onto the fuselage and sucked in mouthfuls of air. His paddle was floating near the wing. Waiting until he could breathe normally he reached out to retrieve it. The crocodile's head broke the surface within inches of his fingers and the wood disappeared in a flash of teeth and angry foam. The turbulence abated and the green covering of the water began to knit itself together.

Poynter changed his position and Regan screamed. From the thigh down his legs were covered with leeches, plum red and swollen like ugly blood blisters. Her eyes travelled to her own legs and her hand jumped to her mouth.

'Leave them,' said Poynter. 'They'll drop off.'

She wondered at the calm in his voice; but then she understood. If the horror failed to break you it had to become an inoculation against itself.

Poynter took the remaining paddle and waited. By the time they reached the main river the sky was black and the rain coming down in torrents.

FORTY EIGHT

Von Graben looked down the river towards the dark horizon. The latticework of haze that indicated heavy rain was clearly visible. Soon the rain would sweep upstream to where they stood at the foot of the rapids. The return journey would be even more difficult. It had taken two hours of hacking through dense bush and scrambling over slippery rocks to arrive where they were now. He felt sad and exhausted. What had he expected to find here? Surely no craft could have survived the pounding force of the angry white water.

He knew and accepted that a duty had turned into a compulsive quest. The game of fox and hounds, the personal vendetta; both had been overtaken by something far more powerful, something in which Regan O'Donnell had become inextricably involved. Maximilian von Graben listened to the muted roar and knew that the river spreading out before him carried his destiny with it.

'Masta!' One of the Yaundes was calling from the water's edge. An eddy spun slowly beneath a steep bank and a half-submerged object turned listlessly at its centre. Von Graben launched himself into the water. He recognized Regan's dress. His hands snatched at the material and tore it from the water. The impression of a human form had been given by the air trapped beneath the folds.

Schutz stood on the bank and looked at von Graben strangely. In his glowing, wild boar eyes a dangerous comprehension was dawning.

Down river, a dug-out canoe was approaching. One tall, reedlike native stood in the stern, a second paddled. Both men were naked save for a patch of cloth at the crutch. Their nasal septa had been transfixed by pigs' tusks so that they appeared as stubby white moustaches.

202

Von Graben threw the sodden dress ashore and beckoned to one of the Yaundes. 'Do you understand these people?'

'If they are Yorubas, yes masta!'

'Ask them if they have seen any bodies in the water.'

The Yaunde inclined his head and started to shout across the tide. Although they responded, the men in the canoe came no closer to the shore.

Their interchange continued and von Graben stared into the Yaunde's eyes as if trying to read a translation in them.

'What are they saying?'

'They have seen no dead bodies, masta. But when they were setting traps in the reeds they saw a strange boat go past with a white man and a white woman in it.'

'When?' Von Graben dismissed his own question with a wave of the hand. The natives did not understand time. 'Tell them that we need two canoes and that they must show us where they saw the white people.'

There was a glint of triumph in Schutz's eyes but von Graben did not see it. He had other things on his mind.

FORTY NINE

It was evening when they came to the island. The Dove was almost completely waterlogged and the water hissed like the surface of a boiling saucepan. The sky was a grey sponge squeezed tight above their heads and they could barely see the banks through the oppressive gloom. Exhausted and with their tattered clothing in danger of being washed from their backs by the continuous downpour, they made out an open space between the reeds and let the Dove carry them aground. There were mooring posts here and it seemed that the reeds had been cleared by men and the bank prepared as an anchorage.

Poynter dragged the Dove ashore and staggered up the slight rise. Through the rain and gloom some huts were visible, mere outlines against the grey. Night was falling fast and the light draining away with the streams of water that ran about his feet. He waited for Regan and took her hand, drawing her after him. Together they stumbled towards the huts, fighting the sensation that death had already overtaken them and that they were in some kind of purgatory. Surely there could be no life attached to these mean, windowless dwellings, shedding their thatch as a mangy dog sheds fur. Poynter fell on his knees to enter one and felt the spiders' webs damp against his face. The hut was empty and the rain had purged it of its familiar smells. Either the village was only used by fishermen or the inmates had retired to higher ground. There was wisdom in such a move. Already the feather-topped grasses near the mooring posts were under water.

When Poynter tried to rise he found his limbs locked by cramp and fatigue. At least there was some shelter from the rain here. Regan crept in beside him and immediately he drew closer to her body. His stomach felt as if its sides had become fused together. Water dripped onto his face from a hole in the leaking roof but he was almost too tired to move. He must sleep. Tomorrow they would press on. Inside his feverish head the earth rolled and memories crowded his mind. When he touched Regan it was not her body that he felt but the companion of so many long days and nights beneath the stars. Once again he was stretched out inside the crib of the rails and it was with Smith's arms around him that he fell asleep.

Regan felt the warmth stealing through her body and stared out into the night. She was not thinking of Poynter.

FIFTY

It was Schutz who saw the Dove first. Hunched up in the prow of the lead canoe like an intimidating figurehead, he had been sweeping his torch low across the water as the paddlers zig-zagged from side to side of the broad river. It had stopped raining but the clouds still hung low shutting out the moon. The only light came from clouds of fireflies encircling bushes along the bank, so that they seemed like illuminated Christmas trees.

In the two canoes were nine men. Four reluctant Yorubas conscripted by fear of the white man's weapons to serve as paddlers, von Graben, Schutz and the three remaining Yaundes.

The broken, twisted wires of the Dove glistened and her clumsy, half-beached shape contrasted with anything else seen in the night.

Schutz's canoe squelched against the mud and he extricated himself with difficulty, grunting with pain as he held his wound. The native soldier with him moved quickly up the slope and returned to whisper that there were huts ahead. Schutz watched von Graben's canoe gliding from the darkness and turned towards the Dove. Given the full possession of his strength he would have liked to have kicked it to pieces. Denied that simple pleasure he could at least ensure that it departed from his sight for ever. Placing his boot against the shattered nose, he thrust with all the force that he could muster and the Dove reluctantly slid backwards and half sank below the water. Another thrust and the current picked her up and began to carry her down river. She twisted slowly as if trying to turn back towards the land.

Von Graben came ashore and instantly gauged the situation. The river was rising fast, the Yorubas apprehensive. If left alone with the canoes they would surely make off. He called Schutz to heel and gave orders for a Yaunde to accompany the rest of the party.

Warily, von Graben, Schutz and the three Yaundes spread out with the four Yorubas huddled before them like a nervous flock of geese being shepherded to market. The huts loomed out of the darkness and the men's shadows were thrown across them by the light of the fizzling torches. Von Graben spoke to a Yaunde and one of the trembling Yorubas was forced to crawl inside the opening of a hut. No sooner had the soles of his feet disappeared than he was scrabbling backwards and waving his arms in silent pantomime. One hand pointed, the other held two fingers aloft.

Schutz went through the flimsy wall of the hut as if it was rice paper. Von Graben glimpsed two bodies close together as Schutz grabbed his pistol from its holster and pressed the muzzle against Poynter's temple as if trying to penetrate it.

'Halt!' Von Graben commanded. For a second it seemed that Schutz would disobey. Then his arm dropped.

Regan shrank back. Schutz was a bomb about to explode, a finger pressure away from blowing their brains out.

Poynter started to rise and Regan saw the Luger nestling by his shoulder. Her hand darted out but a Yaunde was quicker. His bare foot sent the pistol spinning across the hut.

'Nein!' Von Graben interceded again as Schutz's arm straightened.

'You see!' There was triumph in Schutz's cry. 'She tries to do it again.'

Regan spoke softly. 'I shot you because you were raping me.' The words followed each other with the harsh measured finality of nails thumping into a coffin lid.

Von Graben looked into Schutz's face and knew that it was true. He felt humiliated; not as a German officer but as a man. His hand stretched out. 'Give me your pistol. You are under arrest.'

Disbelief slowly gave way to a truculent smile. 'I see. You want the Engländerin for yourself.'

Von Graben's expression did not flicker. 'Your pistol.' He continued to hold out his hand whilst the two Yaundes gaped at each other and the shivering Yorubas wondered what strange ritual the white men were enacting whilst the great and powerful bore was preparing to drown the land they were standing on.

Poynter's eye was drawn past Schutz's legs into the night. A shadow had moved.

Schutz's smile changed to a look of surly viciousness. 'No,' he said.

One of the Yorubas cupped his hand to his ear and began to gabble excitedly as the others gesticulated downstream. The Yaundes took up the refrain. Above the eruption of voices came the noise of distant thunder. The bore was coming.

'The canoes.' Von Graben had taken one step from the hut when he stopped. A small bedraggled figure stood in the darkness covering him with a Mauser. Smith.

A Yaunde swung up his rifle but Smith fired first. The man crashed backwards with the sound of the shot. Instantly Smith flicked open the bolt and drove another round into the breech. The expended cartridge rolled across the damp ground trailing a wisp of cordite. Schutz slowly unclenched his fist and let the pistol drop from his fingers.

Poynter, his face alight with incredulity and joy, scrambled to his feet and stared at a ghost. '*Smith!* How in God's name did you get here?'

Smith's eyes did not leave the Germans. 'I clung to the Dove's wing. When that broke up I had to follow the river. Lost my way dozens of times. I was dozing in the reeds when this lot went by. Then I saw the Dove.'

Poynter listened. The roar was getting louder. 'Any more guards to worry about?'

Smith patted the Mauser. 'Only the one who had this.'

'We must get to the Dove.'

'She's gone. There's only a couple of canoes. I'll get 'em away from the river.' He thrust his Mauser into Poynter's hands and picked up Schutz's pistol before running into the darkness with the Yorubas clamouring at his heels.

Poynter nodded to Regan. 'Collect their weapons.' He was thinking of the Dove. Gone? It was as if he had lost a limb. The mounting roar jerked him back to the immediate danger. Every second it was coming closer. He saw the Yaundes flinch. A weird sibilance screeched in his ears, the wild water sweeping through the reed beds building to a swooshing, hissing crescendo. In the darkness he could hear the Yorubas shouting and glimpsed their glistening bodies as they dragged the canoes towards higher ground. Then thunder wiped out their voices and a surge of white water broke from the night and raced across the open ground snatching at their feet and slapping the walls of the flimsy huts. For a second it threatened to engulf them and then swept on upstream with the sound of booming cannon fire. The reeds swayed. The earth glistened.

Smith appeared, panting and dripping wet. The canoes were safe. 'Are we going to take this lot with us?'

Regan moved closer to von Graben. He looked into her eyes and then turned to face his captors. There was no plea for mercy in the proud gaze.

'We can't leave them here and we daren't let them go. We'll have to take them.' Poynter looked at Schutz. 'Don't give me an excuse to kill you,' he said quietly.

Schutz continued to glare like a wounded water buffalo waiting to charge.

They set off immediately. The next bore would reach them in about nine hours if the gap between the last two was a guide and there was no knowing how far they had to go. The Yorubas replied with blank, uncomprehending stares to the word 'Douala'.

Already the strong tidal nature of the river was sucking the water towards the ocean where it would brood, boil and fester until the next great wave brought it charging up the funnel, hell-bent on destruction.

The shrinking island disappeared behind them and a wind sprang up. Von Graben, Schutz and the surviving Yaunde were in the leading canoe with two Yorubas. The paddlers had been told to keep a safe distance between the dug-outs and reminded that Smith's Mauser would be covering them. Poynter sat behind Regan and Smith in the second canoe with the two Yorubas at prow and stern. Reunited with Smith, he felt his capacity to survive multiplied. A bright light of hope and expectancy cut through his tiredness.

They travelled in silence, the river moving faster and faster with the Yorubas only having to make a sudden dab of their paddles to change direction or avoid a floating object. Sometimes they passed over drowned reed beds, sometimes millraces of angry water poured in from left or right. It was as if every river, creek and stream in the Cameroons was rushing down to swell the turbulent flood.

A hole appeared in the sky and the moon shone down, turning the edges of the black clouds silver and throwing an eerie, dazzling light across the water. The moon was round and fat as a pumpkin and revealed a strange floating landscape in which whole islands of reed, some studded with bushes and small trees, floated down the stream jostling and turning like cogs in some great, mad machine, bent on its own destruction.

More hours passed and the paddlers began a slow monotonous chant: 'Ee-yah, ee-yah, ee-yah', each phrase punctuated by the paddles digging down into the water. The torches had long since spluttered out and the Yorubas' lean, muscled bodies gleamed like twists of black wax in the moonlight. Smith had handed over the rifle and he and Regan lay as though unconscious against Poynter's legs. Ahead, the other canoe was a dark shape sometimes indistinguishable from the floating logs. Poynter cradled the Mauser across his lap and peered ahead. The moon disappeared behind clouds but his eyes kept boring into the night.

Dawn came up not as a blaze of colours illuminating the eastern sky but as a thin grey light that turned darkness into murk and eventually dissolved into grudging day. It began to rain steadily.

Now they were all thinking about the bore. The river was still running fast and the water tasted brackish. In places there were moving log jams of trees that looked as if they had been swept up on the crest of the last incoming wave and then been outstripped by it. Sooner or later the fast-ebbing river would collide with what amounted to a tidal wave driving a small forest before it.

All ears were strained for the first rumbling roar and the Yorubas paddled close to the widening reed-girt shore, their fearful eyes searching for side channels that could be taken in an emergency.

But increasingly there was no land visible. Only great beds of weeds sometimes beaten down for hundreds of yards before they rose straight and serried again. Poynter's tired eyes peered up every channel and scanned every shore. How far could Douala be? There was a shout from ahead and he turned to gape. Three hundred yards away a long grey shape was emerging from a channel. It was a trim motor launch and in silhouette he could recognize a three-pounder gun mounted on the prow. Relief flooded over him. A British gunboat. Thank God! Their ordeal was over. He saw Smith's head turn towards him and wondered why the man's eyes were dead. Then he saw what hung from the stern of the vessel they were approaching. A white flag with a black cross on it.

Like a man reading his own name on a gravestone, Poynter picked out the neat gold lettering on the prow: *Herzogin Elisabeth*. It was a German ship.

FIFTY ONE

'An extraordinary stroke of good fortune.' Von Graben was too racked by cramp and exhaustion to do more than nod as the Kapitän continued. 'We came up from Kribi to lay mines across the entrance to Douala harbour under cover of darkness. A British light cruiser saw us but that would have presented no great problem had we not developed engine trouble. The *Herzogin Elisabeth* can make thirty knots. We would have outrun them easily. As it was we were forced to hide in the mouth of the river. We'd just made good the damage when you appeared.'

Von Graben watched the four freed Yorubas paddling away towards a gap in the reeds with all the strength they could muster.

'Are you returning to Kribi?'

'At nightfall. The cruiser cannot come in here after us and no gunboat will find us in the reeds. When night comes we'll slip away. They'll be lucky if they even hear us.'

'But the bore?'

The Kapitän raised a calming hand. He was a handsome young man with a down of hair on his cheek bleached white by the sun. 'With our speed harnessed to that of the river we can cut through it like a knife through butter. I can leave a glass of schnapps on the ward-room table and it will not be disturbed.'

'You have done this before?'

The Kapitän patted his arm reassuringly. 'In these tidal waters it is an everyday necessity. Fear not, my friend, you are no longer in a canoe.'

Von Graben knew that he was being patronized but it was of no concern to him. Looking about him he felt as if he had entered another world. How spruce the sailors seemed with their black ribbons tumbling from their caps, their pale flesh unsullied by suppurating bites and sores, their faces shaven. They, in turn, returned his gaze with something near apprehension. He and the other exhausted husks of men who had clambered aboard must look like visitors from another planet.

Von Graben thought of Regan, alive and safe, and felt a surge of tenderness and relief. She had been taken below but Smith and Poynter were still on deck. Smith stood defiantly with his arms folded across his chest, looking at Schutz like a Yorkshire terrier daring a bull mastiff to yawn at it.

Von Graben stiffened. Schutz had recovered his pistol.

'Herr Kapitän –' The words had barely escaped von Graben's lips when there was a violent blast on the ship's whistle. The helmsman swung the wheel over and the engines began to roar into full life. Ahead, the great river widened out into the infinity of the Atlantic Ocean, a rapacious mouth about to swallow the scattering of islands before it. In the distance, a bar of light against the horizon was taking on a grey menacing shape. The bore was coming. Sailors ran to their stations and the wake began to boil as the launch surged forward. Von Graben braced himself and then nearly pitched on his face as their speed was cut dramatically. There was a terrifying whining screech of tortured metal and men began to run towards the stern. Von Graben joined them and looked down. He saw a pale black cross and half-submerged tentacles of frayed fabric. Then a mass of rusting wire wrapped round the vessel's propeller. With a start of horrified recognition he knew what he was looking at.

'The Dove,' breathed Smith. 'My God. She was here to meet us.' He raised his head to von Graben and Poynter and for a second the three men were united in a gaze of awe and wonder. Then their eyes jerked away. The bore was approaching at the speed of an express train. Islands were swept from their sight like raindrops on a window pane and a great, swelling comber of water overlapped each bank. Men scurried to and from the engine room as the captain shouted at the helmsman to keep the launch head-on to the approaching wave. But the current was fast and treacherous and the *Herzogin Elisabeth* without power. A floating island of vegetation bunted her side and started to push her inexorably across the tide. Ratings thrust with boat-hooks and hung from the stern trying to break the Dove's stranglehold on the propeller. Calm and order had exploded into panic.

And all the while the bore thundered nearer, seeming to suck the ebbing river into its mouth in order to render itself more powerful. The noise attacked the eardrums with a great booming roar and logs danced like matchsticks on the foaming white crest.

Von Graben saw that Schutz had disappeared. A new fear seized him and he started to run towards the companionway. The vessel slewed into a trough and he lost his balance and slid across the deck. On hands and knees he reached the stairway and pulled himself upright. Ahead he could glimpse a wall of grey water capped with white like the side of a snow-covered house. He launched himself down the stairs as he heard Regan scream.

Schutz was leaning against a tilting bulkhead holding his side with one hand and slowly raising his pistol with the other. Von Graben tore open his holster. It was empty. He snatched a bayonet from the weapon rack at his side and hurled himself forward. A shot rang out.

The *Herzogin Elisabeth* was lying broadside to the tide when the bore hit her and she rose in the air like a shuttlecock. The wave knocked her backwards and then swept her before it until it seemed that she must disappear for ever. Then her bottom showed through the angry white foam and she careened on, spilling out men and ballast. One hundred yards, two hundred yards, three hundred yards. The gunboat was almost at the bank before the bore tired of playing with her and swept on to wreak more destruction. As the whirlpools and eddies smoothed into streaky brown, the sleek craft began to settle ignominiously in a few feet of water near the reed beds.

Schutz dragged himself up the drowning companionway as the water poured past him. The bayonet was still in his back. He stumbled to his knees and then staggered to the edge of the sinking deck, rising water swelling over his ankles. Below the stern he saw the wires bunching and spreading and he threw back his head and cursed them until he coughed blood. He lost his footing and toppled forward into the water. The wires gently closed round his struggling body and the Dove drew him down with her to her final resting place.

Poynter's head broke the surface and he sucked in great mouthfuls of air as the river surged and fell. His body was bobbing up and down like a fishing float. He struggled to tread water. Around him bodies and flotsam were strewn over an area of a quarter mile. Some men were swimming, some were drowning, some were clinging to logs or spars, some were already floating corpses.

A log dawdled by as if uncertain whether to float upstream or down and Poynter swam a few clumsy strokes and flung his arms across it.

Hardly had he made contact than there was a triumphant blast on a ship's siren and his stinging eyes turned towards the mouth of the estuary. A vessel was approaching under full steam. At her mast flew a white ensign.

Poynter's head dropped forward against the log and he closed his eyes. A hand closed about his and an arm rested on his shoulder. His friend trod water beside him. Bleeding, battered, alive.

Von Graben saw the British gunboat arriving as he staggered ashore. He fell to his knees amongst the sagging bed of reeds and buried his head in his hands. When he looked up it was to find himself staring at Regan's feet. She dropped to her knees and rested a hand on his head. 'Are you all right?'

'Have you come to take me prisoner?' he said.

She seemed to consider the question seriously. 'No, no, I wouldn't be capable of doing that, would I?'

'No,' said von Graben firmly.

'A man like yourself would have very clear ideas about what he was going to do next.'

Von Graben looked again at the approaching British gunboat and at the waterlogged path that led away through the battered reeds. The *Herzogin Elisabeth* was grounded a hundred yards away, her bows tipped forward and the muzzle of her three-pounder gun symbolically dipped beneath the surface. There was no sign of life from her and the nearest German could be heard calling out from a spar three hundred yards away. The voice getting fainter.

'I will find a German unit and join up with them.'

'Spanish Muni lies to the South. It's neutral.'

'Why do you say that?'

'Do you always ask questions you know the answers to?'

They looked into each other's eyes and then he opened his arms and she came in close, against his body. 'Thank God you're alive.'

'And you.'

'I love you.'

'*Ich liebe dich.*' She drew back. The British vessel had weighed anchor in mid-stream and was lowering a boat.

He smiled ruefully. 'I could keep you as my prisoner.'

'Not any more. We're equals now, you and I.'

'And when the war is over —'

Regan pressed a finger against his lips. 'Go now, my darling. I don't want you to see me crying. May God keep you for me.' They clung and kissed and he tasted her tears. 'I *will* find you again.'

'Go.' She watched him walk away until he was swallowed up by the reeds and she could hear the rhythmic slapping of the oars echoing across the water.

FIFTY TWO

'Capital drop of port, don't you think?' said the First Officer. 'Pity your lady friend isn't here to enjoy it.'

Poynter smiled politely. He was tired of wardroom jokes about his relationship with Regan but now found it easiest to ignore them. 'I don't think she's left her cabin all day,' he said. 'Fever.'

He returned his attention to the small, bulbous glass and raised it to his lips. The rich ruby liquid seemed thicker than the crystal that enclosed it. He sipped and watched it glide slowly down the glass. Like blood.

All survivors of the *Herzogin Elisabeth* had been transferred to the light cruiser *HMS Challenger*. The vessel was bound for England, having disembarked reinforcements for the Douala garrison. Men who would join the force setting off to destroy the German stronghold at Ndinga Mountain. Poynter had volunteered to follow his information ashore, but it had been felt that with all the newly released mines floating in the harbour it would be safer if the *Challenger* continued on her passage back to England.

' 'Spect you'll be glad to be getting back to the real war,' said the Second Officer who was not quite certain what Poynter was doing in the wardroom. 'They say it'll be over by Christmas.'

'They always say that,' said the Chief Engineer, a dour Scot in the best tradition of the breed, who held his nose over his port glass as if suspecting that somebody might have replaced its contents with dyed liquid paraffin.

'Don't be so pessimistic, Mac,' said the First Officer. 'Now that the Bosch have dug themselves in we've got them cold. What's this place in Flanders – begins with Y?'

Poynter listened to the voices and took another sip of port. His body felt as if it belonged to somebody else. He did not live in this plump carcass filled with good food and wine. Perhaps it was the clothes he had been lent. Nothing seemed to fit very well. But then his own skin did not seem to fit very well either.

'Winkle them out of those trenches in no time, don't you think, Mr Poynter?'

He realized he was being addressed again. 'I hope so,' he said.

'You're probably going to get a gong, you know,' said the Second Officer. 'You and that other chap, the rating, what's his name?'

'Smith,' said Poynter.

'That's right,' said the Second Officer. 'Smith. It would have to be, wouldn't it?' He laughed and the others, with the exception of Poynter, joined in. 'Funny little man. No doubt the embodiment of the bulldog breed.'

Poynter's chair scraped back and he stood up. 'Excuse me, gentlemen.' His eyes made a cursory circuit of the table. 'I'm turning in. Good night.' He placed his glass in the centre of his place setting and strode past the advancing waiters to the drinks tray where he selected a bottle of brandy and two glasses before continuing to the door.

'What an extraordinary fellow,' said the Second Officer, not waiting until the door had closed.

'Looks like Wellington, don't you think?' said the First Officer.

'Just as damned haughty.' The Second Officer tapped his temple. 'If you ask me, I think the jungle's got to him.'

The Chief Engineer pulled the decanter towards him and filled his glass. 'Perhaps he finds you insensitive and rather boring,' he said. 'Of course, it would only be his opinion.'

The sound of someone cheerfully whistling 'It's a long way to Tipperary' came to Smith as he lay on his bunk in the bowels of the ship staring at the ceiling. He sat up as Poynter appeared carrying his bottle and the two glasses.

'What's your name?' Poynter asked.

Smith looked at him as if he were mad. 'Smith, sir '

'Your *whole* name.'

'Oh, George Albert Smith.'

Poynter put down the brandy and stuck out his hand. 'I'm delighted to make your acquaintance, George Albert Smith. My name is John Eustace Merivale Poynter.'

'You're drunk,' said Smith.

'Only slightly. And I'd like you to join me.' Poynter slopped generous measures of brandy into the glasses. 'We'll drink a few toasts to absent friends.' He produced Cunningham's silver flask and tossed it on the bunk.

'Cunningham and the Dove,' said George Albert.

'Cunningham and the Dove,' repeated John Eustace Merivale raising his glass. 'God bless them both.'

In her cabin, Regan O'Donnell dreamed her private dreams and in the wardroom they were talking about raising pheasants. The Chief Engineer had gone to bed.